"Are you serious... really expected to conduct an investigation while important evidence is withheld from me?"

My colleagues found something of absorbing interest on the Curia ceiling and studied it intently. Obviously, there was only to be the form of an investigation, not its substance. State Security! The meaning was clear: Senatorial reputations were at stake, and the most junior member of the elected government was being sent out to sweep the whole untidy mess into a dark room and close the door after it.

"We serve the Senate and People of Rome," Rutilinus said, when I had calmed a bit.

I cursed piously as I left the Curia. It was not shaping up into a good day. There were days when I had had to investigate ten murders before noon, but a hundred ordinary homicides were preferable to one which involved high personages.

There was also the little matter of my career, which could come to an abrupt and premature end should I mishandle this matter. So, I reflected, could my life.

SPQR

JOHN MADDOX ROBERTS

AVON BOOKS ◆ NEW YORK

SQPR is an original publication of Avon Books. This work has never before appeared in book form. This work is a work of fiction, and while some portions of this novel deal with historic occurrences, actual events, and real people, it should in no way be construed as being factual.

AVON BOOKS
A division of
The Hearst Corporation
105 Madison Avenue
New York, New York 10016

Copyright © 1990 by John Maddox Roberts
Maps by Loston Wallace
Published by arrangement with the author
Library of Congress Catalog Card Number: 90-92990
ISBN: 0-380-75993-4

First Avon Books Printing: September 1990

AVON TRADEMARK REG. U.S. PAT. OFF. AND IN OTHER COUNTRIES, MARCA REGISTRADA, HECHO EN U.S.A.

Printed in the U.S.A.

RA 10 9 8 7 6 5 4 3 2 1

For
Martha Knowles and Ken Roy
Good friends, fine historians and
GREAT company!

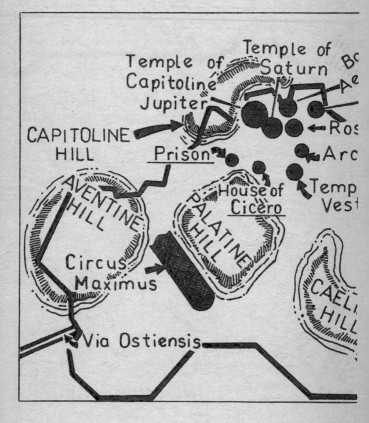

silica
milia

Curia

stra

hive

le of
ta

SUBURA
DISTRICT

QUIRINAL HILL

VIMINAL HILL

ESQUILINE
HILL

AN

W   N

S   E

ROME c.70 B.C.

by: Loston Wallace

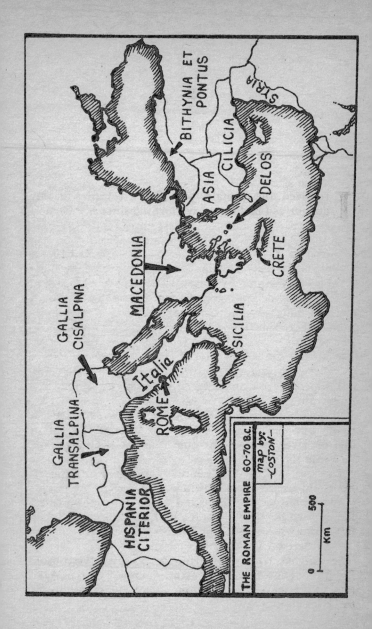

THE ROMAN EMPIRE 60-70 B.C.
map by: —LOSTON—

Km
0   500

HISPANIA CITERIOR

GALLIA TRANSALPINA

GALLIA CISALPINA

ROME
Italia

MACEDONIA

SICILIA

BITHYNIA ET PONTUS

ASIA

CILICIA

SYRIA

DELOS

CRETE

I

I received the captain of the ward vigiles in my atrium, as I had on every morning since my election to the Commission of Twenty-Six. I am not an early riser by nature, and the office had no more onerous duty for me. It was still dark and even my few clients had not yet begun to arrive. The squad of vigiles sat sleepily along a bench against the atrium wall, their leather buckets at their feet, while my aged janitor served them cups of watered, sour wine, hot and steaming.

"No fires in the night, Commissioner," the captain reported. "At least, not in this ward."

"May the gods be thanked," I said. "Anywhere else?"

"There was a big one over near the Circus. We could see it clearly from the crest of the Viminal. It may still be burning."

"Which way is the wind blowing?" I asked, alarmed. If it was one of those oil warehouses between the Circus and the river, the fire could be all over the city by noon.

"From the north."

I let out a relieved sigh and vowed a goat to Jupiter if he would keep Boreas blowing today. "Anything else?"

"Two householders reported break-ins"—the vigile stifled a yawn—"and we found a body in the alley between the Syrian apothecary and Publius's wineshop."

"Murdered?" I asked.

"Strangled. With a bowstring, it appeared. We rousted Publius out and he said the man was named Marcus Ager, and he'd been renting a room above the wineshop for the last two months."

1

"Freeborn or freedman?" I asked.

"Must be freedman, because a couple of my men said they recognized him as a Thracian daggerman who used to fight under the name of Sinistrus. He hadn't fought in the last two years, though. Maybe he saved enough to buy his own freedom."

"Small loss, then. Was he with Macro's gang, or one of the others?"

"Not as I know," the vigile said, shrugging.

"Just more trouble for me. Now I'll have to search the dole rolls to verify his residence in the district, then try to track down his former owner. He may wish to take charge of the body." I don't approve of manumitting gladiators, as a general thing. A man who has spent several years as a licensed killer is not likely to settle into the role of responsible citizen easily. Usually, they squander their savings within a few months of manumission, enroll on the grain dole, then drift into one of the gangs or hire on as a strong-arm man for some politician.

Still, I was grateful that there had been only one murder to investigate. After a night when the gangs were restless, it was not unusual to find a dozen or more bodies in the back alleys of the Subura. We had just celebrated the Plebeian Games, and the city was usually quiet after a big festival. For a day or two, at any rate.

You must understand, whoever you are, that in those days Rome, mistress of half the world, was a place as savage as a village of Nile pygmies. Roman soldiers kept the peace in hundreds of cities around our sea, but not a single soldier patrolled the streets of Rome. Tradition forbade it. Instead, the city was controlled by street gangs, each under the protection of a powerful family or politician for whom it performed tasks liable to criminal prosecution.

I dismissed the vigiles to their long-awaited sleep, then hastily received my clients. This was at the very beginning of my career, you understand, and my clients were few: a couple of family freedmen, a discharged soldier from the legion I had served in briefly, and a householder from a rural plebeian family traditionally under the protection of the Caecilii. I might have had none at all, but my father had insisted that a man starting out in public life had to have a few clients dogging his steps in the morning to lend him dignity. They saluted me as patron and inquired whether I required any services of them that day. It would be several years before I should actually *need* an entourage of clients, but it was customary.

My janitor brought them small gifts of food which they wrapped up in their napkins, and we all set off to visit *my* patron. This was my father, Decius Caecilius Metellus the Elder, bearer of a proud and ancient name, but known to all and sundry as Cut-Nose because he had taken a Cimbrian sword across his face at Raudine Plain while serving under General Marius. He never stopped talking about the campaign and took a good deal of credit for the great victory. Sometimes, after a few cups of wine, Father would admit that Marius deserved some recognition.

Father, old Roman to the core, kept his janitor chained to the gatepost, although anyone could see that the chain link attached to the man's ankle-ring was just a hook, which the fellow could detach at any time.

"Decius Caecilius Metellus the Younger," I announced, "and his clients, to pay our respects to the patron."

The slave let us into the atrium, which was already crowded with Father's other clients, of which he had a prodigious mob. He was an Urban Praetor that year, an office of great dignity. He would be standing for the Consulate in two years, and a man who must make innumerable long-winded speeches needs a sizable cheering section. Many of the men present that morning had permanently hoarsened their voices by cheering every point made and every clever turn of phrase during Father's career as a lawyer pleading before the court. This was a court day and Father's lictors were there, leaning on their rod-bundled axes. At least, this year, Father would be presiding rather than pleading; a relief to every ear and larynx present.

The room was abuzz with the usual city gossip; the lowborn chattered of races and swordsmen, the better-bred concentrating on politics and foreign affairs and the deeds of our over-adventurous and squabbling generals. Everybody traded the latest omens, and applied them to the doings of charioteers, gladiators, politicians and generals. There was much talk of the fire near the Circus. All Romans live in mortal terror of fire.

Eventually, the great man appeared. His toga was as white as a candidate's except for its broad purple stripe. Unlike most modern politicians, Father was not accompanied by a bodyguard of riffraff such as the late Marcus Ager. He said it demeaned the dignity of a Senator to walk as if in fear of his fellow citizens. On the other hand, he had few political or personal enemies, so he was in no real danger. After greeting a few of his more prominent clients, he signaled for me to approach him. After we exchanged greetings, he clapped me on the shoulder.

"Decius, my son, I've been hearing good reports of your work on the Commission of Twenty-Six." The old man had been most disappointed in my lack of aptitude and interest in a military career. I had served the bare minimum necessary to qualify for public office and used a minor wound as an excuse to go back to Rome and stay there. Now that I was embarked on my civil career, though, Father was willing to acknowledge me again.

"I try to do my duty. And I find that I have a flair for snooping."

"Yes, well"—Father waved a hand as if dismissing my comment—"you have subordinates for that sort of thing, you know. You really should confine your activities to those commensurate with your rank: arresting those who are a danger to the community and making a report of your investigation to the Senate."

"Sometimes wealthy or highborn people must be questioned, Father," I explained. "Often I find that such persons will talk to a noble in a way they would never do with some state freedman."

"Don't try to gull me, young man," Father said sternly. "You enjoy it. You've never overcome your taste for low company and disreputable pursuits." I shrugged in acknowledgment.

Perhaps I should explain something here: In this modern age of blurring social distinctions, the significance of this exchange might be lost. We Caecilii Metelli are an ancient and incredibly numerous family of great distinction, but our ancestor arrived in Rome just a bit too late to qualify for patrician status. We are of the plebeian nobility, which to my taste is the most desirable status: qualified to hold the highest public office without the ceremonial restrictions endured by patricians. In practical career terms it meant only that we were barred from certain priesthoods, which was all to the good. Sacerdotal duties are the bane of public life, and I never held a priesthood I didn't loathe.

Still standing, Father ate his breakfast from a tray held by a slave. Breakfast consisted of a crust or two of bread sprinkled with salt and helped down with a cup of water. This is a custom rich in staunch old Roman virtue, no doubt, but deficient in the fortifying nourishment required by a man who will spend a full day on the work of the Senate. It was my own practice to have a far more substantial meal in bed. Father always assured me that this was a barbaric practice, fit only for Greeks and Orientals, so perhaps I played an unknowing part in the downfall of the Republic. Be that as it may, I *still* have my breakfast in bed.

Luckily, since this was a court day, Father did not require us all to accompany him to the levee of *his* patron, the advocate, great orator and thoroughgoing scoundrel, Quintus Hortensius Hortalus. Instead, we merely accompanied him to the Basilica, preceded by his lictors, and made sure that his entrance was properly solemn and dignified before the day's uproarious litigation began. As soon as he was ensconced in his curule chair, I made

my way back out to the Forum for my customary round
of meeting and greeting prior to embarking upon the
business of the day. This could be time-consuming. As a
junior civil servant, I was of little personal importance,
but my father was a praetor who might well be Consul
someday, so I was sought out by many.

In all of the great and varied city of Rome, I love the
Forum best. Since childhood, I have spent part of nearly
every day there. During my few and unwilling absences
from the city, it was the Forum that I longed for most.
At the time of which I now write, the Forum was a marvelously jumbled mass of temples, some of them still
wooden; market stalls; fortune-tellers' booths; speakers'
platforms; monuments of past wars; dovecotes for sacrificial birds; and the general lounging, idling and
gossiping-place for the center of the world. Now, of
course, it is a marble confection erected to the glory of
a single family instead of the ancient tribal gathering-
place and market that I loved. I am happy to report,
though, that the pigeons decorate the new monuments
just as they did the old.

Remembering my vow of the morning, I made my way
to the Temple of Jupiter on the Capitoline. Word had it
that the fire was under control, so I had downgraded my
sacrifice to a dove. My personal income was small, and
my office was not one which attracted many bribes, so it
behooved me to take care with my expenditures.

I pulled a fold of my toga over my head and entered
the dim, smoky interior of the ancient building. In this
temple I could almost believe myself in the presence of
the old Caecilii who had lived in the wood-and-thatch
village of Roma which had stood on these hills, and had
performed their rituals in this temple. I speak, of course,
of the temple as it was before the present restorations
which have turned it into a second-rate copy of a Greek
temple to Zeus.

I gave my dove to the priest on duty and the bird was
duly killed to the presumed satisfaction of Jupiter. While
the brief ritual was performed, I noticed a man standing

next to me. With his toga pulled over his head, I could see only that he was a youngish man, perhaps about my age. His toga was of fine quality, and his sandals had the little ivory crescent of the patrician fastened at the ankles.

As I left the temple, the man hastily followed, as if he wanted to speak to me. Outside, on the broad portico which has the finest of all views of the city, we uncovered our heads. His face seemed familiar, but it was the thinning hair above his still-youthful face which jogged my memory.

"I greet you, Decius of the illustrious Caecilii," he said, embracing me and bestowing upon me the kiss which all Romans in public life must endure. It seemed to me that this normally perfunctory salute was given with more warmth than was absolutely necessary.

"And I greet you, Caius Julius Caesar." Even through the veil that separates us, I can detect your smile. But the most trumpeted name in Roman history was not famous then. In those days, young Caesar was known only for the astonishing number and variety of his debaucheries, and for his extravagant debts. However, to everyone's amazement, he had suddenly displayed a civic conscience and was standing for a quaestorship as a champion of the common man.

His new democratic ideals raised no few eyebrows, since the ancient Julian gens, although it had produced no men of public distinction in many generations, had always been of the aristocratic party. Young Caius was breaking with family tradition in siding with the *Populares*. True, his uncle by marriage was Marius, that same general in whose service my father had earned his nickname. That murderous old man had terrorized Rome in his last years as Consul and leader of the *Populares*, but he still had many admirers in Rome and throughout Italy. I also reminded myself that Caesar was married to the daughter of Cinna, who had been Marius's colleague in the Consulate. Yes, young Caius Julius Caesar was definitely a man to watch.

"May I inquire after the health of your esteemed father?" he asked.

"Healthy as a Thracian," I answered. "He's in court today. When I left him, the Basilica was packed with Senators suing to get back their property confiscated by Sulla."

"That's a business that'll take years to sort out," Caesar said wryly. When he had been a very young man and Sulla was Dictator, Sulla had ordered him to divorce Cornelia, Cinna's daughter. In a rare moment of personal integrity, Caesar had refused and was forced to flee Italy until Sulla's death. That act of defiance had made him celebrated for a short time, but those had been eventful days in Rome, and most of the survivors had nearly forgotten him.

We descended the Capitoline, and Caesar asked my destination. He seemed oddly interested in my affairs. But then, when he was running for office Caius Julius could be as amiable and ingratiating as a Subura whore.

"Since I'm so near," I answered, "I might as well look in on the Ludus Statilius. I have to investigate the death of a man who may have come from there."

"A gladiator? Does the demise of that sort of trash really rate the time of a public official?"

"It does if he's been freed and is a citizen on the grain dole," I said.

"I suppose so. Well, let me accompany you, then. I've been meaning to make the acquaintance of Statilius for some time. After all, you and I will one day be aediles, in charge of the Games, and we'll need these contacts." He smiled and clapped me on the shoulder, as if we had been dear friends for life instead of virtual strangers.

The Statilian training school consisted of an open yard surrounded by barrack-buildings arranged in a square. There were three tiers of cells for the fighters, and the school maintained nearly a thousand at any one time. The Statilian family was devoted to the sports of the amphitheater, and the school was run so tightly that even during the slave rebellion of the three previous years, the school had remained open, supplying a steady stream of expert swordsmen for the public Games.

We stood for a while in the portico, enjoying the practice of the fighters in the yard, where the beginners fought the post and the more experienced fought each other with practice weapons. The veterans fenced with real swords. I have always been a devotee of the amphitheater and the Circus, and I had even taken some sword instruction myself at this school, before my military service. The Ludus Statilius stood where the Theatre of Pompey now stands, and it now comes back to me, after all these years, that we must have been standing that morning almost on the spot where Caius Julius died twenty-six years later.

The head trainer came to greet us, an immense man in a coat of bronze scales with a helmet the size of a vigile's bucket under his arm. His face and arms bore more scars than the back of a runaway slave. Obviously, a champion of years past.

"May I help you, my masters?" he asked, bowing courteously.

"I am Decius Caecilius of the Commission of Twenty-Six. I wish to speak to Lucius Statilius, if he is here." The trainer shouted for a slave to run and summon the master.

"You are Draco of the Samnite School, are you not?" Caesar said. The trainer nodded. I knew the name, of course, it had been famous for years, but I had never seen him without his helmet. "You had ninety-six victories when I left Rome ten years ago."

"One hundred twenty-five when I retired, master, and five *munera sine missione.*" Allow me to explain this term, which has fallen out of use. Before they were forbidden by law, *munera sine missione* were special Games in which as many as a hundred men fought until only one was left on his feet, sometimes fighting in sequence, sometimes all against all. This man had survived five such, besides his one hundred twenty-five single combats. This may help to explain why I prefer that such men be confined except when employed in their official public capacity. While we waited for Statilius, Draco and Julius chatted about the Games, with the swordsman predictably lamenting the sorry state to which the art of mortal combat had fallen since his day.

"In the old days," he said, smiting his chest with his fist and making the scales rattle, "we fought in full armor, and it was a contest of skill and endurance. Now they fight with the breast bared and the fights are over before they fairly begin. Soon, they will just push naked slaves out into the arena to kill one another with no training at all. There's no honor in that." It has been my observation that even the most degraded of men have some notion of honor which they cling to.

Statilius arrived, accompanied by a man in Greek dress who wore a fillet around his brow, plainly the school's resident physician. Statilius was a tall man, dressed in a decent toga. He introduced the physician, who rejoiced in the grandiose name of Asklepiodes. Briefly, I asked Statilius about Marcus Ager.

"You mean Sinistrus? Yes, he was here for a while. Just a third-rate daggerman. I sold him a couple of years ago to someone looking for a bodyguard. Let me consult my records." He hurried off to his office while Caesar and I conversed with the trainer and the physician.

The Greek studied my face for a moment and said: "I see you've been in battle against the Spaniards."

"Why, yes," I said, surprised. "How did you know?"

"That scar," he said, indicating a jagged line along the right side of my jaw. It's still there, and has plagued my barbers for the sixty years since I received it. "That scar was made by a Catalan javelin." The Greek folded his arms and waited to receive our awestruck applause.

"Is it true?" Julius asked. "When was that, Decius? Sertorius's rebellion?"

"Yes," I admitted. "I was a military tribune in the command of my uncle, Quintus Caecilius Metellus. If something hadn't attracted my attention and made me turn my head, that javelin would have gone right through my face. All right, Master Asklepiodes, how did you guess?"

"I did not guess," the Greek said smugly. "The marks are there to see, if one knows what they mean. The Catalan javelin has a serrated edge, and that scar was made by such an edge. It traveled at an upward angle. The Catalans fight on foot, and this gentleman is clearly of a rank worthy to go into battle on horseback. Furthermore, he is of the right age to have served as a junior officer in the campaigns of Generals Pompey and Metellus in Spain of a few years ago. Hence, the gentleman was wounded in Spain in recent years."

"What's this?" I said, vastly amused. "Some new form of sophistry?"

"I am compiling a work describing the infliction and treatment of every imaginable warlike injury. With my staff of surgeons, I have worked and studied in the ludi of Rome, Capua, Sicily and Cisalpine Gaul. I have learned more in this way in a few years than twenty years with the legions could have taught me."

"Most sagacious," Caesar said. "In the arena fights, you get to see the effects of many kinds of foreign weapons without having to take the time and trouble to visit all those places in time of war."

This discussion was interrupted by the return of Statilius. He held some scrolls and wax tablets and proceeded to display them to us.

"Here is what you want." He opened the tablets and unrolled the scrolls. There was the bill of sale, stating that Statilius had bought a healthy Gallic slave who had all his teeth and was about twenty-five years of age. His name was something unpronounceable and he had been given the slave-name Sinistrus. Another scroll held the man's school and amphitheater records. He had shown little aptitude for the sword and spear, and had been enrolled in the Thracian School as a dagger fighter. His record in the arena had been undistinguished except for his survival: a couple of wins, two adjudged ties and three defeats in which he fought well enough to be spared. He was wounded frequently.

One tablet was a record of a sale to the steward of one H. Ager. There was much official documentation to go with the transfer of ownership. I remembered that that had been a year of the slave rebellion, and the sales of slaves, especially males of military age, had been under severe restrictions. While I studied the documents, Caesar proceeded to ingratiate himself with Statilius, spoke of his future aedileship and asked for "something different" in the way of combats for the Games he intended to sponsor. Five years later, I was to witness this "something different," and it was to be the biggest sensation in the history of the Games.

"Here's where he got his freedman's name," I remarked. "With your permission, Lucius, I would like to keep these for a while, until my investigation is finished. This is a trivial business, so I should be able to return them by one of my freedmen in a few days."

"Please feel free," Statilius said. "Now that I won't be buying him back, I'd probably just destroy the records, except for the bill of sale, in any case."

We bade goodbye to Statilius and the Greek and retraced our steps toward the Forum, I to check the records at the Grain Office and Caius Julius to continue his politicking. It seemed that even this item of dull routine was to be interrupted. A Senate messenger was standing on the base of the rostra, scanning the passing throng. He must have had eagle eyes, for he spotted me almost as soon as I entered the Forum along the Via Capitolinus. He hopped to the pavement and ran up to me.

"Are you not Decius Caecilius Metellus of the Commission of Twenty-Six?"

"I am," I said resignedly. The arrival of such a messenger always portended some unpleasant task.

"In the name of the Senate and People of Rome, you are summoned to an extraordinary meeting of the Commission of Three in the Curia."

"No rest for one on the business of Senate and People," said Caius Julius. I took my leave of him and made my way the short distance to the Curia. With the Senate messenger preceding me, nobody sought to detain me for conversation.

I have always felt a certain awe for the Curia. Within its ancient brick walls had occurred the debates and the intrigues that had brought us victory over Greeks, Carthaginians, Numidians and a score of other enemies. From the sacred precincts had issued the decisions and orders that had changed Rome from a tiny village on the Tiber into the greatest power in the world that borders the inland sea. I am quite aware, naturally, that it is also a sewer of corruption and that the Senate has brought Rome to near-ruin at least as often as it has decided nobly and wisely, but I still prefer the old system to that currently, and I hope temporarily, prevailing.

The great Senate chamber was empty and echoing, unoccupied except for the bottom row of seats, where sat my two colleagues on the Commission of Three, and beside them Junius, the Senate freedman who acted as secretary. As always, Junius had stacks of wax tablets beside him and a bronze stylus tucked behind his ear.

"Where have you been?" asked Rutilius. He was Commissioner for the Trans-Tiber district, a cautious and conventional man. "We've been waiting since the second hour."

"I was sacrificing at the Temple of Jupiter and then conducting an investigation into a murder in my district. How was I to know an extraordinary meeting was called? What has happened that requires such prompt attention?"

"What murder?" asked Opimius. He was my other colleague, in charge of the Aventine, Palatine and Caelian districts. He was a supercilious little climber who came to a bad end several years later.

"Just some freed gladiator who was found strangled this morning. Why?"

"Forget the scum for the moment," Rutilius said.

"There is a matter demanding your immediate attention. You've heard about the fire down near the Circus last night?"

"Who talks of anything else this morning?" I said, annoyed. "We're Police, not Fire Control. What has the fire to do with us?"

"The fire started in a warehouse on the river. There is every appearance of arson present." Opimius spoke with the indignation which Romans reserve for fire-raisers. Treason is treated much more leniently. This was serious, indeed.

"Please go on," I said.

"The fire, of course, was in my district," Opimius continued, "but it seems that the owner of the warehouse lived in the Subura."

"Lived?" I said.

"Yes. A messenger sent to notify the man of the fire found him in his lodgings, dead. Stabbed."

"Peculiar, isn't it?" said Rutilius. "Junius, what was the fellow's name?"

Junius glanced at one of his tablets. "Paramedes. An Asian Greek from Antioch."

"Just a moment," I said, sensing a chance to shift the whole business to someone else. "If the man was a foreigner, this case properly belongs to the Praetor Peregrinus."

"There seem to be complications," Opimius stated, "that hint of a certain"—he made wavy gestures with his hands—"delicacy to the affair."

"It has been determined," Rutilius said, "that the investigation should be carried out at a lower level, with as little public disturbance as possible." It was plain that ours was not the first meeting to be held that day. Some very frantic conferences had been convened uncommonly early in the morning.

"And why all this intrigue?" I asked.

"There are international implications here," Rutilius explained. "This Paramedes, or whatever his name was, was not just the importer of wine and oil that he pretended to be. It seems that he also had contacts with the King of Pontus." That was indeed something to ponder. Old Mithridates was a thorn in the Roman side and had been for many years.

"I take it that the fellow's been under investigation for some time. Who's been in charge of the investigation? If I must handle this, I'll want to see all the records and documents that have been compiled on this man to date."

"Ah, well," Opimius said, and I feared the worst. "It seems, ah, that, since these matters touch on state security, those documents have been declared secret. They are to be put under Senate seal and deposited for safe-keeping in the Temple of Vesta."

"Are you serious?" I barked. "Am I really expected to conduct an investigation while important evidence is withheld from me?"

My colleagues found something of absorbing interest on the Curia ceiling and studied it intently. Obviously, there was only to be the form of an investigation, not its substance. State security! The meaning was clear: Senatorial reputations were at stake, and the most junior member of the elected government was being sent out to sweep the whole untidy mess into a dark room and close the door after it.

"We serve the Senate and People of Rome," Rutilius said, when I had calmed a bit.

"Exactly," I said. "All right, Junius, tell me whatever scraps of information I am permitted to know."

"The late Paramedes of Antioch," Junius droned, "was an importer of wine and olive oil and owned a large warehouse, now incinerated, on the Tiber, near the Circus."

"Wait," I interjected as he paused for breath. "If he was a foreigner, he couldn't have owned property in the city outright. Who was his citizen partner?"

"I was just coming to that," Junius sniffed. "As title holder for his city property, Paramedes had as partner one Sergius Paulus, freedman."

That was more like it. That man Junius so blithely dismissed as S. Paulus, freedman, was one of the four or five richest men in Rome at that time. Paulus, once a slave of an illustrious family, had risen to the position of steward while in servitude. Upon his master's death, he was willed his freedom and a generous sum of money. With this stake, he had put his freedman's expertise to work and made many shrewd investments, quickly multiplying his wealth. At this time, he owned so many farms, ships, shops and slaves that there was really no way to calculate his wealth, except that it was fairly certain that he was not quite as rich as General Marcus Licinius Crassus, who was as rich as a Pharaoh.

"What's a moneybags like Paulus doing in partnership with a petty Greek importer?" I wondered aloud.

"No opportunity for making money is too small for base cash-breeders like Sergius Paulus," Opimius said with contempt. No patrician, no plebeian noble, can match the snobbery of a jumped-up commoner like Opimius.

"I'll call on him this afternoon," I said. "Junius, be so good as to send a Senate messenger to the house of Paulus and tell him to expect me. Do you think I could pry a lictor loose to accompany me?" Nothing impresses a Roman with one's power and *gravitas* more than a lictor bearing the fasces. It is truly amazing how a simple bundle of rods tied about an ax can invest a simple mortal with the majesty and might of the Senate, the People of Rome and all the gods of the Pantheon.

"They're all assigned," Junius said. I shrugged. I'd just put on my new toga and hope for the best. The meeting broke up. Opimius was to get a full report on the fire, which was, of course, in his district. I was to look into the murder of Paramedes, which had occurred in my district, and call upon Sergius Paulus, who likewise lived in my district. Rutilius was going to flee back to the Trans-Tiber and hope that none of this would touch him.

I cursed piously as I left the Curia. I would loiter a few minutes to allow the messenger time to reach Sergius's house, then proceed there myself, stopping at my house on the way to change into my new toga. It would be a long trudge and I would have to forgo my customary bath and midday meal. It was not shaping up into a good day. There had been days when I had had to investigate ten murders before noon, but a hundred ordinary homicides were preferable to one which involved high personages.

There was also the little matter of my career, which could come to an abrupt and premature end should I mishandle this matter. So, I reflected, could my life.

II

The house of Sergius Paulus stood on a back street in the Subura, flanked by a pair of tremendous tenements. I was resplendent in my new toga, whitened with fuller's earth and only a little dirtied by my progress through Rome's unsanitary winter streets.

The janitor conducted me into the atrium and I studied the decorations while a slave ran to fetch the master. In contrast to the squalid streets outside, all within was rich and sumptuous. The mosaics were exquisite, the lamps were masterpieces of the bronze-worker's art, the walls were covered with frescoes superbly copied from Greek originals. All the stone in evidence was fine marble and the roof-beams smelled of cedar.

I had not expected this. While it is true that freedmen often possess great riches, they seldom have taste commensurate with their wealth. I speculated that Paulus had had the sense to buy a good Greek decorator, or perhaps he had a wellborn and educated wife.

Sergius himself arrived with commendable promptness. He was a portly man with a round, hospitable face. His tunic was of plain cut, but its material and dye probably cost more than my whole house and its contents and, probably, its occupants.

"Decius Caecilius Metellus, how honored I am to make your acquaintance!" He grasped my hand and his grip was firm despite the pudginess of his hand. His palm had never suffered manual labor or practice of arms. "You look starved. I know you must be here because of that terrible business this morning, but do let me offer you a bite of lunch before we get down to serious matters." I accepted gladly and he led me through his lavish peristyle and into the dining room. There was something instantly likable about the man.

I realize that this may sound strange coming from a member of the nobility, a class with a traditional contempt for the new-rich who have made their wealth from commerce and speculation, instead of decently through inheritance, but in this as in many another attitude, I have always differed from the general run of my class. My beloved Rome is made up of a multitude of human types, and I have never sought to banish any of them from my company on a basis other than personal behavior or poor character, or, sometimes, because I simply didn't like them.

Sergius's "bite of lunch" consisted of a banquet that would have done the Senate proud at the reception of a new ambassador. There were pickled peacocks' tongues and sows' udders stuffed with Libyan mice, deep-fried. There were lampreys, oysters, truffles and other rare, exotic delicacies in endless profusion. Whoever handled Sergius's interior decoration did not moderate his table. It was ostentatious and vulgar and utterly delicious. I did my noble best to do justice to the meal, but Sergius, a notable trencherman, surpassed me easily. Father would have been shocked. The wines were as lavish as the food, and by the end of the meal I was most unprofessionally jovial.

"Now," I began, "the matter touching which the Senate has sent me here to make inquiry about." I stopped abruptly and repeated the sentence mentally, to see whether it made any sense.

"I won't hear of it," Sergius protested. "I would be a poor host were I not to offer you a bath. After all, your business is detaining you from attending the public baths. It happens that I have a modest bath right here in the house. Would you care to join me?"

Nothing loath, I followed him to the rear of the house. A pair of sturdy slaves flanked each of us to prevent accidents. They seemed well-drilled in the art of getting master and guests from table to bath without unpleasantness. Bath attendants divested us of our clothing at the entrance of the bath. Predictably, Paulus's "modest bath" proved as much of an understatement as his "bite of lunch." Private baths were still rare in those days, but since they are now common I will not bore you with an account of its size and appointments, except to note that the bath attendants were all young Egyptian girls. Sergius was making up for his years as a slave in great style.

"Now, my friend Sergius Paulus," I said as we relaxed in the hot pool after a brief plunge in the cold one, "I really must get down to business. Serious business. Murder, sir, and arson, and a partner of yours who happens to be newly dead." Suddenly, one of the Egyptian girls was beside me in the water, naked as a fish and handing me a goblet of wine that gleamed with droplets of condensation. Sergius was flanked by two such, and I refrained from speculating about what their hands were doing under the water. I took a drink and forged ahead.

"Sergius, what have been your dealings with the man called Paramedes of Antioch?"

"On a personal level, almost none at all." Sergius leaned back and put his arms around the wet shoulders of his two attendants. Their hands were still beneath the water and he wore a blissful expression. "On a business level, he was just a foreigner who needed a city patron. He wanted to buy a warehouse to store his imports; oil and wine, I believe it was. I have a number of such foreign clients in the city. They pay me a percentage of their annual earnings. I don't believe I ever saw the man except on the day he came to me and we went before the Praetor Peregrinus to legalize the arrangement. That must have been about two years ago. Pity the fellow's dead, but Rome is a dangerous city, you know."

"I know better than most." One of the fetching little Egyptians took my half-empty cup and gave me a full one. I certainly couldn't fault the service.

"This business about arson at the warehouse, though,

that does disturb me, even though my quasi-ownership is purely a legal formality. Nasty business, arson. I hope you're able to apprehend the felon responsible and give him to the beasts in the amphitheater."

"Responsible for the arson, or for the murder?" I asked.

"Both. I should think the two were connected, shouldn't you?"

He was a shrewd man, and I obviously wasn't going to trick him with leading questions. We left the hot bath and the attendants oiled us, then scraped us clean with strigils, then back into the hot bath for a while, then to the massage tables. No wispy Egyptians at the tables, though. Instead, the masseurs were great strapping blacks with hands that could crush bricks.

"Do you know," I asked Sergius when I had breath again after the Nubian pounding, "whether Paramedes had an arrangement of *hospitium* with any Roman citizen?"

Paulus seemed to think for a while. "Not that I recall," he said at length. "If he'd had one, that family will be claiming the body for burial, as is customary. But then, if he had a *hospes* in the city, he wouldn't have needed to come to me for patronage, would he?" It was a good point. Another possible lead eliminated, then.

Sergius saw me to the door, with an arm across my shoulders. "Decius Caecilius, I am most happy that you have paid me this visit, even under such distressing circumstances. You must most certainly come visit me again, just for the pleasure of your company. I entertain often, and if I send you an invitation, I hope you will be good enough to attend."

"I should be more than honored, Sergius," I answered sincerely. Besides, my financial condition was such in those days that I could not afford to pass up such a meal as Sergius would undoubtedly provide.

"Although this was an official visit, it has become much more a social one, so allow me to bestow this parting guest-gift." He handed me something heavy discreetly wrapped in linen and I thanked him courteously as I stepped out onto the street.

I walked, somewhat unsteadily, toward the little Temple of Mercury at the end of the street. The priest hailed me from the top of the steps and for the next half hour I had to listen to his complaints about the shocking state of the temple, of its desperate need for repair and restoration. Such projects are usually undertaken by wealthy men rather than the state, and I suggested that he approach his well-fixed neighbor down the street. As I glanced that way, I noticed an elaborate palanquin had been set down before the street door of Sergius's house. As I watched, someone came from the house, heavily veiled, and climbed into the palanquin.

The slaves, a matched team of Numidians, closed the curtains and picked up the litter. By the time they passed the temple, they were moving at a smart trot, with the skillful broken step that makes for a comfortable ride. I watched closely, partly because I hoped someday to be able to afford such fine transportation myself, but also because I was curious about who might be leaving the house of Sergius Paulus thus clandestinely. I was able to make out little except that the palanquin was embroidered in the Parthian fashion, with silk thread. Very costly.

Like any other citizen, I made my way home on my own sore feet. There, I changed from my new toga into the one I had begun the day with and unwrapped the guest-gift. It was a cup of massive, solid silver, richly worked. I pondered it for a while. Was it a bribe? If so, what was I being bribed for? I locked the cup away in a chest. My day was not over yet. I still had to view the body and effects of Paramedes.

Mercifully, the house occupied by the late Paramedes was not far from my own. Truthfully, Rome is not a very large city compared with others such as Alexandria and Antioch. Its population is large, but stacked in layers in the towering *insulae*, which makes for efficient use of space at some considerable sacrifice of comfort, beauty and, above all, safety.

Paramedes's house was the ground floor of a tenement, quite decently appointed. Usually, in such houses the running water reaches no higher than the first floor, so that the wealthy occupy the desirable ground-floor apartments, the artisans live on the second and third levels, and the poor eke out their miserable lives crowded into tiny rooms beneath the eaves.

The door was guarded by a hired watchman, who stepped aside for me when I displayed my Senate seal. The house was like a thousand others in Rome. It seemed that the man had owned no slaves, and there was little in the way of housekeeping equipment present beyond a few jugs and plates. Any papers the man had had were already taken. The body was sprawled in the bedroom, as if he had been awakened by a sound from the front of the house, had gone to the bedroom door to investigate and had been met by the assassin's dagger. There was a gaping rent slanting from the breastbone to the side, and the floor was awash with blood. Something about the wound seemed peculiar, although I knew I must have observed hundreds of such injuries in war, in the arena and in the Roman streets.

I turned my attention to the little pile of personal effects that had been left on a table. There was an old dagger, not very sharp. A statuette of Venus and one of Priapus; a set of dice, loaded; and an amulet of cast bronze shaped like a camel's head. The reverse side of the amulet had lettering engraved in the bronze, but the light had grown too dim to make it out. I swept the items into my napkin and tied them up.

I informed the watchman that I was taking the effects into my keeping for the nonce. He said that the undertaker's men would come for the body after sunset the next day. If nobody claimed the corpse within the customary three days, it would be buried at state expense in the common burial-ground, along with the corpses of slaves and of other foreigners without patrons. These mass burial pits, which made the whole city redolent in summer, occupied the ground now covered by the beautiful gardens of Maecenas. This is one improvement of the old city of which I have always thoroughly approved.

On the way home, it struck me that I had neglected my obligations in not scavenging some scraps of Sergius's sumptuous meal for my slaves. That was what I should have been carrying in my napkin instead of the possessions of the unfortunate Paramedes. I considered stopping at a wineshop and buying some sausages and cakes, but the shutters were already closed for the night wherever I looked. I shrugged and continued on my way. They would just have to be content with kitchen fare. The good cheer of the afternoon was fading and my head was beginning to throb.

Cato, my janitor, opened the gate at my knock. He shook his head in disapproval of my behavior. Cato had been a gift from my father when I set up house in the Subura. He and his equally aged wife, Cassandra, did what modest housekeeping I required. Needless to say, both had been adjudged too old and feeble to be of use in Father's household.

Cassandra brought me a dish of fish and wheat porridge, supposedly a sure guardian against the chill of winter, along with heated wine, heavily watered. After the luxurious delicacies of Sergius's table, it was plain fare indeed. But I felt the better for having downed the mess, and quickly collapsed into bed, still in my tunic, and fell asleep.

It was perhaps two hours before dawn when I awoke to find someone in the room with me. It was black as Pluto's privy, of course, but I could hear scuffling and the sound of breathing.

"Cato?" I said, not quite awake. "Is that—" A dazzling white light flashed inside my head. When next I was aware of the outside world, it was to hear Cato reproving me.

"This is what comes of moving from your father's fine mansion to this Subura crib," he was saying, nodding in agreement with himself. "Thieves and housebreakers all over. Maybe now you'll listen to old Cato and move back ..." He went on in this vein for some time.

I was unable to dispute with him because my head was swimming and my stomach heaving. It was not the effect of my excesses of the day before; I had been soundly bashed on the head by the intruder.

"You are lucky to be alive, master." This was Cassandra's voice. "You owe a cock to Aesculapius for your escape. We must wait till full light to find out what's been stolen." She was ever a practical soul. That was a question much on my own mind.

Before I could investigate the matter, though, there was still the tiresome routine of the morning report of the vigiles, and my clients' morning call. All were properly shocked and speculated upon the new depths to which the city had fallen. I am not sure why anyone should have been shocked that my house was broken into, since the crime was so common in the Subura, but all men are baffled when the prominent are victimized along with the poor.

When the light was sufficient, I went through my bedroom to see what was missing. It had already been determined that the intruder had been in no other part of the house. I first unlocked the safe-chest and made sure that everything was there, including Sergius's silver cup. There was little about that might tempt a thief, and nothing seemed to have been disturbed.

Then I noticed the little pile of personal effects left behind by Paramedes of Antioch prior to his journey to the Styx. Most of the items still lay on my unfolded napkin, resting on a bedside table. They were in some disarray, and the little figurine of Venus lay on the floor. I gathered the items together and at first thought that they were all present. Then I remembered that there had been an amulet of some sort. That was it, an amulet in the shape of a camel's head, flat on the reverse side, with lettering. It was gone.

That the thing should be missing was mystery enough,

but what manner of cat-eyed thief could unerringly find so small an item in such utter blackness? Sorcery came immediately to mind, but I dismissed it. Supernatural explanations are a crutch for those who won't take the trouble to puzzle out a logical answer.

Despite my ringing head I attended my father's rising; then we all went to the house of Hortensius Hortalus, since it was a day when official business was forbidden. Hortalus was a large man with a profile of immense dignity. He always seemed to be regarding something to one side of him, so as to present the world with his most gratifying aspect.

When Father presented me, Hortalus clasped my hand with power and sincerity, just as he would have the hand of a street sweeper whose vote he wanted.

"I have just heard about your narrow escape from death, young Decius. Shocking, utterly shocking!"

"Not all that great a matter, sir," I said. "Just a break-in by some—"

"How terrible," Hortalus went on, "should Rome lose her young statesmen through her lamentable lack of civic order." Hortalus was a mealymouthed old political whore who was responsible for at least as much of the city's violence as any of the gang leaders. "But, to lighter things. Today I sponsor a day of races, in honor of my ancestors. I would be honored if you and your clients would attend me in my box at the Circus." At this, my spirits rose considerably. As I have said, I am passionately fond of the Circus and the amphitheater. And Hortalus, for all his bad qualities, owned the finest box in the Circus: on the lowest tier, right above the finish line. "You Caecilii are supporters of the Reds, are you not?"

"Since the founding of the races," my father said.

"We Hortensii are Whites, of course, but both are better than those upstart Blues and Greens, eh?" The two self-styled old Romans chuckled away. The Blues and Greens in those days were the factions of the common men, although their stables were greater than those of the Reds and Whites, and their charioteers better and more numerous. It was a notable sign of the changing times that a rising young politician like Caius Julius Caesar, of an ancient patrician family which traditionally supported the Whites, ostentatiously favored the Greens whenever he appeared in the Circus.

A slave passed out vine wreaths for us, somewhat brown and wilted at this season, and we all trooped gaily to the Circus. All thoughts of official business were forgotten for the moment, with the prospect of a day's racing ahead of us. The whole city was flocking toward the flats by the Tiber where the wooden upper tiers of the Circus reared against the sky.

The carnival atmosphere lightened the dismal season, and the open plaza around the Circus was transformed for the day into a minor Forum with traders, tumblers and whores competing for the coins of the audience, turning the air blue with raucous shouts and songs. It is at such times, I think, that Rome turns from being mistress of the world and reverts to her true character as an Italian farm town in which the folk have left their plows for the day.

Father and I were honored by being seated next to Hortalus, while our lower-ranking clients took the lesser seats higher in the box. Even those seats were better than any others in the vast stadium, and I saw my soldier, freedman and farmer preening themselves, the envy of all eyes, trying to act as if these privileged seats were their customary lot.

To keep the people entertained and in good humor while the first race was being readied, some swordsmen were going through their paces with wooden weapons. Those of us who were fond of gladiatorial exhibits, which is to say nine tenths of the spectators, took a keen interest in this mock fighting, for these men were to fight in the next big Games. Throughout the stands, handicappers wrote furiously in their wax tablets.

"Do you favor the Big Shields or the Small Shields, young Decius?" Hortalus asked.

"Give me a Small Shield every time," I said. Since boyhood, I had been a keen supporter of the men who fought with the little buckler and the short, curved sword or the dagger.

"I prefer the Big Shield and the straight sword, the Samnite School," Hortalus said. "Old soldier and all that. Those were the arms we fought with." Indeed, Hortalus had distinguished himself as a soldier in his younger days, when some patricians still fought in the ranks on foot. He pointed to a big man with a shield such as the legionaries bear, which covered him from chin to knee. "That's Mucius, a Samnite with thirty-seven victories. Next week he fights Bato. I'll put a hundred sesterces on Mucius."

I looked about until I saw Bato. He was a rising young fighter of the Thracian School and was fencing with his little square shield and short, curved practice-sword. I could see no signs of injury or other infirmity. "Bato has only fifteen victories to his credit," I said. "What odds?"

"Two to one if the Thracian fights with the sword," Hortalus said, "and three to two if he uses the spear." The small Thracian shield gives a man more freedom to maneuver a spear than does the big scutum of the legions.

"Done," I said, "If Bato wears thigh armor. If he wears only the greaves, in a fight with swords, then I want five to three in his favor. If he uses the spear, the bet stands as you've made it."

"Done," Hortalus said. This was a fairly simple bet. I've known real devotees of the fights to argue for hours over such fine points as whether their man wore simple padding for his sword arm, or bronze plate, or ring armor, or scale, or mail, or leather, or fought with the arm bare. They would quibble over the exact length and shape of sword or shield. The superstitious would shave points over such matters as the colors of his plumes, or whether he wore a Greek-style crest in a quarter-circle, a square Samnite crest or paired feather tubes in the old Italian style.

There was a flourish of trumpets and the gladiators trotted from the arena. Their places were taken by the charioteers, who made their way around the *spina* in a solemn circuit while the priests sacrificed a goat in the tiny temple atop the *spina* and examined its entrails for signs that the gods didn't want races that day.

The priests signaled that all was propitious and Hortalus stood, to tremendous applause. He intoned the ritual opening sentences, and it was a joy to hear him. Hortalus had the most beautiful speaking voice I ever heard. Cicero on his best day couldn't match him.

He dropped the white handkerchief into the arena, the rope barrier fell, the horses surged forward and the first race was on. The charioteers dashed around the *spina* with their customary recklessness for the seven circuits. I believe a Green was victor in that first race. They showed equal elan for the rest of the twelve races that made up a regular race-day at that time. There were some spectacular crashes, although there were no deaths, for a change. The Reds won heavily that day, so my financial condition was bettered at the expense of Hortalus and his fellow Whites. Hortalus took his losses in good part, making me instantly suspicious.

As we left the Circus, I saw the troop of gladiators marching in formation back to the Statilian school. Accompanying them was the Greek physician, Asklepiodes. I excused myself from my party after promising to attend dinner at Hortalus's house that evening. I crossed the plaza, which was still heavily redolent of the previous day's fire, and stopped the Greek, who greeted me courteously.

"Master Asklepiodes," I said, "your skill at reading wounds has been much on my mind of late. I am investigating a murder, and something about the death-wound bothers me. Lacking your skill, I can't decide what it is that is so singular."

"A murder?" said Asklepiodes, intrigued. "I have never heard before of a physician being consulted on a police matter. But then, why not?"

"You understand," I went on, "I can't ask this of you officially, because today is a holiday. However, you must view the body before it is taken away for burial this evening."

"In that case, young master, consider my expertise to be at your service." I led him through the dismal streets to the house of Paramedes, where I had to bribe the guard to let us in. Since I could not be on official business that day, he did not have to admit me. Petty power is a truly pernicious thing.

Due to the chilly weather, the smell was not overpowering and the body had not bloated. The stiffening had worn off and Paramedes looked almost freshly killed, except for the blackened blood. Asklepiodes examined the corpse quickly, pulling back the edges of the wound to look inside. When he was finished, he straightened and gave me his analysis.

"Knife wound, from right hipbone almost to the sternum. Done with a *sica*."

"Why necessarily a *sica*?" I asked.

"The curvature of a *sica* blade keeps the point from piercing the inner organs. The wounds on this man's organs are clean cuts, with none of the ripping characteristic of the straight-bladed *pugio*. Also, only a man of extraordinary strength could drag a straight blade upward through a body like that, while the curved *sica* blade makes such carving easy." He though a moment. "Also, this blow was delivered by a left-handed man."

Of course. That was what had bothered me about the wound. Nine out of ten wounds one sees are on the left side when delivered from in front by a right-handed assailant. An armorer had once told me that helmets are always made thicker on the left side for that very reason.

We left the importer's house and strolled toward the Forum. We passed through a small side-market and there I bought a gift for Asklepiodes: a hair-fillet made of plaited silver wire. He thanked me profusely and begged me to call on his services at any time I thought he might aid my investigations. I would have to see whether I could get Junius to reimburse me for the fillet out of the Senate's semiofficial bribe fund. He was sure to refuse, the officious little Greekling.

I stopped at a favorite wineshop and sat at a bench sipping warmed Falernian and studying the murals of Games twenty years past while many facts sorted themselves out and many disturbing associations raised ugly questions. I knew that my wisest course would be to turn in the mere form of an investigation. Tomorrow, I should report that Paramedes had been killed during a botched robbery, that the arson at his warehouse was a coincidence, probably ordered by a jealous competitor. (The Senate is made up primarily of landowners, always willing to attribute the basest motives to businessmen.) I could leave it at that. Marcus Ager need not come into it. The break-in at my house need not come into it.

I make no claim to be more honest than other men. I have not always observed the very letter of the law. There may have been times when a generous gift has swayed my judgment on some trifling matter. But this was a matter of murder and arson within the city. My city. And there was a likelihood of collusion with an enemy of Rome. This went far beyond ordinary, petty corruption.

I had certain standards to live up to. The Caecilii Metelli have been servants of the state since Rome was no more than a village. Members of our family were Consuls at a time when few but patricians ever held that office. The first Plebeian Censor was a Caecilius Metellus. Metellans were generals in our wars with Macedon, Numidia, Carthage.

These were evil times, the previous years having been marred by civil wars, insurrections, rebellions of provincial governors, the actions of self-seeking generals, even a massive slave rebellion. There had been proscription lists, dictatorships, the unprecedented seven Consulships of Gaius Marius. Within my own lifetime soldiers had actually fought within the city, and there had been bloodshed within the sacred precincts of the Curia.

Yes, they were evil times, but in my long lifetime I have come to see that the times have always been evil, and the idyllic old days of nobility and virtue never really occurred, but are only the fantasies of poets and moralists. Many men involved in the politics of my younger days used this supposedly unique depravity of the times to excuse unconscionable behavior, but I could not.

Very well, if there was little virtue to be found in public life, there was still duty. I was a Caecilius Metellus, and no member of that family had ever betrayed Rome. As long as there was even the appearance of a danger to the city, I would pursue this case to its very depths and bring the guilty parties to justice.

I sat back feeling greatly relieved, now that the decision had been made. Even the wine tasted better. So what did I have?

Paramedes had been murdered. Paramedes had been the owner of a warehouse which had burned down on the night of his murder. The fire had been a result of arson. He had been in partnership with one of Rome's wealthiest men. He was rumored (ah, those evasive rumors!) to have connections with the King of Pontus. At the highest levels of the Senate there was concern, a virtual panic, about this case. Important information concerning the doings of Paramedes had been seized and sequestered in the Temple of Vesta.

Marcus Ager, formerly known as Sinistrus, had been murdered on the same night. Paramedes had been killed with a *sica*. There was nothing unusual in that. The *sica* is the favored weapon of the common street-killers. Its curved blade makes it easy to wear concealed in a sheath beneath the armpit. It is so common among cutthroats that it is considered infamous, and soldiers will only use the straight-bladed *pugio*, an honorable weapon.

The *sica* is also the weapon of the Thracian gladiators.

Marcus Ager had been a Thracian daggerman. Paramedes had been killed by a left-handed man. Marcus Ager had fought under the name Sinistrus. And Sinistrus, of course, means left-handed.

III

The next morning, after my routine duties were taken care of, I went to examine the site of the fire. The ruins of the warehouse formerly owned by Paramedes stood on a piece of riverside property with docking facilities on the bank. These were always desirable properties, since barges coming up from Ostia could make their deliveries directly instead of having the goods off-loaded and hauled by wagon or porter to their destination. So valuable, in fact, that now, two days after the fire, the ruins were being cleared away and new construction was beginning.

Heat from the burning oil had been such that the warehouse had burned right down to its foundations and the wharf had been destroyed. Luckily, the wind that night had blown most of the sparks out onto the river, and the blaze had been confined to the warehouse. Gangs of slaves were employed in clearing away the wreckage while surveyors took sightings with their instruments to lay out the foundations of a new building. I made a mental note to look into the question of ownership.

A brief inquiry among the idlers lounging about to watch the work in progress elicited a few facts: Some men had been seen to rush into the warehouse in the early morning hours (there are always sleepless persons who observe such things), there had been crashing sounds from inside and shortly thereafter the structure had burst into flames. For all its fearsome aspect, arson was only slightly less common than a head cold in Rome. Vigiles could do little more than douse the odd kitchen-fire or lamp flare-up. The fabled General Crassus had built a good part of his fortune with his private fire-fighting squad. They would rush to the site of a fire, fight off other fire fighters, and Crassus would make the owner an offer for the still-burning property. The unfortunate owner would naturally accept any offer and then Crassus would send in his men to put out the fire while his new property was still salvageable. It was rumored (ah, those rumors!) that other employees set the fires for him. He was always first at the site, at any rate. Scandalous, and highly profitable.

Perhaps it was a sign of the times that such behavior did not prevent Crassus from being elected Consul for that year. As a balance, his colleague as Consul was Pompey, his rival general. Ruling on alternate days, the two neatly canceled each other's effect, which suited everybody, and it meant that they would both be out of Rome for an extended period when their year in office was over. That was better yet.

However, just then my business was not with such high personages. Now I had to go see someone nearly as influential, but not quite so respectable. This was a matter calling for extreme circumspection. I went to question Macro.

Macro controlled the most powerful gang in Rome at that time. He was the terror of the whole city, and relatively immune from prosecution because of his political connections. He was a supporter of the *Optimates* and a particular client of Quintus Hortensius Hortalus. He was not, as one might infer, the sort of client who called upon the great man every morning. Macro's clientage made Hortalus's elections a foregone conclusion.

Macro's house was a minor fortress in the Subura surrounded by tenements owned by Macro and his cronies. It fronted on a narrow street lined with wineshops and fishmongers' stalls. A nearby *liquamen* factory added the pungency of its product to the general reek of the neighborhood. The street entrance of the house was flanked by a pair of louts with the telltale bulges of *sica* handles showing beneath their arms.

I had to demand the presence of Macro himself before the daggermen would let me in. After a considerable period of bickering during which my official dignity suffered mightily at their insolence, Macro finally arrived. He took one look and began to bark: "Don't you fools know a Commissioner when you see one? Let the gentleman in!" With ill grace, the thugs admitted me.

"I must apologize for those two," Macro said. "You understand, it's hard to get good boys these days. Not like in the old days." Everybody was lamenting the decadence of the times.

"Those two arena-cheaters had better not appear before me in court," I remarked affably. "The Sicilian sulfur mines are shockingly understaffed, I hear."

"Probably a good place for them," he said. Macro was about forty-five years old, big and bald-headed and covered with more scars than I ever saw on a man who wasn't an old veteran of the legions or the arena. We had had dealings in the past. His connections protected him and my office protected me, so we could talk easily.

"I trust your father is well," he said.

"Perfectly," I answered. "I understand that your man Aemilius will be up before him just after the Nones."

We came to the peristylium, open to the blue sky, where incense burned continuously to combat the smells from outside. We reclined at a table and a slave brought wine and sweetmeats. The wine was Caecuban. Macro could afford the best.

"I'd been meaning to look you up on that matter," Macro said. "A good word from the right quarter might keep the boy out of the ludus." I had been hoping to hear that. I needed a bargaining point. I said nothing. "Much as we always enjoy each other's company," Macro went on, "I presume this is more than a social visit."

"As a matter of fact, I am investigating a number of matters in which you might be able to assist me."

"I am always at the service of Senate and People."

"And very grateful we all are," I said. "What might you know concerning a fire at the warehouse belonging to one Paramedes of Antioch?"

Macro spread his hands and shrugged. "Just another fire, as far as I know."

"And the murder of Paramedes?"

"He was murdered?"

"And the murder of one Marcus Ager, once known as Sinistrus?"

"Marcus who?"

"Enough of this!" I snapped. "Nobody cuts a purse or a throat in this district without your knowledge. I'm not after you, I just want to clear up some matters that fall within my jurisdiction. If you can help me, do so. If not, then I may not be able to help you with young Aemilius."

Macro brooded in his winecup for a minute. "All I can tell you, Decius Caecilius, is that these are matters I would prefer not to be associated with." This was disturbing news, indeed. For a matter to be so foul that Macro wanted nothing to do with it portended something truly awesome.

"However," he continued, "I shall make inquiries. Anything I can find I shall put at your disposal. If," he amended hastily, "I can do so safely."

That was better than nothing. "I would like to have the information as soon as possible," I said. "It isn't long until the Nones."

"We all depend upon political favor, Decius Caecilius. I shall do for you what I can without endangering mine. I want to save Aemilius, he's my sister's boy, but neither for him nor for you can I commit suicide."

"No need to," I assured him. "Do me this favor: Sinistrus was bought from the Ludus of Statilius Taurus by someone who identified himself as the steward of someone named H. Ager. The slave rebellion was in full swing two years ago, so if someone bought this slave under false pretenses, one of your colleagues must have had a hand in it. Find out who bought him and send me the name, as secretly as you like. I'll try to prevail on my father to go easy on your nephew."

"I shall have the name by this time tomorrow," Macro said.

"Oh, one more thing." I told him of the break-in at my house.

He thought it over for a while. "I have heard nothing of this. Why anyone should want a bronze amulet I cannot imagine, unless it had some magical power. As for the thief—how did he come in? Over the roof and into the peristylium?"

"So I suspect. There was no forcing of doors or windows."

"A lightweight, then, to come in over rooftiles without making noise. That would go with the eyesight, too. Few can see so well in the dark past the age of fifteen. I think your intruder was probably a young boy."

I massaged my scalp, wincing. "He hit hard, for a child."

Macro nodded. "We learn to hit very hard, very young, in this part of Rome."

An hour later, I was on the Campus Martius. Except for walking about the city, I had not exercised for weeks. I have never made a cult of physical activity, but dining with the likes of Sergius Paulus and Hortensius Hortalus made me feel like a fat Oriental potentate. Someone like, now that I thought of it, Mithridates of Pontus.

At the side of the field, near the shrine of Pollentia where the running-track began, I paid an urchin a quadrans to watch my toga and sandals. Stripped to my tunic, I started to run. Before I had gone a quarter-circuit I new how out of practice I was, and made one of my customary vows to go there every day and run for an hour until I had worn away the effects of soft living. Running is marvelously effective for ordering one's thoughts, though, and since some god had seen fit to put Mithridates in my mind, I reviewed what I knew of him. There was always some rogue of that name troubling the eastern world, kings of Parthia or Pontus. The one giving

us so much trouble that year was the King of Pontus, the
sixth Pontine king of that name. He was something of a
marvel, because he had been no more than eleven years
old when he inherited the throne from his father (Mithridates V, naturally), had been a prize troublemaker for
every minute of his reign and was still alive at sixty. Romans of his disposition seldom survived for a decade.

While still of tender years he had clapped his mother
in prison for trying to seize power, then eliminated his
brother (another Mithridates, too inconsequential to rate
a number). Over the next half-century he had repeatedly
invaded, often successfully, the small but rich kingdoms
that make up that part of the world. This brought him
into conflict with Rome, since we had possessions in his
path, and alliances with some of his rival kings. He tried
to expel all Romans from Asia, but was defeated by Sulla
and Fimbria. Some years later our General Licinius Mu-
rena took it into his head to invade Pontus and was
soundly drubbed for his pains. There was a spell of
peace, then the Consul Aurelius Cotta tried his luck and
was beaten. Most recently, Lucius Licinius Lucullus was
having a go at Mithridates, and enjoying some success.
If Mithridates had a philosophy, it seemed to be that any
enemy he could not defeat in battle he would outlive.

He was said to be a huge man, a champion with all
weapons, the fastest foot-racer in the world, a superb
horseman, a poet and more. It was said that he could
speak twenty-two languages and that he could outeat,
outdrink and outfornicate any ordinary human being.
But then, it is always the Roman tendency to ascribe he-
roic qualities to someone who has repeatedly bested us.
We did the same, briefly, for Hannibal, Jugurtha and
even Spartacus. It would be too humiliating to admit
that our most successful foe was probably some disgust-
ing little Asiatic hunchback with a squint and a hanging
lower lip.

Puffing and sweating, I went to the javelin range and
took a weapon from the rack. Casting the javelin was the
only martial exercise in which I excelled, and it be-

hooved me to be good at something, since service with the legions was a requirement for anyone running for office.

Standing at the stone marker, I cast at the nearest target. The javelin spun properly, arched upward prettily and plunged downward, skewering the target dead center. I worked my way out to more distant targets, trotting out onto the field from time to time to gather up my javelins. After one such trip, I glanced up to admire the full splendor of the Temple of Jupiter on the Capitoline, looming above the ominous crag of the Tarpeian Rock. It was then that I noticed someone was watching me.

Below the temple, below the rock, below the tumbling vista of tenements and palaces, right at the edge of the field, stood a veiled lady, attended by a serving-girl. The day was cloudy, but the lady wore a wide hat of plaited straw. She was being careful of her complexion or her identity or both. Since she stood near the javelin-rack, I would have to approach her, a not-unpleasant prospect except for my disheveled and sweaty condition.

"Good day, my lady," I said as I began to replace the javelins. Except for a few runners around the periphery of the field, the Campus Martius was almost deserted. It was always thronged in the spring.

"Greeting," she said formally. "I was admiring your skill. So few wellborn men bother with martial exercise anymore, it is good to see someone keeping up the tradition."

Were I a vain man, I would have been flattered to know that she could discern my innate nobility even though I was dressed in my tunic with no mark of rank. However, even in my young and innocent days I was not stupid.

"Have we met, my lady? I confess, your veils defeat me."

She swept the veil aside, smiling. Her face was definitely that of a highborn Roman lady, with the slightly tilted eyes that spoke of Etruscan ancestry. The tilted eyes bore the only cosmetics she used. Indeed, she needed none. She was, I think, the most beautiful woman I had ever seen. So she seemed to me that day, anyway.

"We have, Decius Caecilius." She continued to smile, provocatively.

I took up the game. "But surely I would remember. You are not the sort of lady I forget easily."

"And yet I was quite taken with you at the time. It was at the house of your kinsman, Quintus Caecilius Metellus Celer, at the time of my betrothal."

"Claudia!" I said. "You must forgive me. You were only twelve then, and not half so beautiful as you are now." I tried to remember what year that had been. She had to be nineteen or twenty by now. There was some speculation within the family as to why the marriage had not yet taken place.

"You haven't changed. But then, you have. That was before you left for Spain, and you've acquired a scar since then. It's very becoming."

"There are others," I told her, "but not so dignified." I noticed that the serving-girl was studying me coolly, without the downcast-eyed modesty expected of domestic slaves. She was a wiry creature of about sixteen, and I thought she looked more like an acrobat than a lady's maid.

"You intrigue me," Claudia said.

"Wonderful. No one has ever called me intriguing before. I assure you, there is nobody I would rather intrigue." Smitten young men speak like that.

"Yes, it intrigues me that you would rather serve Rome through the plodding routine of office instead of dashing military glory." I couldn't tell whether her tone was gently mocking or seriously mocking.

"Plodding but relatively safe. Military shortcuts to power and authority shorten one's life."

"But nothing is safe in Rome these days," she said, quite seriously. "And our illustrious Consul Pompey has done rather well out of his military adventures."

"Spared himself some of the drudgery of office, at any rate," I agreed. Early in his precocious career, the boy-

wonder general had secured consular command of an
army without having served even as a quaestor. He was
now Consul at the age of thirty-six. He and his partner,
Crassus, had secured election to the Consulate by the
simple expedient of encamping their legions within sight
of the city walls.

"Well, you may be odd in these times, but I think it's
admirable. I was on my way home from the Capitol when
I saw you practicing here. I decided to come over and
extend an invitation."

"An invitation?" I seemed to be attracting a lot of those
lately.

"This evening my brother and I host a banquet in
honor of a visitor. Will you pay us the honor of attending?"

"I am flattered. Of course I'll come. Who is the guest?"

"A foreign nobleman, a *hospes* of my brother's. I'm not
supposed to noise his name about, because he's supposed to have enemies here in the city. Claudius made
me promise not to tell. You'll meet him tonight."

"I'll look forward to meeting this mysterious traveler,"
I said, not greatly caring. Foreign potentates were common in Rome, and one more unpronounceable name
failed to pique my interest. I would, however, be happy
to put up with some boring Egyptian or Numidian in
order to see Claudia again.

"This evening, then," she said, resuming her veil. The
slave girl studied me solemnly until her mistress said,
"Come, Chrysis."

I decided that I had time to go to the public baths,
then home to change clothes before the banquet, where
I would arrive fashionably late.

I went to one of my favorite establishments, a small
bathhouse near the Forum that boasted no palaestra or
lecture halls and therefore was mercifully free of grunt-
ing wrestlers and droning philosophers. It provided towels and oils and its *caldarium* was a good place to stew in
hot water and ponder.

I was still astonished that Claudia had grown into such

a beautiful woman. I had heard her spoken of, naturally. She was fast building a reputation as a scandalous young lady, but in those days a woman could be scandalous just by speaking her mind in public. She had done nothing really reprehensible so far.

The Claudians were a strange and difficult family, one of the oldest patrician gens, Sabine in origin but with a strong infusion of Etruscan blood. This Etruscan element was credited for that family's occasional forays into mysticism and odd religions. The family's history was sprinkled with famous patriots and notorious traitors. One Claudian had built the fine road to Capua and then named it for himself. Another had drowned the sacred chickens and in consequence lost a sea battle with the Carthaginians. They were fairly typical of the breed. However, at this time I had just one Claudian on my mind.

Bathed, shaved, freshly dressed and perfumed, I presented myself to the janitor at the town house of Publius Claudius Pulcher, a fine structure that had once belonged to a wealthy Senator who had been executed during the Sullan proscriptions. Publius himself greeted me in the peristylium. He was a handsome young man of stocky build and he welcomed me warmly.

Publius was known as a headstrong, violent youth, soon to live up to the worst of his family's reputation. But that was the future, and on this evening I was interested only in his sister. The guests included a number of the rising young men of the time. Caius Julius was there, never one to pass up a free meal and a chance to establish powerful contacts. The formidable Cicero was there as well, fresh from his celebrated prosecution of Verres. He was one of the "new men," that is to say, men of non-Roman birth who were beginning to come to prominence at that time, as the old Roman families died out through civil war or lack of interest in procreation.

There was also a plump-faced young man whose beard was trimmed in the Greek fashion and who wore Greek clothing. This, I decided, had to be the mysterious guest.

Ever since Alexander squashed them under his heel, all the Asiatics want to be imitation Greeks. I lost interest in him when Claudia entered.

I took a cup from a passing slave and was about to monopolize Claudia when another of the guests made it plain that he wanted to speak with me. I groaned inwardly. It was Quintus Curius, an extraordinarily dissipated young Senator, a man to whom virtually every crime short of treason had been imputed. He was to add that one before his short career was done. We went through the customary greetings.

"Odd gathering here, isn't it?" he said. With him there, I could not but agree. "That Cicero, for instance. How does an odious little nobody like that come out of nowhere to Rome and make a name for himself in public life?"

"Actually," I said, "he's from Arpinum."

Curius shrugged. "Arpinum is nowhere. Caius Julius, of course, he's a comer, and almost respectable. Lucius Sergius Catilina, that's a man to keep your eye on. And this Greekling, now. Who do you think he might be?"

It was my turn to shrug. "Eastern princes with Greek tutors are no rarity. Someone young Claudius took hospitality with in his travels, I presume." Gratefully, I saw that Claudia was coming to my rescue.

"Curius, I must borrow Decius for a while," she said, taking my arm. When we were safely away, she said, "When I saw you standing there looking so distressed, I just had to do something. Isn't he a horrid bore? I don't know why my brother invited him."

"He doesn't entirely approve of your guest list," I told her. "Cicero, for instance."

"Oh, I rather like Cicero. He's a brilliant man and afraid of nothing. Married to the most abominable woman, though."

"So I've heard," I said. "I've not had the pleasure of the lady's acquaintance."

"We should all be so lucky. Now you must meet our guest of honor." The young Asiatic turned at our approach. "Decius Caecilius Metellus, I present Tigranes, Prince of Armenia." So that was it.

"The son of the magnificent King of Armenia does Rome great honor by his presence here."

"I am dazzled to be in your wondrous city," he said with a perfect Greek accent. He could not have been terribly dazzled by Rome, coming from his father's fabulous new royal city, Tigranocerta. But perhaps it was power that dazzled him rather than beauty.

"I only wish," he continued, "that I could make my visit more public. The state of relations between us, alas, is not the best." He had reason to be discreet about his presence. Rome was very nearly at war with Armenia. "However, rest assured that, unlike my father, I am a firm friend of Rome." And running for your life from the old man's wrath, I thought.

"Rome's admiration for the ancient kingdom of Armenia is unbounded," I assured him. "Envy" might have been a better word. Old Tigranes in those days was King of Kings, a title originally held, I believe, by the King of Persia. Since then, the title was held by the Oriental tyrant who had the most subject-kings licking his sandals. Tigranes the Elder was unthinkably wealthy, and every one of our generals was itching to have a go at him. The sack of Tigranocerta was certain to net the richest haul since we took Corinth. Every legionary would be able to retire to a villa in the country with a hundred slaves.

"My generous friend Publius Claudius and his gracious sister have most kindly extended their hospitality to me for the duration of my stay here in the capital of the world."

"And you could not be in better hands, I assure you." It seemed to me that he looked at Claudia with more than mere admiration.

"So I believe," he said. "The Lady Claudia is, I believe, the most remarkable woman I have ever met."

Claudia smiled at the compliment, bringing out a tiny dimple at the corner of her mouth. "Prince Tigranes and

I have discovered a mutual fondness for the Greek Lyric poets."

"Would you believe that she has all of Sappho by heart?" Tigranes said.

"She is famed as a lady of wide accomplishments," I assured them both. I could well believe that she was something new to him. It had only recently become fashionable for wellborn Roman women to be educated. In the East, women were never educated, and if they were intelligent, they were careful to hide the fact.

"Is this a pleasure visit?" I asked, knowing full well that it was not.

"Of course, it is the greatest pleasure to visit Rome, and one I shall treasure all my life. I do, however, wish to confer with your distinguished Consuls concerning my troublesome neighbor to the northwest." This could only mean the redoubtable Mithridates, whose name, even if merely implied, seemed to be everywhere lately.

"As I understand it," I said, "he may not be troublesome much longer. Last I heard, General Lucullus had him on the run." Something struck me and I turned to Claudia. "Isn't your sister married to Lucullus?"

"She is," Claudia affirmed. "Lucullus has promised Publius a staff appointment as soon as Publius can join him in the East."

"Ah, so Publius is about to enter public life?" I said heartily. The thought of Publius Claudius in a position of military authority made one tremble for the fate of Rome. The only reason I could conceive that he would risk his aristocratic hide in a campaign was to accumulate enough military time to run for office.

"The call to public duty comes to all men in our family," she said.

"Let's see," I mused, "a couple of years in the East, and Publius will be old enough and have the qualifications to stand for a quaestorship, will he not?"

"He wishes to be a tribune of the people," she answered.

This was a bit of a shock, although it should not have been. "Then he will become a Clodius?" I queried.

"Exactly. And, since my brother and I do everything together, I shall become Clodia."

"I beg you to reconsider, Claudia," I said, very gravely. "This is not a step to be taken lightly."

Tigranes was looking from one to the other of us in great puzzlement. At that moment, a slave ran up to Claudia and told her than an important guest had arrived. She turned to me.

"Decius, the prince is puzzled by all this. Perhaps you can explain some of our quaint old customs to him while I take care of my duties as hostess."

"I confess," Tigranes said when she was gone, "that I don't understand what you meant—about Publius, I mean."

This was a subject that could be confusing even among Romans, but I did my best to enlighten this foreigner. "You are aware of our distinction between patrician and plebeian?"

He nodded. "At one time, I thought that it meant the same as noble and commons, but I've found that is not quite the case."

"True. The patricians were the founding families, and they still have certain privileges, mostly concerning ritual duties and such. At one time, they had all the high offices, but no longer." Slaves came by bearing trays of sweetmeats and we helped ourselves. "There were some rather nasty civil wars fought over plebeian rights, long ago, but the fact is, the patrician families have long been dying out and plebeians have had to take over their duties. We now recognize a plebeian nobility. These are families that have had Consuls among their ancestors. Is this clear?"

"I think so," he said, very doubtfully.

"For instance, my own family, the Caecilii Metelli, has had many Consuls. By far the largest number of the senatorial families these days are plebeian. There are still some patrician families." I looked over the room. "For instance: Over there is Caius Julius Caesar, a patrician. So is Sergius Catilina. Both of this year's Consuls, Crassus and Pompey, are plebeians. Cicero over there is not even from Rome, but everybody expects him to be Consul someday. Is this clear?"

"I think so," he said, nibbling on a sugared fig.

"Good. Because now it gets complicated. Our host and hostess belong to the very ancient Claudian gens. This family is unusual in having *both* patrician and plebeian branches. The patricians are usually called Claudius, and the plebeians are usually named Clodius. Certain members of this family have chosen, for political reasons, to switch from patrician to plebeian status. To do this, they arrange to have themselves adopted by a member of the plebeian family and then change the spelling of their name."

Tigranes looked slightly stunned. "But why should anyone want to change from patrician to plebeian?"

"That is a shrewd question," I admitted. "Partly, it's to curry favor with the mob, which is entirely plebeian. Partly, it's constitutional. Only plebeians can hold the office of tribune."

"I thought tribunes were military officers," he said.

"Military tribunes are low-ranking officers, appointed by the Senate, who continually embarrass our generals with their inexperience and clumsiness." Having been one, I could speak with authority. "Tribunes of the people are elected by the plebs and have had considerable power, including the power of veto over a senatorial decree."

" 'Have had'?" Tigranes said, with an excellent grasp of Latin tenses.

"Well, yes," I said, floundering somewhat because I was so puzzled myself. "Actually, under the Sullan constitution, which still stands, the tribunes of the people have been stripped of most of their old powers." Sulla, one need hardly point out, had been a patrician.

"And yet Claudius wants to be a tribune," Tigranes said. "Will this be difficult?"

"Well, let me see. He'll have to have a plebeian sponsor, which is no problem since so many of his kinsman are Clodians. There will be legislation to force through the Senate. They are always reluctant to see such social fluidity. It can be complicated."

"I marvel at this multiplicity of governmental voices," Tigranes said. "In my homeland, the Great King says what is to be, and it is."

"We've done well out of our system," I assured him. At that moment, the new guest entered. It was none other than my father's patron, Quintus Hortensius Hortalus. Everybody expected a sudden clashing of guests, because Hortalus had defended Verres, whom Cicero had prosecuted with such spectacular success. However, the two men remained quite civil, in that odd fashion that lawyers have.

I excused myself to go to the privy. Actually, I only needed a few moments to ponder the makeup of the night's odd gathering. Upon reflection, I realized it was not so disparate after all. Virtually every man present was a supporter of Pompey. Within a month, Pompey and Crassus would step down from consular office to take up proconsular command. One of the Consuls for the next year was none other than Quintus Hortensius Hortalus.

Now, while Pompey and Crassus were technically equal in rank, Crassus was not one tenth the general Pompey was. It was clear to everyone that Pompey coveted the eastern command now held by Lucullus. It would be the spectacular crown to Pompey's brilliant military career to add the eastern kingdoms to Rome's holdings. The problem was, it looked as if Lucullus was going to do exactly that before Pompey had the chance.

Perhaps I should say something about Lucullus here. He was an altogether admirable man whose reputation had suffered of late because he did not belong to the all-important family we all know so well. He is remembered now because of his later writings on the nature of the good life and because of his patronage of the arts, but in those days he was our most brilliant general. He was one of the few genuinely fine Romans I ever knew, able in political and military life, a patron of the arts, ferocious in battle, magnanimous in the moment of victory. I know it sounds like the praise of a lackey, but we were not related and I never owed him anything, so you may take it as true. Unlike so many of our generals who bought the goodwill of their soldiers by allowing them great license, especially after a battle, Lucullus was a strict disciplinarian, and as a result his troops had little affection for him when the campaigning was rough.

It is an oddity of soldiers that they will hate most officers who beat them and discipline them strictly, but will worship others for the same qualities. In my lifetime I have known two generals whose soldiers reveled in the strictness of their rule. One was Germanicus, beloved nephew of our First Citizen. The other was Caius Julius, who had that wonderful facility for persuading men to do those things directly contrary to their own interests but ideal for his. I do not by this mean to equate Caesar with Germanicus, for the latter is a splendid man, if somewhat dim of apprehension, while Caius Julius was the most brilliantly cold-blooded schemer Rome ever produced.

But I am getting ahead of myself. At that moment, on that night, I had only Tigranes and Publius and Claudia on my mind. Especially Claudia. It pained me that she would contemplate lowering her social status, but that would have no bearing on our personal relationship. It was the knowledge that, when Publius Claudius changed his status and became Clodius, he would instantly become a figure of controversy and acrimony. That meant that he would be a target for assassins, and so would she, if she persisted in backing his fortunes.

I returned to find the guests being conducted into the dining room. We all crawled onto the couches, a rather undignified procedure dictated by tradition, and slaves took our sandals and passed out wreaths: laurel, I noted, probably in honor of the foreign guest's Greek tastes.

The dinner was arranged in the old style, with three couches arranged around three sides of a square table, three guests to each couch.

Publius had a difficult problem of precedence to contend with, having both a visiting prince and a Consul-elect among his guests. Had Hortalus been in office, the right-hand position on the central couch would have been his by right, but Publius had given that place to Tigranes as a distinguished foreign guest. Hortalus had the next-highest place, in the center of the middle table, with Publius taking the left end.

The rest of us were seated in no particular order, since birth and office were so oddly mixed in this group. I had the upper position on the right-hand couch, putting me next to Tigranes, with Claudia to my right and Caius Julius next to her. Opposite us on the third couch Curius, Catilina and Cicero reclined. It was still a new custom for women to recline with the men at dinner, but Claudia was nothing if not up-to-date. In earlier days, women sat in chairs, usually next to their husbands. Nobody on this occasion seemed upset by Claudia's presence on the couch. I certainly wasn't. The banquet itself was perfectly decorous, probably out of respect for Hortalus's status as Consul-elect.

There were no flamingos' tongues or dormice rolled in honey and poppy seed or other culinary curiosities such as delighted Sergius Paulus. To begin, the servers brought in various appetizers: figs, dates, olives and the like, along with the inevitable eggs. Before anyone reached for these, Hortalus intoned the invocation to the gods in his matchless voice. Then we all set to.

"Ever since I reached Italy," Tigranes said to me, "every dinner has begun with eggs. Is that a custom here?"

"Every formal dinner begins with eggs and ends with fruit," I told him. "We have an expression, 'from eggs to apples,' meaning from beginning to end."

"I've heard the expression, but I never knew what it meant." He eyed a dish of hard-boiled pheasant's eggs doubtfully. Apparently, eggs were not esteemed among his countrymen. He found the next courses more to his liking: roast kid, a vast tuna and hares boiled in milk. Throughout this there was little but small talk. The latest omens were discussed, as usual.

"Four eagles were seen atop the Temple of Jupiter this morning," Hortalus said. "This must portend a good year to come." It would, of course, be the year of his Consulate.

"I've heard that a calf was born three nights ago in Campania," Curius contributed, "with five legs and two heads."

Cicero snorted. "Monstrous births have no bearing on the affairs of men. They are nothing but the sport of the gods. I think the stars are of greater significance in our lives than most of us realize."

"Oriental mummery," Hortalus pronounced, "begging our royal guest's pardon. I think that the only omens of significance for us are those officially recognized and handed down to us by ancient custom: the auguries and the haruspices."

"Those being?" Tigranes asked.

"Auguries are taken by the officials of the college of augurs, of whom there are fifteen," Caesar explained. "It is a great honor for one of us to be elected to that college. They interpret the divine will by observing the flight and feeding of birds, and by determining the direction of lightning and thunder. Favorable omens come from the left, unfavorable omens from the right."

"Haruspices, on the other hand," Cicero said, "are determined by observing the entrails of sacrificial animals. This is carried out by a professional class, mostly Etruscans. Official or not, I consider it to be fraudulent."

Tigranes looked confused. "Just a moment. If you regard the left side as favorable and the right as unfavorable, why do Roman poets often speak of thunder from the right as a sign of the gods' favor?"

"They are following a Greek custom," Claudia said. "The Greek augurs faced north when taking the omens. Ours face south."

"Speaking of lightning," Catilina said, "I don't know whether it came from right or left, but this morning a bolt struck the statue of Lucullus by the wharf at Ostia. I heard this from a bargeman at the Tiber docks today. Melted him into a puddle of bronze."

There was much chatter about this omen. No official augur was required to interpret this one as unfavorable to Lucullus.

"This sounds most ominous," Hortalus said. "Let us hope that it doesn't presage some terrible defeat in the East." The statement had a hypocritical ring to it, but then Hortalus always sounded that way. If he told you the sun had risen that morning, you would go outside to see, just to make sure.

"There are no few here in Rome who would rejoice to see Lucullus recalled," Curius commented.

"But the Senate would never recall a successful general," I said, not liking the sound of this.

"Not as long as he's successful," Publius Claudius said, smiling. "And my brother-in-law has been *very* successful." He picked up a skewer of grilled lamb and gnawed at it daintily.

"Mark me," Catilina said, "that man is building himself an independent power base in the East, currying favor with those Asian cities by bankrupting half of Rome." Sergius Catilina was one of those red-faced, red-haired men who looked and sounded angry all the time. He referred to Lucullus's slashing of the Asian debt. When Sulla was Dictator, he had levied a tremendous assessment on the cities of the province of Asia, which they could pay only by borrowing at usurious rates from Roman financiers. To save the cities from utter ruin Lucullus had forgiven much of the debt and had forbidden high interest, earning him the undying enmity of our moneylenders.

"Perhaps Publius will be able to point out the error of his ways when he sails to join Lucullus next year," Claudia said airily. She seemed to want to lighten the conversation and quickly changed the subject. Soon the main course dishes were cleared away and we all observed a few moments of silence as the household gods were brought in. Officiating as household priest, Publius drew his toga over his head and sprinkled the little gods with meal and wine lees. When the gods were carried out, the dessert was served.

During this time, Tigranes paid me inordinate attention, asking me to explain this or that concerning Roman custom, law or religion. He showed extraordinary interest in my career and plans for future officeholding. I might have been flattered at such interest from a man who might one day be King of Kings, but at the time I felt more annoyed that he prevented me from devoting my time to Claudia. As a result, Caesar received most of her conversation, for which I envied him.

Claudia excused herself from the drinking-bout that followed dessert, and I decided that I had better moderate my intake of wine. It had come to me during dinner that I was in the company of men with whom it would be unwise to speak carelessly. They were the sort of men who played the power game for the very highest stakes. Such men usually die by violence, and of those present at that drinking-bout, only Hortalus enjoyed a natural death. Of the nature of my own demise, I am not yet qualified to write. The politics of that time shared some aspects in common with the *munera sine missione* of which I wrote earlier.

Taking little part in the drinking, I watched my fellow guests with interest. Curius was well advanced in drunkenness from what he had sipped during dinner. Sergius Catilina had the sort of red face that grew redder as he drank. His voice loudened and coarsened as well. Hortalus remained as calm and jovial as always, and Cicero drank moderately, his voice never slurring.

Caius Julius was named master of revels and he decreed that the wine be mixed to a strength of only one part water to two of wine, a strong mix considering the potency of the Falernian that Publius served. I was grateful that Caesar refrained from decreeing one of those

bouts where every guest had to down a specified number
of cups. For instance, we might have been required to
drink a cup for every letter in the name of the guest of
honor. Tigranes would not have been a bad choice, but
we all would have been on the floor before getting to
the end of Quintus Hortensius Hortalus. Instead, we were
to drink as we pleased, although a server made sure that
our cups never stayed empty.

"Tonight," Caius Caesar said, "since we have so many
guests of such high standing in the world, we will discuss
the proper uses of power, both civil and military, in the
service of the state." This was another Greek custom chosen to flatter our foreign guest. When Romans settle
down to serious drinking, philosophical discourse is
rarely chosen for entertainment, on the grounds that nobody the next day will remember what was said anyway.
Wrestlers, acrobats or naked Sardinian dancers would be
more like it.

"Marcus Tullius," Caesar said, "be so good as to open
the discussion. Mind you, you are not arguing before the
bar, so keep your remarks brief and concise, so that men
half-drunk can follow the thread of your reasoning."
Caesar himself was the very soul of tipsy good-fellowship,
although I was certain that he was perfectly sober.

Cicero thought for a moment, marshaling his argu-
ments. "We Romans," he began, "have created something new in the world. Since expelling the last of our
kings more than four hundred years ago, we have constructed our Republic, which is the finest instrument of
statecraft ever devised by man. It is not an unruly, shout-
ing rabble such as the old Athenian republic, but rather
a system of duly constituted assemblies, headed by the
Senate and presided over by Consuls. With apologies to
our honored guest, this is far superior to the outmoded
system of monarchy, for we have laws instead of arbitrary will, and all positions of power within the state are
apportioned according to merit and service, and all are
subject to recall upon proof of incompetence or corruption.

"As such, power is properly wielded, for the good of the state, by those men specially trained in the laws and usages of state governances. Military command should only be given to those who have spent years in the civil branch, lest commanders be capable of thinking only in military terms, and seek out wars to enrich themselves rather than undertake military action only for the good of the state." This was a none-too-subtle jab at Pompey, who had attained generalship with almost no public service and then, through military power, had assumed the highest office.

"Sergius Catilina," Caesar said, "share your thoughts on the subject."

Catilina was bleary-eyed, but his voice was sharp. "While none of us, of course, would wish to see a restoration of the monarchy, our esteemed Marcus Tullius totally neglects the value of good birth in selecting those who should wield power. Those who are raised up from the dregs have no sense of duty to the state, but only a lust for personal aggrandizement. It takes centuries of breeding to produce the innate qualities of character that go into true nobility, and this is, regrettably, becoming a rare quantity. Every day, I see the sons of freedmen sitting in the Senate!" Like Publius, Catilina was a man who thought he deserved high office because of his birth. He certainly had no other qualifications. "I would propose that public office and military command be restricted to patricians and to the plebeian nobility. Then we would not have so many mere adventurers in positions of power."

"Admirably put," Caesar said dryly. "Now, since Quintus Curius has withdrawn himself from the discussion"—the gentleman had passed out and was snoring—"let us hear from our Consul-elect for the coming year."

"I am not a political philosopher," Hortalus intoned, "but a mere lawyer and dabbler in the arts of statecraft. While I would never want to see a Roman king, yet I am a friend to kings." Here he bowed to Tigranes. "And while I agree that arbitrary power wielded by a single

man is a menace to order, yet we have the admirable
practice of dictatorship for those emergencies when only
the quick decisions of a single commander can preserve
the state. As for the military"—he gestured eloquently
with his winecup—"I think that we have for some time
allowed far too much latitude in our generals abroad.
There is now a tendency among them to forget that they
owe their commands and all else to the Senate, and thus
come to regard themselves as virtual independent rulers
within their areas of operation. We all remember Sertorius, and earlier this evening Sergius Catilina made some
remarks of this nature about General Lucullus." It was
typical of Hortalus to use someone else's statement to
make his own point. "Perhaps it will soon be time to
introduce legal proceedings spelling out the duties of
our generals, and limiting their powers."

"Excellent points," Caesar said. "Now we shall hear
from our host."

Publius was well gone in wine, but still marginally co-
herent. "I am soon to join my brother-in-law, the glori-
ous Lucullus, in the war against Mithridates. Military
service is essential in one who would serve the state. Always said so. But power resides here, in Rome. If a man
wants to have supreme power, it's not to be had con-
quering Spaniards or Egyptians. Power comes from the
Roman people. *All* of the Roman people, patrician and
plebeian both. The Senate passes ultimate decrees, but
power rests in the Popular Assembly as well. One who
would wield power is deceiving himself if he thinks that
a mere Senate majority is enough. A popular following
is also essential, and not just in the assemblies, but in
the streets."

"Most interesting," Caius Julius said when the rather
disjointed harangue seemed to be over. "But now, for a
different perspective, let us hear from our visiting
prince."

"First," Tigranes said, "you must allow me to express
my unbounded admiration for your unique Roman system, which chooses from among its best people those fit

to govern half the world. However, I fear that it would never be suitable for my part of the world. Here you are steeped in Greek culture, and have a long tradition of elected government. My people are for the most part primitive Asiatics, unused to any but autocratic government. To them, their king is a god. Take away the king, and they lose their god as well."

He smiled at all the guests gathered around the table, as if we were the best friends he had ever known. "No, I believe that the East will always be ruled by kings. And I think you will agree that they should be kings who are friends of Rome. Few share my views on the matter in the East these days." Still angling for Papa's throne, I noted.

"A point most excellently taken," Caesar said. "Now we must hear from Decius Caecilius Metellus the Younger, who has recently begun his public career, is the son of our esteemed Urban Praetor and the scion of a distinguished line."

I had drunk little, yet I felt light-headed. Perhaps it was my preoccupation with Claudia. I had promised myself not to speak injudiciously, but something about Caesar's fulsome introduction caused me to depart from the bland address I had planned. Also, there was something in the air, something that had been nagging at my mind all evening. It was the way that everything that had happened since the murders of Sinistrus and Paramedes, everything said or hinted by nearly everyone I had spoken to, and especially everything said at this dinner, had circled around two names: Lucullus and Mithridates, Mithridates and Lucullus. I knew that if I pried hard enough, I could wrench this tangled heap of lies and secrecy open, exposing everyone's guilty interest in those two powerful men. I had the level to pry with: the power of the Senate and People of Rome. But as yet I had no fulcrum upon which to rest my lever.

"As the most junior member of the government," I began, "I scarcely dare speak in such distinguished company." They all looked at me, smiled and nodded, except for Curius, who snored softly. Servers padded about on bare feet, keeping the cups brimming.

"But in the course of this fascinating discussion a few things have occurred to me, and I will share them with you." Still, they smiled. "It seems to me that what is more important than birth or origin, more important even than experience or ability, is loyalty to Rome, to the Senate and People. As my patron Hortalus and my friend Sergius Catilina have pointed out, a victorious general who fights only to enrich or glorify himself is no servant of Rome. Neither is a magistrate who sells his decisions or a governor who robs his province." At this, Cicero nodded vigorously. He had prosecuted Verres for exactly that. "And no one," I went on, "is a loyal Roman who deals secretly with foreign kings for his own gain, or who conspires against a Roman commander in the field for envy of his glory."

Cicero nodded again, mouthing silently the word "True." Catilina looked sour as ever, but it was a look of boredom. The face of Hortalus retained its joviality, but his smile had gone stiff. Publius glared at me angrily, and Tigranes looked into his winecup as if afraid of what his face might reveal.

"Excellent," Caesar said, with a look of approval. It meant nothing. Caius Julius was the most controlled man I ever knew. He could smile at a man he was about to kill, and he could smile at a man he knew was about to assassinate him.

The talk continued, and the wine was drunk for a while longer, but nothing of consequence was touched upon for the balance of the evening. In time Hortalus called for his sandals, as did Cicero and Caesar. Catilina, Curius and Publius were carried off by their slaves. Tigranes spoke animatedly and drunkenly for a space; then he, too, nodded off. The household slaves bore him off and I found myself alone amid unsettling thoughts.

I had not brought a slave, so I found my own sandals and prepared to let myself out. Just outside the dining room, I found Claudia waiting for me. She was dressed in a gown so sheer that the lamplight behind her shone through it, displaying her form perfectly. This was the crowning blow to my already disordered sense. In my father's country house near Fidenae there had stood an ancient sculpture of the Greek Artemis, said to be the work of Praxiteles. She was dressed in the brief chiton of a hunter, poised on the toes of one foot as she pursued her quarry. When I was a boy, she represented my ideal of female beauty with her slim, supple limbs and lithe hips, her small, high breasts and long-necked grace. I never acquired a taste for the wide-beamed female form personified by the Junos and Venuses favored by most Roman men. Claudia was the image of my marble Aphrodite.

"Decius," she whispered, "I am happy to find you still on your feet and not swaying."

"I wasn't the best of company tonight," I said. "I couldn't get into the spirit of the evening."

"I know. I was listening."

"Why would you want to listen to a pack of power-addled drunks? You must have been terribly bored." I tried to will the lamps brighter, so that I could see her better, then gave it up. I was going to see no more of her than she wished me to see.

"It is always good to know what men of power are saying in Rome these days. And while Hortalus was the only man present tonight who wields real power, the rest show great promise for the future."

"Even Curius and Catilina?" I asked.

"Men don't have to be intelligent or capable or of good character to play an important role in the high affairs of state. It is quite sufficient to be bad and dangerous." These were strange words from a half-dressed woman speaking privily in the night to a man who was not her husband. I was willing to overlook the oddness of the situation in order to stay with her longer.

"And I?" I asked. "Am I one of these men of promise?"

She stepped closer, just as I had hoped. "Oh, yes. You

have everything they spoke of tonight: ability, birth, loyalty . . . there is no position you can't achieve."

"In time," I said. "These things must be accomplished slowly, in regular succession."

"If you are content to have it so," she said. "Bold men are not afraid to speed the process."

I could see where this was leading. "Bold men have been beheaded in recent years, or been hurled from the Tarpeian Rock or dragged by the hook into the Tiber."

She smiled, but it was a smile of scorn. "The same has been the fate of the timid. The difference is that the bolder ones staked their lives on something worth having. Pompey and Crassus haven't waited on seniority and the ladder of office. They are Consuls now."

"Hortalus has been more careful," I said, "and he'll die in bed. Not those two."

Her smile went away. "I misjudged you, Decius Caecilius. I had thought you made of better material." She stepped very close, the tips of her breasts just brushing my tunic. "You might have spent this night with me. Now I think you had best spend it alone, as you deserve. Only the best deserve the best."

I summoned up my remaining shreds of dignity and said, "All the bolder souls have left or passed out. I had better take my leave as well. Some of them are undoubtedly more deserving of the best." Her face froze as I walked past her.

Outside, it was dark as only a moonless night in Rome can be dark. I knew it would be more than tactless to go back inside and ask for a torch or lantern. Besides, while a light would make walking easier, it would make it even more dangerous than usual. The thieves who lurked everywhere were always on the lookout for those staggering home full of wine. A light would draw them like moths. It would be preferable to risk stumbling or stepping into unpleasant substances. I did a great deal of both before I reached home and collapsed exhausted into bed, worn out by one of the longest, strangest days of my life.

IV

Morning came, as usual, far too early. I will never understand how we came to think it a good idea to rise while it is still dark. I think our moralists find it virtuous because it is so unpleasant. They always speak approvingly of beginning work at "gray dawn," as if that were somehow superior to a bright blue morning. Perhaps it reminds them of campaigning in the field, where soldiers are awakened an hour before dawn. I never saw any good in that, either. Only an idiot would fight at such an hour. The reason soldiers are roused at such an hour is that most centurions are cruel and brutal men who enjoy seeing their underlings suffer. Because of that, Senators, praetors and Consuls rise when they cannot even see to dress themselves and feel thereby more virtuous than those who prefer to start the business of the day only after they are fully awake. I wonder how many wars we have lost because the Senators who planned them were nodding off in the dim, early light of dawn.

Nonetheless, I was up and hearing the vigile's report while still yawning and trying to force some breakfast into my fatigue-paralyzed stomach. Mercifully, there had not been a single murder in my district that night. You have to live in the Subura to understand how glad that made me. Especially considering that it might have been my own murder that was reported. All the way home the night before, I had thought I heard the faintest of footsteps behind me. My condition and the darkness of the night were sufficient to make the most skeptical see ghosts, though, so I might have had the whole city to myself.

After the vigiles I received my clients. There was also another visitor, a very tall, strikingly handsome young man dressed in the sort of blue tunic favored by sailors. He smiled when I greeted him, exposing perfect teeth and an attitude friendly but just short of insolence.

"I come from Macro," he said. "He told me to speak with you privately."

My clients looked him over suspiciously. "Speak your piece openly, boy," said Burrus, my old soldier. "Our patron was assaulted a short time ago, and we'd not have it happen again."

The youth threw back his head and laughed loudly. "Then you need have no fear of me, old man. I never have to attack a man twice."

"I think I am safe enough," I told them, ignoring their scandalized looks. "Wait for me in the peristyle; we go to the praetor's this morning." To the youth: "Come with me." I led him to my writing-room, which I had altered to have large windows and a skylight of glass panes. I wanted a better look at this alarming young man. He walked with a loose, easy sway, at once casual and athletic.

I sat behind my desk and studied him. He had curly black hair and straight, clean features that the Greeks might have considered excessively heavy but were the embodiment of the Roman concept of manly beauty. His body was that of a young Hercules. I have never been tempted by pederasty, but in this youth I could understand the attraction some men feel to the practice. I put on my stern public face.

"Do you always call on public officials without putting on a toga first?"

"I'm new in the city," he said. "I don't even own one yet."

"Your name?"

"Titus Annius Milo, from Ostia. I am now a resident, with Macro as my sponsor."

On my desk was an ancient bronze dagger, found in a tomb on Crete. The man who sold it to me swore, naturally, that it had belonged to the hero Idomeneus. Every old bronze weapon I ever saw was supposed to have belonged to some Iliadic hero. I picked it up and tossed it to him. "Catch." He caught it easily, only his arm moving. His palm was so hard that it actually made a clicking sound when the bronze struck it.

"Rowers' guild?" I asked. Only rowers have hands like that.

He nodded. "Three years in the navy, chasing pirates. The last two rowing barges between Ostia and Rome." The rowers' guild is so powerful that it is forbidden to use much cheaper slave labor. Young Milo was a splendid example of what a man could look like if he rowed ships for a living but was paid decent wages and could afford to eat like a free man.

"And what has Macro to communicate to me?"

"First," he said, "the boy who broke in and knocked you on the head is not local." He tossed the dagger back upon the pile of papyrus it had been weighting.

"Can he be sure of that?"

"To break into an important man's house only to steal a paltry bronze amulet means a special hire, and all of the break-in boys are accounted for that night. They all report to a ward master and all the ward masters report to Macro. No one would seek to conceal such a crime."

"Go on."

"Sinistrus was almost certainly killed by an easterner. The bowstring garrote is an Asian technique. Romans prefer the *sica*, the *pugio* or the sword."

"Or the club," I said, rubbing my still-sore scalp. "All these homicidal foreigners are awfully convenient for Macro. I've suspected him of many things, but never of innocence."

"Even a man like my patron can't be guilty of everything." He grinned infectiously. "Finally, this H. Ager who bought Sinistrus is the overseer of a farm near Baiae.

It may take a few days to find out to whom the estate belongs."

"Very good," I said. "Tell Macro to report to me as soon as he has the name of the estate holder. And tell him, when he has something to communicate, to send you. You are not nearly as objectionable as most of his men."

"I'm flattered. Have I leave to go?"

"Just one more thing. Tell Macro to buy you a decent toga."

He flashed his teeth a last time and was gone. Indeed, he was a definite improvement upon the usual street scum and freed gladiators who thronged the gangs. I liked his easy manner and quick intelligence. I was always on the lookout for valuable contacts in Rome's underside, and I had a feeling that young Milo would go far in the city, if he lived.

As we trooped to my father's house, I brooded on this new information. The origin of my attacker and the murderer of Sinistrus was of minor interest, save that the same person could not have done both. A boy had broken into my house, and only a strong man could have throttled a powerful trained killer like Sinistrus. The hint of Asian origin was tantalizing, but hints are not facts.

Another question bothered me far more: Why did H. Ager come all the way from Baiae in Campania to buy a fighter and then free him? I thought of the men I knew who owned villas near Baiae. Caesar had one. So did Hortalus. So did Pompey. Truthfully, that meant nothing. It was the most famous resort in the world. Everyone who could afford a villa at Baiae owned one. I intended to own one myself, as soon as I was rich enough. It had a wonderful reputation for luxury, loose living and immorality. Moralists loved to rant about decadent Baiae. It sent people flocking there.

On our way to my father's house, there occurred one of those common, trifling events that somehow turn out to have, not so much consequences, but reverberations later. An all-white litter came by, carried by men in the white tunics of temple slaves. Immediately, we halted and bowed low. Inside the litter was one of the vestal virgins. These ladies, consecrated to the goddess of the hearth, have prestige second to none in Rome. They are so holy that, should a felon being led to execution encounter a vestal in his path, he is immediately freed. This puts little hope in the hearts of malefactors. Vestals do not leave the temple very often, while criminals are executed by multitudes.

When she was past, we went on. I had not recognized her. The Temple of Vesta is frequented mostly by women, and the vestals were chosen from girls of good family not yet in their teens. I knew personally only a single vestal, an aunt who, after her term of service was over, had very sensibly declined to leave the temple for the dubious advantages of a middle-aged marriage and had chosen to remain a vestal for life. The term of service is thirty years: ten to learn the duties of a vestal, ten to practice them and ten to teach the novices. A life like that does not prepare a woman for life in the outside world.

We did not get as far as my father's house. Instead, we almost collided with him as he and his whole crowd of clients strode toward the Forum.

"To the Curia," my father said. "A messenger has arrived from the East. Important news from the war." I had wanted to speak with him about the odd occurrences of the day before, but now that would have to be postponed. As we neared the Curia the crowds grew dense. In the almost magical fashion I knew so well, word had spread throughout the city that there was important news from the East. We reached the Forum to find a veritable sea of close-packed humanity. Father's lictors strode forward with their fasces and the crowd parted before them like water before a warship's ram.

The mob smelled of garlic, *garum* and rancid olive oil. Questions were shouted at us as if we knew more than they did. Rumors flew back and forth in the immemorial fashion: victory for Rome; defeat and disaster for Rome;

plague approaching Rome; even a revival of the slave insurrection. And, of course, everybody talked about the latest omens: Fifty eagles circled the Capitol last night; a child was born with a snake's head in Paestum; the sacred geese had spoken in human tongue, prophesying doom for the city. Sometimes I think there is a town in Italy where the only occupation is to think up and disseminate omens.

Praetors in their purple-bordered togas filed into the Curia while their attendants crowded the steps and portico outside. The lictors stood to one side, and as we ascended the steps Father summoned them.

"Get this mob into some kind of order," he told them. "The citizens will soon hear an important announcement, and I want them looking and behaving like Romans when they do."

"Yes, Praetor," said Regulus, the chief of the lictors. He shouted for the heralds, and as we entered the Curia we could hear them calling for the citizens to assemble by tribes.

Inside, the Curia was utterly packed. Sulla had nearly doubled the size of the Senate in order to fill it with his cronies and reward his followers, but he had not seen fit to build us a larger Curia to accommodate them. Pompey had given the two Censors for the year, both adherents of his, the task of weeding out corrupt and unworthy Senators, but this had alleviated the situation only slightly. My father went to sit with the praetors while I made my way to where the rest of the committee members stood, in the rear of the house.

Down in front, before the theater-style tiers of benches, sat the Consuls side by side in their curule chairs. Pompey, the most illustrious soldier of the age, still looked absurdly young for the office he held. He was, in fact, not constitutionally qualified for the Consulate, nor for any of the higher military commands he had wielded. He had never been quaestor, aedile or praetor and, at thirty-six, he was still not old enough to be Consul. Still, much may be forgiven a man who has an army at the gates, and there he sat. His main ambition was to own all the military glory in the world, but he was not a total political dunce like so many military men, and some aspects of his Consulate had been exemplary. The purge of the Senate I have already alluded to, and he had reformed the courts so justly that only the corrupt and venal could complain, which they duly did.

Crassus was a different matter. He had all the political qualities for the office but was sadly lacking in the military department. This was due to bad luck more than anything else, for the commands he had been assigned following his domestic office tenures had been lacking in opportunities. While Pompey had been winning glory in the civil wars in Italy, Sicily and Africa, and in Spain against Sertorius and Perperna, Crassus had been fighting slaves. Even then, Pompey had taken some of what little glory there is in a servile war, for he had smashed the force under the Gallic gladiator Crixus that had left Spartacus to make its own way home. Crassus had made up for some of his disappointment with a memorable gesture. He had crucified six thousand captured slaves all along the Appian Way from Capua to Rome. As rebels they were now useless as slaves, and they served as an example to other malcontents. It also let everyone else know that Marcus Licinius Crassus was not a man to be trifled with.

Crassus envied Pompey's glory and Pompey envied Crassus's incredible wealth. Both itched for Lucullus's eastern command. It made for a volatile combination and Rome was edgy as a result. Everyone would breathe a little easier when the two stepped down in less than two months to leave Rome and take up their proconsular posts elsewhere. Hortalus and his colleague Quintus Metellus, another amiable hack, terrified nobody. (This was not the kinsman under whom I served in Spain, but another Quintus Caecilius Metellus, later surnamed Creticus.)

At a gesture from Pompey, a young man came forward and stood nervously before the now-silent assembly. He

was a military tribune, still dressed in a travel-stained
tunic of the sort that is worn beneath armor. By ancient
custom, he had surrendered his weapons and armor at
the city gate, but he retained his military belt with its
pendant, bronze-studded straps and his hobnailed military boots, which crunched loudly on the marble floor.
I did not know him, but resolved to make his acquaintance when this session was over.

Hortalus stood from his seat at the lowest tier and
turned to address the Senate. He was dressed in a toga
of dazzling whiteness, draped gracefully in a new fashion
he had devised. It was so impressive that tragic actors
had begun to imitate it.

"Conscript Fathers," began the beautiful voice, "this
tribune, Gnaeus Quintilius Carbo, has come from the
eastern command with a communication from General
Lucullus. Please give him your fullest attention." Hortalus sat and Carbo took a scroll from its leather tube.
Unrolling it, he began to speak, at first hesitantly and
then with confidence.

"From General Lucius Licinius Lucullus to the noble
Senate and People of Rome, greeting.

"Conscript Fathers: I write to you to announce victory
in the East. Since defeating Mithridates in the great battle of Cabira more than a year ago, I have attended to
administrative duties here in Asia while my subordinate
commanders have reduced the king's strongholds and
fought the guerrillas in the hills. I send by the same messenger a detailed account of this campaign. I now have
the honor to announce that Pontus, Galatia and Bithynia
are totally under Roman control. Mithridates has fled
and taken refuge with his son-in-law, Tigranes of Armenia."

At this, Lucullus's faction, a considerable part of the
Senate, leapt to their feet, applauding and cheering. Others showed their approval with more restraint, while the
financiers and his political rivals sought not to show their
anger and disappointment. One could not, after all,
openly condemn a Roman victory. I cheered as loud as

anybody. The jubilation died down and Carbo resumed his reading.

"While this is a significant victory, the East will never be safe for Romans while Mithridates lives and is at large. Tigranes has shown defiance of Rome by granting Mithridates asylum, and in the new year I propose to enter Armenia with my legions and demand of Tigranes the surrender of Mithridates. If he refuses, I shall make war upon him. Long live the Senate and People of Rome."

At this, the anti-Lucullan faction erupted in fury. For Lucullus to make war on a foreign ruler without a formal declaration from the Senate would be a serious breach, indeed. There were calls for his recall, even for his execution. At length Hortalus stood, and all fell quiet. By custom, neither Consul would speak until the Senate had its say.

"Conscript Fathers, this is unseemly. Let us consider what General Lucullus has actually said." Like the lawyer he was, Hortalus began to tick off the cogent points. "He has brought a guerrilla campaign to a conclusion; he does not petition for permission to celebrate a triumph. Second, he does not say he will enter Armenia, he 'proposes' to, thus leaving leeway for orders to the contrary. Third, he does not say he will invade, but rather that he will 'enter' the country." How one enters a foreign country with an army and without permission and not be invading it remains a mystery to me, but Hortalus was a hairsplitter.

"Fourth, he does not propose to attack the forces of Tigranes, but simply to demand the surrender of Mithridates. How can we condemn the justice of this, after the injuries that pernicious king has done to Rome? Let us rather take satisfaction in what has been done so far, and send representatives to General Lucullus to discern his intentions and convey the will of the Senate to him. There is no need for urgency. His legions will remain in winter quarters for at least three more months. The campaigning season in Asia begins in March. Let us not be carried away by partisan passions. Let us rather rejoice that once again Roman arms have prevailed against the barbarians."

Cicero stood. "I agree with the distinguished Consul-elect. Let us declare a day of public rejoicing in honor of a Roman victory." This proposal was carried by acclamation.

Now Pompey stood. It was his day to wield the imperium, and Crassus sat silent, savoring his rival's discomfort. Nobody had the slightest difficulty in reading Pompey's thoughts. His clenched jaw said it all. He knew there was a real danger that Lucullus would destroy both Mithridates and Tigranes, leaving no enemies in the East to capture and plunder. There would be nothing left but Parthia, which had given us no cause for belligerence. Besides, the Parthians fought as mounted archers, and it was doubtful that even a master tactician like Pompey could overcome them without terrible losses. We Romans excel in infantry and siege tactics, not in the lightning, will-o'-the-wisp campaigning of the steppe warriors.

"Of the legality of General Lucullus's proposed penetration of Armenia"—a nice bit of phrasing, I thought—"I shall refrain from speaking. I shall not hold this office when he marches. For now, I decree a day of public rejoicing, with sacrifices of gratitude to all the gods of the state. All further public business is forbidden for this day. Let us address the people."

With a cheer, we made our way outside. I found myself jostling Sergius Catilina and could not resist a jab. "Not bad for a man whose statue was destroyed by lightning, eh?"

He shrugged. "The story's not yet over. Plenty can happen between now and March. If you ask me, some piddling guerrilla campaign isn't much cause for rejoicing."

It was one of Rome's besetting evils that, in order to petition the Senate to celebrate a triumph, a general had to have a smashing, spectacular victory that accomplished three things: end the war, extend the boundaries of Roman territory and carpet the ground with several thousand dead foreigners. Along with desire for loot and political power, the lust of our generals to celebrate a triumph got us into far too many unjust wars.

Outside, the scene was incredibly transformed. The jabbering mob we had pushed through was gone, replaced by as orderly an assembly as one could ask for. The lictors and heralds had got the populace to form up in the ancient manner, by tribes. In front, facing the Rostra, were the neatly ranked members of the Centuriate Assembly, the Plebeian Council and the Equestrian Order. Before all stood the tribunes of the people. I was gratified to see that the members of these assemblies had rushed home to don their best togas for the occasion. All stood in perfect order, ready to receive news of victory or disaster with *dignitas,* as befitted citizens. Moments like that made one proud to be a Roman.

The Consuls, Censors and praetors mounted the Rostra and stood beneath the bronze beaks of enemy ships. In utter silence, Pompey stepped forward. Beside him was the chief of the heralds, a man with the most amazingly loud voice I ever heard. At intervals through the crowd stood other members of the guild, ready to relay his words to those yet farther back. Pompey began to speak, and the herald amplified his words, and the citizenry learned of the events in the East.

Great shouts of joy went up at the conclusion of the address. Mithridates had slaughtered Roman citizens and allies all over Asia, and was probably the most hated man in the Roman world. It is characteristic of people to concentrate all their fears and hatreds on a single man, preferably a foreigner. These people were in far more danger from their own generals and politicians, but that would never occur to them. At any rate, everyone felt that it was all up for Mithridates. Pompey said nothing publicly about Lucullus's intention to invade Armenia, merely that he would demand the surrender of Mithridates from Tigranes.

In honor of the occasion, Pompey decreed an extra distribution of grain and wine, and a day of races to take place in one week. Even louder cheers greeted this, and the assembly began to break up as the people went off to the temples to observe the sacrifices. Quite aside from their genuine love of ritual and gratitude to the gods for a Roman victory, there would be plenty of meat for everybody that night as the carcasses of the sacrificial animals were cut up and distributed.

As the crowd around me began to thin, I caught sight of the young tribune, Carbo. He was alone now, his brief moment of glory past, when he had the sole attention of the most powerful deliberative body the world had ever known. He looked lonely standing there, and I had already determined to make his acquaintance, so I walked over to him.

"Tribune Carbo," I said, "my congratulations on your safe return. I am Decius Metellus, of the Commission of Twenty-Six."

"The praetor's son?" He took my hand. "I thank you. I was just about to go to the Temple of Neptune, to give thanks for my safe sea voyage."

"That can wait," I assured him. "All the temples will be jammed with people today. You can go in the morning. Will you be staying with your family while you are here?"

He shook his head. "I'm from Caere. I have no family here in the city. Now my duty is done, I suppose I'd better see about quarters for the night."

"No sense being put up in some tiny officer's cubicle on the Campus Martius," I said. "Come stay at my house while you're in the city."

"That is most hospitable," he said, delighted. "I accept gladly."

I confess I was not motivated by a pure spirit of gratitude to one of our returned heroes. I wanted information from Carbo. We walked down to the river docks and arranged for a porter to carry his baggage to my house. First he removed a clean tunic from his pack and we went to one of the public baths near the Forum, where he could wash off the salt and sweat of several weeks of travel.

I did not wish to burden him with serious discussion while he was relaxing, so I confined myself to city gossip while we bathed and were pounded by the masseurs. Meantime, I studied him.

Carbo belonged to one of those families of the rural gentry in which the military obligation was still taken very seriously. His arms, face and legs had the deep tan of long service in Asia, and there was a broad welt on his forehead and a small bald spot on his crown from the incessant wearing of the helmet. He had all the marks of hard training with arms. I liked the look of him, and it gave me hope to see that we still had such soldiers in Roman service.

We were both hungry after the baths, but there would be only lean pickings at my house, for the markets would all be closed. So we retired to a delightful little tavern run by a man named Capito, a client of my father's. It was on a side street near the Campus Martius, with a beautiful courtyard surrounded by a vine-arbor that provided cool shade in summer. The arbor was rather bare at this time of year, but the day was clear and warm, so we elected to sit at an outside table. At my order, Capito brought us a platter heaped with bread, cheeses, dried figs and dates, and another piled with tiny, grilled sausages. He and his wife and servers made much over Carbo, the hero of the hour; then they retired to let us eat in peace. We tore into this minor banquet with great appetite, washing it down with a pitcher of excellent Alban wine. When I judged that we were safe from death by starvation, I began to sound him out.

"Your general has done splendidly so far. Do you foresee equal success in the coming campaign?"

He thought awhile before answering. This was a thing I was to note about him. He never spoke quickly on weighty subjects, but always considered his words carefully.

"Lucius Lucullus is as fine a general as I have ever served," he said at last. "And he is the finest administrator I have ever known, by far. But he is not popular with the soldiers."

"So I've heard," I said. "A hard one, is he?"

"Very strict. Not foolishly so, mind you. Two generations ago, his discipline would have been esteemed by everyone. But the legionaries have grown lax. They still fight as hard and as expertly as ever, and they can take hard campaigning, but the likes of Marius and Sulla and Pompey have spoiled them. I mean no disrespect, but those generals bought their men's loyalty by allowing them to loot at will after a victory, and letting them live soft at the end of the campaigning season."

He dipped a scrap of bread into a pot of honey and chewed slowly, considering further. "Nothing wrong with allowing the men a little loot, of course. The enemy's camp, or a town that persists in resisting after it's been offered good terms, or a share of the money when the prisoners have been sold off, those things don't harm good order and discipline. But those generals I mentioned have let their men plunder whole countrysides and extort money and goods from the locals during an occupation. That's bad. Bad for discipline and bad for public order. And it makes Rome hated wherever the legions are quartered."

"But Lucullus doesn't allow it?" I asked, refilling both our cups.

"Absolutely not. Flogging for extortion or taking bribes, beheading for murder. He allows no exceptions."

"And the men grumble against him?"

"Certainly. Oh, it's to be expected in a long war. Lucullus has been out there for nearly five years, and some of us were in Asia under Cotta, before Lucullus arrived. Men want to go home, and too many are being kept on after their terms of service have expired. No real danger of mutiny yet, but who knows what will happen when they learn that there's to be another hard campaign, this time in Armenia. He keeps them drilling and training hard, even in winter quarters, and they don't like that, either."

"He should relent a little," I said. "Promise them the loot of Tigranocerta."

"That might be best," Carbo agreed, "but it might turn out to be a disappointment. From what I've heard, Tigranocerta may not be the fabulous royal city everyone talks about. Some say it's just a big fort: hard fighting and little loot."

"That would be unfortunate," I said. "But I fear that things may be about to get worse for General Lucullus."

Carbo's look sharpened. "What do you mean?"

"Gnaeus, are you loyal to Lucullus?"

He seemed somewhat offended. "Loyal to my general? Of course I am. What reason have you to doubt it?"

"None at all. But all generals have enemies, and sometimes those are on their own staffs."

"Lucullus is the best general I have served. I will be loyal to him as long as he is loyal to Rome."

"Excellent. You will be returning to the army before the new campaigning season?"

"Yes. From here I will go to spend some time with my family, then I return to the East."

"Good. Gnaeus, I am about to tell you something in strictest confidence, and I want you to convey this to General Lucullus. He does not know me, but he will know my father, the Urban Praetor, by reputation at least. It concerns the actions of his enemies, actions which I think to be not only hostile to Lucullus, but, even worse, pernicious to Rome."

Carbo nodded grimly. "Tell me. I will tell him."

I took a deep breath. This had the feeling of conspiracy, or at least slanderous trouble-making, but I could not ignore my instincts in this matter. "Sometime in the next year, Publius Claudius Pulcher will sail to Asia to join Lucullus as a tribune. He is the general's brother-in-law. Publius is a bad man, and lately he has been keeping company with the enemies of Lucullus here in Rome. I suspect that they have persuaded him to join Lucullus in order to undermine his command. Publius has no real interest in serving, but he wants to enter politics. I believe he is currying favor with a number of highly placed men by undertaking this."

Carbo's eyes narrowed. "I will tell him, never fear. And I thank you for taking me into your confidence."

"I don't know whether it is all a part of this or a mere coincidence, but Publius is now entertaining as his house-guest none other than Prince Tigranes, son of the King of Armenia. Do you know anything of him?"

"Young Tigranes? Just that he and the old man are on the outs. The boy felt he wasn't being given enough power or some such and tried to raise a rebellion. He failed, naturally, and had to run for his life. That was last year. So he's in Rome now? I'll never understand why those eastern kings always want to breed so many sons, the way they always turn into rivals. No family loyalty over there—among the royalty, at any rate."

This was a very true observation. A few years before, the King of Bithynia, Nicomedes III, had been so disappointed with his possible heirs that he actually *willed* his kingdom to Rome, as a bequest. It was the only province we ever acquired in so unorthodox a fashion. It was not totally bloodless, however. To nobody's surprise, Mithridates found a supposed son of Nicomedes whose claim he could champion and tried to annex Bithynia to Pontus. He allied himself with Sertorius, who had made himself a sort of independent king in Spain and provided Mithridates with ships and officers. For a while he was successful, even defeating an army under Cotta, but that was when Lucullus took the field against him. Lucullus defeated Mithridates in a sea battle that time, and recovered Bithynia for us. All because an eastern king had no use for his family. The world is truly a strange place, and Asia is stranger than most parts of it.

I did not know what sort of trouble it might lead to, but I felt better for having passed on my warning. My only alternative would have been to write a letter to Lucullus, and such written documents are always dangerous things. They can fall into the wrong hands; they can resurface years later when political realities have been

utterly transformed, only to be used as evidence in a trial
for treason or conspiracy. He who would keep his head
in Roman politics must be extremely careful of all such
documents.

Well-fed and somewhat somnolent from the wine, we
decided to walk around the city to clear our heads.
Carbo, who had never been in Rome on a holiday,
wanted to go to the great Temple of Jupiter to watch the
ceremonies, which were famed for their elaborate spectacle. We went to my house so that I could lend him a
toga and we climbed the long way to the old temple. He
was not disappointed, despite the throngs of garlanded
celebrants that crowded the Capitol. Romans never need
much excuse to celebrate, and they throw themselves into
it with a will. Coming back in the dim light of evening,
we wandered in the streets awhile, accepting wine from
the jars and skins that were passed promiscuously about.
At that time, public officials were still expected to min-
gle with the people during holidays, without regard to
rank or status. Aristocrat and bath attendant, patrician,
plebeian, public official and common guildsman were all
equal on a holiday. Today even Crassus and Pompey
should be out in the temples or in the streets, pretending
that they were just ordinary citizens like the rest of us.
Well, perhaps not quite like the rest. They would have
their bodyguards handy. Being good Roman citizens did
not make them fools.

As darkness came, we wended our way to my house.
Cato and Cassandra had prepared a room for Carbo.
They were delighted to have a guest to fuss over, and I
had brought them a bag of pastries and a jar of wine to
keep them cheerful during his visit. They had the un-
killable sentimentality of old house slaves, and treated
Carbo as if he were a general come home to celebrate a
triumph, having defeated all the barbarians in the world
single-handed.

As he staggered wearily off to his bed, Gnaeus Carbo
turned to me and said something terribly obvious but
unexpected and weighted with much trouble to come.

"Decius, my friend, let me tell you something: If the Senate thinks· Lucullus will wait until March to invade Armenia, they are wrong. He ordered me to return to my legion no later than the end of January, even though that means a sea voyage at the worst season. He will strike before March, while the Senate dithers here."

I bade him good night and retired to my own room to think. What he had just said was almost certainly true. One thing our generals knew above all else was that the Senate could debate forever. They dithered with Hannibal at the gates and they would dither while Lucullus made an unsanctioned invasion of Armenia. If he were successful, he would say that he had informed the Senate of his intentions and they had not forbidden him to act. With the loot of Armenia in his purse and his army at his back, the Senate would grant him a triumph, give him a title, perhaps Asiaticus or Armenicus or some such, and that would be that. Should he fail, he would be condemned and exiled, although in all likelihood one of his subordinates would probably murder him, as Perperna had murdered Sertorius. As I have said, politics was a high-stakes game in Rome in those days.

V

The next two days were mercifully uneventful.
Rome is usually very quiet the day after a public
holiday, and the first day was no exception. The
second was devoted to an annual religious ceremony of
the Caecilian gens. All of the oldest families have these
private rites, and it is forbidden for a family member to
describe them outside the family. On the third day,
things began to happen again.

While it was yet early in the day, I returned from my
morning calls to find Gnaeus Carbo packed and ready
to set off on the next leg of his journey, to his native
Caere. Before he left, he took a small pouch from his
belt and shook out two identical bronze disks.

"Would you do me the honor of accepting one of
these?"

He handed them to me and I examined them. Each
was embossed on one side with the face of Helios,
pierced just above his crown so that the charm could be
worn on a chain or thong. On the reverse side had been
carved both our names. They were tokens of *hospitium*.
They represented a very ancient custom of reciprocal
hospitality. This meant far more than a friendly over-
night stay. The exchange of these tokens imposed a most
solemn obligation on both parties. When one visits the
other's place of dwelling, the host is obliged to provide
the guest with all necessities, to render medical attention
if the guest falls sick, to protect him from enemies and
give him aid in court, and to provide him with a funeral
and honorable burial should he die. To underscore the

sacred nature of *hospitium*, below our names was carved the thunderbolt of Jupiter, god of hospitality. We would incur his wrath should we violate the requirements of *hospitium*. We could pass these tokens to our descendants, who would be obligated to honor them long after we both should be dead.

"I accept, gladly," I said, touched by the gesture. It was just the sort of old-fashioned honor I could have expected from an old-fashioned man like Gnaeus Carbo.

"I will take my leave, then. Farewell." With no more ceremony, Carbo shouldered his pack and walked out of my house. We remained good friends until he died many years later in Egypt.

I took the token to my bedroom and placed it in the little wooden box of carved olive wood inlaid with ivory where I kept many such tokens, some of them going back for generations and entitling me to hospitality from families in Athens, Alexandria, Antioch, even one from Carthage, a city that no longer exists. As I put it away, something about the token tickled a memory at the back of my mind, but it failed to elicit any great insights. Just then I had too much on the front of my mind to pay much attention to phantom memories lurking at the back.

Foremost in my thoughts, getting in the way of all rational consideration of my very real problems and dangers, was Claudia. Try as I might, I could not drive the woman from my mind. I kept remembering her as I had last seen her, with the lamplight making a corona around her. I tried to think how I might have acted differently, but I could not. I tried to think of a way to make things right between us, but I could think of nothing. These were bad thoughts to be entertaining when I was concerned with murder, arson and the likelihood of a treasonous conspiracy involving highly placed Romans and a foreign king who was the sworn enemy of Rome.

Men, especially young men, do not think clearly when their passions come into play. Philosophers have always assured us of this. Many of Rome's fortune-tellers offered as a sideline a potion guaranteed to rid one of this morbid fixation on a particular woman. I even considered consulting one of them. But then I had to admit to myself that I did not *want* to be free of my infatuation. Why young men actually enjoy this sort of suffering is a great mystery, but it is undeniable that they do.

Cato interrupted these musings. "Master, there is a woman to see you. She won't state her business."

I thought it might be one of the nuisance visits every public official dreads, but I needed some sort of distraction. "I will see her in my reading-room."

I put on my toga and went to sit behind my desk, which was stacked with enough parchment to make me look very busy, indeed. In truth, these were mostly personal papers and letters, since I left all my official writings in the Archives, where there were public slaves to keep track of them. A few minutes later Cato showed in a young woman who looked vaguely familiar. Then I remembered. It was Claudia's serving-maid, the wiry little Greek girl.

"Chrysis, isn't it?" I said coolly. Ordinarily, slaves do not call upon public officials, save to deliver messages from the freeborn. Cato would never have let her in had he known her status. But then, when they don't dress like slaves, how is one to tell?

"I am Chrysis." Her face was widest at the cheekbones, tapering to a small, pointed chin. With her cool green eyes and russet hair, she resembled a malicious little vixen. She moved as if her limbs had multiple joints.

"Why did you not identify yourself as Claudia's slave to my man?"

"Because I'm not a slave," she said. Her name was Greek, but her accent was not. I couldn't place it, but I had heard its like recently. My fixation with her mistress was doing terrible things to my memory.

"Then what are you to Claudia?"

"Her companion." She used the Greek word, probably to avoid the Latin equivalent, which also means "prostitute" when applied to a woman.

"Well, Claudia is an unconventional woman. What did you wish to see me about?"

Her lips quirked up at the corners. "My Lady Claudia wishes to see you." This was what I both hoped and feared she would say.

"When last we spoke, Claudia did not seem to want to see me again, ever."

Still wearing her enigmatic smile, the strange little woman walked around my desk. Hands demurely behind her back, she made her hips move as fluidly as a python's spine. Somehow she invested the simple act of walking with an indescribable lewdness. Standing now beside me, hands still behind her back, she bent until her face was inches from mine.

"But my lady often speaks from anger, rather than from her heart. She finds you a very pretty gentleman. She burns for you and cannot sleep."

At least it was clear why she did not wish to commit such a message to writing. Why she should entrust it to this astonishing little slut was less so. Of course, I had doubts whether the message was sincere, but it so mirrored my own feelings that I tried to convince myself that it was.

"Well, we can't very well let your mistress go sleepless, can we? How does she propose to resolve this dilemma?"

"She wishes you to come to her tonight, to a house she owns not far from here. She will go there after dark, and I will come here to guide you to her."

"Very well," I said, my mouth strangely dry, restraining myself from wiping sweaty palms on my toga. The combination of my unresolved feelings for Claudia and the aura of sensuality exuded by this rank little animal reduced me to feigning a dignified indifference. I doubt strongly that I fooled Chrysis.

"Until tonight, then," she said. She swayed out of my reading-room as soundlessly as a ghost. So silently that I suspected that she was barefoot, although only a person of uncommon fortitude would brave the Roman streets without sandals.

I released a long-pent breath. There were still many
hours before dark, and I needed something with which
to occupy myself. For a change, I had no official business
to transact, so I decided to draft some letters. I began
one, but could not get past the salutation. Finishing that,
I had forgotten to whom I was writing it. After the fourth
try, I threw my stylus against the wall in disgust. It was a
gesture of pique entirely uncharacteristic of me.

I think better walking than sitting, so I left my house
and began to ramble aimlessly. It was folly to think of
Claudia, so I dragged my thoughts back to the case at
hand. I had so many facts, and so many hints, but nothing with which to tie them all together, as the rods of
punishment are tied around the ax of execution in the
Roman fasces.

I walked through the ancient streets, amid the familiar
sights and sounds and smells of Rome, and I pondered
upon what I might be missing. What did I have? Two
dead men, the unfortunate Paramedes of Antioch and
the wretched Sinistrus. A great fire that might have
burned the city to the ground, had the wind been from
the south that night. I had Publius Claudius and his sister, and a mysterious farm overseer near Baiae named
H. Ager. I had the foreign prince, Tigranes, and I had
the mighty but absent General Lucullus and King Mithridates, the latter now enjoying the hospitality of the Elder Tigranes. I might even throw in the late General
Sertorius, whose rebellion in Spain had brought him to
a bad end. I stopped in mid-step.

What, I thought, had been the connection between
Sertorius and Mithridates? They were separated by the
entire width of the Mediterranean. They were united
only by a dislike for Rome. One may make a distinction
in the case of Sertorius, of course. He was only on the
outs with the then-current government in Rome, the anti-
Marian party. He had claimed to *be* the legitimate government of Rome, in exile, and had even cobbled together his
own Senate, made up of out-of-favor malcontents.

So how had these two enemies of Rome carried on their intrigue? Why, through the only other naval power in the Mediterranean besides Rome. To wit, the pirates. To the astonishment of passersby, I stood there and cursed myself for a besotted fool. Only a few days before, young Titus Milo had mentioned his days in the navy, pirate-chasing. Had my mind been working properly, that alone should have started it working in the right direction, had it not been occupied with lubricious thoughts of Claudia. It is also the nature of young men to blame their own shortcomings on women.

Once Carthage had been the premier naval power on the sea. We had destroyed her fleet. Rather, Carthage had destroyed several Roman fleets, but we kept building new ones and sending them out until Carthage was eliminated as a naval threat. Having done that, we neglected our navy, concentrating as always on our pre-eminence as land soldiers.

Into this naval vacuum had slipped the pirates. They had always been there. In some coastal areas, piracy was still regarded as an honorable profession, as it was in ancient times. After all, had not Ulysses and Achilles blithely raided unoffending coastal villages as they made their way to and from Troy?

The fact was, these pirates operated freely in what we liked to call "our sea." No shipping was safe, but shipping was not the chief victim of the pirates. Mainly, they raided coastal districts for slaves. The great pirate haven on the island of Delos had become the pivotal slave market for the whole Mediterranean world. Those nations that were not clients of Rome got no protection from the pirates. Those that were clients got very little protection anyway.

During the Servile War, Spartacus had contracted with the pirates to ferry his army of slaves and deserters from Messina to freedom somewhere, probably out at the far end of the Black Sea. Crassus had got wind of it and bribed the pirates to betray Spartacus, otherwise that splendid villain might have got away clean. We hated to admit it, but the pirates of the Mediterranean formed a sort of mobile nation, richer and more powerful than most land-based kingdoms.

I looked about me, and found that I was in the warehouse district near the Tiber. Each of us is given, at birth, a *genius*, and in that odd way that these guardian and guiding spirits have, mine had led my steps while my conscious mind was otherwise occupied, and had brought me to the site of the beginning of all my problems. Nearby rose the immense bulk of the Circus Maximus. Before me, construction was well advanced on the new warehouse that was to replace the one owned by Paramedes and destroyed by fire.

It came to me that my *genius* was behaving even more subtly than usual, because this was not merely the Circus and warehouse district. It was also the district where lived Rome's small but wealthy and flourishing Oriental community. Here were to be found the Asiatics, the Bithynians, the Syrians, Armenians, Arabians, Judaeans and the occasional Egyptian. This, I suddenly realized, was exactly where I wanted to be. Here, if anywhere in Rome, I would be able to pry loose some information about the pirates.

I walked another couple of streets, until only one block of tenements and storehouses separated me from the Circus. From each shop front and storehouse came the fragrances of the whole Mediterranean world. Incense and spices were stored here, and rare, fragrant woods. The odors of fresh-sawn cedar from the Levant and pulverized pepper from even farther east mingled with those of frankincense from Egypt and oranges from Spain. It smelled like Empire.

The shop of Zabbai, a merchant from Arabia Felix, stood open, recessed beneath the arches of a shady arcade. Zabbai was an importer of the most precious commodity in the world: silk. So short is human memory that even now men will tell you that Romans first saw silk when the Parthians unfurled their silken banners before the army of Crassus at Carrhae, but this is nonsense. It is true that Romans had never seen silk in such quantity or so brilliantly dyed before beholding those banners, but the cloth had been sold in Rome for at least a hundred years before that, although much adulterated and mixed with threads of lesser fabric.

Zabbai was a typical eastern merchant, rich and polite and oily as an old lamp. Arabia Felix owed its happy title to its geographical location, a place where the land routes from the far East met the Red Sea, with all its African coastal trade, at the spot most convenient for transshipment of goods to the nearby Mediterranean coast.

His clerk rose from a little table and bowed deeply when I entered. "How may I serve you, master?" He didn't know me by sight, but he knew an official when he saw one.

"Summon Zabbai," I instructed him. Minutes later, the man himself emerged from a curtained back room, grinning and clasping his hands together. He wore flowing robes of splendid material and a silken headcloth. His beard was long and drawn to a sharp point. He was an exotic creature, but it was a relief to see an easterner who was not trying to be a Greek.

"My friend Decius Caecilius Metellus the Younger, what honor you do me, how your presence brightens my day, how I rejoice ..." and so on, for quite some time. Oriental effusiveness is a bore to a Roman, but I daresay easterners consider us churlish and uncultured in our direct bluntness.

"My esteemed friend Zabbai," I said when he paused for breath, "I come today not on business, but on a matter of state."

"Ah, politics! Do you stand for the quaestorship?"

"No, I won't be eligible for another six years. This is not a matter of domestic politics, but of foreign policy. With your wide travels and far-flung contacts, and most especially your constant dealings with ships and shipping, I thought you the best man to consult."

He was vastly flattered, or pretended to be. Flinging

his arms wide, he said, "Anything! Anything to be of service to the Senate and People of Rome! How may I serve? No, but first, let us be comfortable. Please, follow me."

We ducked through the curtain and passed through a storeroom in which thin sticks of incense burned constantly to protect the bales of precious silk from the damage of dampness or insects. Beyond that, we emerged into a beautiful courtyard. It was laid out in the traditional Roman manner, with a fountained pool at the center, but with the eastern addition of flower boxes, which sported a few winter blossoms. Arabs come from a desert country, and they love water and growing things even more than do Italians.

Near the pool stood a low table of precious wood with a colorful tiled top, where we seated ourselves on cushions stuffed with feathers and spices. Only an Oriental would think of a luxurious touch like that. Servants brought us dishes of nuts and dried fruits and candied flower petals, along with an excellent wine that had been heavily watered, as befitted the early hour.

When I had partaken enough of his hospitality to satisfy politeness, I got down to business. "Now, Zabbai, my friend, I would like for you to share your knowledge of the pirates who infest our sea."

Zabbai stroked his beard. "Ah, the pirates. I deal with those difficult businessmen many times in a year. What do you wish to know of them?"

"First, some general knowledge. How do you go about your yearly transactions with these romantic fortune-seekers?"

"Like most merchants whose goods move by sea, I find it most convenient to pay a yearly tribute, rather than have to negotiate separately over each seized cargo or factor to be ransomed."

"Yet you say you must deal with them many times each year. How is that?"

"While the greater fleets cooperate, and in most cases a single payment made at Delos is sufficient to buy them all off, yet there are small, independent fleets that obey

no master. These are a special nuisance in the western
sea, especially near the Pillars of Hercules, the coast of
southern Spain and the northern African coast near Old
Carthage. These rogues will take my cargoes and agents,
then give me a certain time in which to ransom them.
Failing that, they will be taken to Delos and sold. It is a
great nuisance."

"Spain, you say?" I mused, speaking half to myself.

"Truly, most of the sea west of Sicily. This is a mere
nuisance, since the great bulk of all trade and shipping,
perhaps as much as ninety percent, is to the east of
Rome. After all, what great cities exist in the West since
the destruction of Carthage? Only Rome. To the east,
there are many great cities and rich islands, all in relatively close proximity. There you will find Antioch, Alexandria, Pergamum, Ephesus, Chalcedon, Crete and
Cyprus, Rhodes and all the other islands. That is where
the commerce is, and so therefore that is where the pirates are most numerous and best organized."

"But to the west," I persisted, "there are independent
fleets. Are these numerous or powerful?"

Zabbai made a very eloquent gesture of the hands, indicating the mutability of all matters pertaining to human affairs. "It is not as if these things were established
by constitution, or even by guild rules or the solemn
agreements of a consortium of businessmen. These pirates are individualistic and whimsical in the extreme. A
group of them will decide to cruise off such and such a
stretch of coast, while others will insist upon betaking
themselves to a strait between two islands, fancying that
the commercial traffic there will be especially heavy and
rich in this season. There is no formal arrangement of
fleets."

"And how do they decide where they want to cruise?"
I asked.

"They may have any of a number of reasons. Dreams
and omens play a part, or they may consult one of the
sibyls. Or they may have harder information, bought
from the factors of shipping merchants. It is best not to

speak too far in advance of the sailing season where one's servants may overhear."

It is a well-known fact that Romans hate the sea. Usually when we need a fleet, we levy one from the Greek allies, put a Roman officer in command and call it a Roman fleet. It is odd that a peninsular people should be so hydrophobic, but there it is. We are also dunces when it comes to commerce, which we perceive as Graeco-Oriental, and faintly disreputable. Respectable wealth comes only from land, agriculture and warfare. The city subsisted on plunder taken in war and tribute levied on the defeated. Our idea of a great financier was the likes of Crassus, who grew rich through extortion. I made a mental note to learn more about these things, even if they were rather un-Roman.

"A few years ago," I said, "you may recall that General Sertorius, who was still in rebellion against Rome, entered into certain treasonous relations with King Mithridates of Pontus. He supplied that monarch with ships and some officers. Did these western pirates act as intermediaries in this process?"

Zabbai's eyes went wide at the obviousness of the answer, but he replied politely. "And how could it be otherwise? To those who have their business on the sea, it was common knowledge that Mithridates sent his request through the pirate chief Djed, and that the accomplice of Sertorius was the equally illustrious sea-brigand Perseus. Djed is an Egyptian and Perseus, I believe, hails from Samothrace. These pirates are a cosmopolitan lot, and men of every maritime nation are to be found among their crews."

"I am curious," I said. "Just how does one go about contacting these pirates? They seem to have no permanent abode, they do not maintain embassies in the various nations of the world. If one has business with them, as did Sertorius and, later, Spartacus, how would one let it be known to them?"

"As I have intimated," Zabbai said, "they are businessmen. They deal in large quantities of goods, most prominently the great lots of slaves they must sell every year. In order to facilitate the sale and transfer of these goods, they maintain business agents in all the major port cities."

I was stunned. "You mean there is a pirate agent operating in Ostia?"

"Oh, but of a certainty. Also in Rome."

"In Rome?"

"Rome is, after all, where many of the wealthiest buyers are to be found," he pointed out reasonably.

"Could you tell me the name of the current agent here in Rome?"

"I wish that I could. Unfortunately, the last agent died and a new one has not yet arrived."

"And who was the deceased agent?" I asked.

"An importer of wine and olive oil named Paramedes of Antioch."

Zabbai must have assumed that I was rather befuddled as I took my leave of him shortly thereafter. However, he was unfailingly polite and insisted that I accept a guest-gift. It was a scarf of saffron-colored silk, nearly two feet square, strong as armor and light as a breath. Since the silk seemed to be unadulterated, it was a gift rich enough to be construed as a bribe, but Zabbai had no cause to bribe me. I decided that he was foresightedly building up goodwill with one who might have a political future. His help and the gift had certainly made me well-disposed toward him, so he must have known what he was doing.

Now I had another link. The late Paramedes had been an agent for the Mediterranean pirates. What else was there that I did not know about this humble Asian-Greek importer? Certainly the hospitable Sergius Paulus had not mentioned any such embarrassing connection. Yet he had been Paramedes's sponsor, so he must have been dipping his spoon into so rich a bowl.

I began to feel profoundly melancholy. The way the Senate had put obstacles in the way of my investigation indicated a foul stew of corruption at the very highest levels. I should not have been surprised. Indeed, I was not surprised. Intrigue, infighting and bribery had been the rule rather than the exception for the past two generations, and the Senate remained a sink of crime and self-seeking despite the periodic attempts by Censors to weed out the worst elements. But Censors are only appointed every fifth year, and they have only a year of power before they must step down. The evil proliferated at a far greater rate than such methods could deal with.

I walked down to the docks and sat on a great wooden bollard, staring out into the swirling, muddy water as if seeking omens there. As painful as the thought was, I had to admit to myself that the Senate was obsolete.

Our system of assemblies with the Senate at the top, with its quaestors, its aediles, its praetors and Consuls and Censors and tribunes of the people, had been a fine arrangement for the city-state that Rome had once been, when every man was a farmer-soldier. The Centuriate Assembly had once been the annual war-hosting where, since every free citizen was present, it was a convenient time to take a vote on matters of public importance. In those days most citizens were farmers or craftsmen. Slaves were rare and free idlers were rarer still. We had dealt honestly with one another and with the neighboring nations.

Now all was changed. It was wealth that got a man into the Senate, not selfless public service. Our generals made war for the sake of loot, not to protect the Republic, and where once Rome had been esteemed everywhere as an ally faithful to treaty obligations, always ready to defend the liberties of a neighboring state, now she was feared as a rapacious predator.

Cicero's famous prosecution of Verres had brought out a telling point. In the course of the trial, a former colleague of Verres had quoted him on his philosophy of administration when he was in the process of looting Sicily. He had said that the profits of his first year he would keep to enrich himself, the second would go to enrich his friends and the third would be for his jury. It was a sign of the times that most people took this as excellent wit rather than as a shocking comment on the quality of Roman provincial administration.

Still, all was not totally lost. The Sicilians had asked Cicero to represent them in court because they had been very pleased with the honesty of his own tenure of office on that island. And Sertorius, despite his excessive loyalty to the Marian cause and his unforgivable raising of rebellion against Rome, had been an administrator of true genius. Of Lucullus's excellent handling of the Asian cities I have already written.

So what was to be done? The old Roman spirit and virtues were still there, even though the citizen body was now a minority, sitting on top of an enormous mass of slaves. There were still good men who could restore the good name of the Republic, although it might require a reform of our governmental system more severe than anything Sulla had ever dared. In the meantime, those charged with such duties must root out the criminals, high or low. That was my task.

I rose from my bollard and saw that the sun was past its zenith. It was time for the baths. Then I would seek out dinner. Darkness came early at this time of year, and when darkness fell, the strange little Chrysis would come to fetch me to Claudia.

I began to walk toward the Forum, feeling lighter with each step.

VI

Other cities grow quiet with the coming of darkness, but the early hours of the night are the noisiest in Rome. This is because, with only minor exceptions, wheeled traffic is forbidden during the hours of daylight. With the fall of night, innumerable wagons and carts come rolling through the gates. These bear farm produce for the morning markets, fodder for the Circus horses, building materials for the incessant construction projects, charcoal and wood for the fires, sacrificial birds for the temples and so on. Some wagons arrived empty. These were headed for the docks, to be loaded with the goods brought upriver from Ostia. Above Rome the Tiber is no longer navigable for the larger vessels, so it is the transshipment point for goods going inland.

During these hours, the streets of Rome are clangorous with the clash of metal tires on paving-stones, the indescribable squeal of crude wooden wheels on the axles of farm carts, the profane shouts of the teamsters, the groans of harnessed slaves, the lowing of oxen and the braying of asses. Silence came only after midnight.

As the great carts rumbled by my door, I waited impatiently for Chrysis to show herself. Nervous and unsettled, I cast about for something to do in order to while away the time. A walk through the dark streets of Rome was not without risk, so I thought I had better arm myself. It was strictly forbidden to bear arms within the city, but most prudent men did, anyway.

I opened the lid of my arms-chest and examined its

contents. Cato kept my weapons and armor clean and oiled against those calls to military service that are the duty of every Roman in public life. In the chest were my crested bronze helmet, the glittering bronze cuirass and greaves that I wore for parade, also my field armor of iron Gallic mail. I picked up my long sword for mounted fighting and my short sword for foot combat. Both were keen and of the highest quality, but they were rather too large to carry thrust beneath a tunic. The broad-bladed *pugio* was a more practical weapon, with its double-edged blade eight inches long. I tucked the sheathed weapon inside my tunic beneath the belt; then something on the bottom of the chest caught my eye. I reached in and brought up a tangled mass of leather strapping and bronze.

It was a pair of *caesti*. Pugilism is the silliest of all combat arts. It consists of taking the human hand, with its multitude of tiny, frangible bones, and smashing it against the human skull, a most unyielding target. The old Greeks had alleviated the damage to their hands somewhat by inventing *caesti*, which in the beginning were mere straps of hide wrapped around the hands and forearms. Later, this dull sport had been livened up by the addition of bits of bronze on the striking surface. Later yet, plates were added. My pair were of the formidable Macedonian type called *murmekes*, also known as "limb-smashers." These were reinforced with a thick strap of bronze across the knuckles. This in turn sported four pyramidal spikes, each a half-inch long. I had won these in a game of knucklebones during my army service, and had lugged them around with me ever since. At last, I thought, I might find a use for them. I dropped one back in the chest and from the other stripped the complicated forearm-straps, retaining only the part that wrapped around knuckles and palm. This I dropped into my tunic on the other side, so that I could slip it onto my left hand as I drew my dagger with my right.

Minutes after I had thus armed myself, Cato came in to tell me that a woman awaited outside. I ignored his reproachful look as I hurried out to join her. We had to wait for an immense hay-wagon to rumble and screech its way by before we could speak.

"Please come with me, sir," she said. She was veiled, but nothing could disguise that insinuating voice or the snakelike way her body moved. There was sufficient moonlight, reflected from the whitewashed walls, to see fairly well.

I had flattered myself that I knew every street in Rome, but she soon had me in an unfamiliar area only a few minutes' walk from my door. Truthfully, no person may truly know all of Rome. The city is large, and areas are leveled by fires or land-speculators and rebuilt along new lines. This was an area of *insulae,* the new type of housing that had come into use as the expanding city crowded up against its ancient walls and there was no way to expand except upward. Five, six, even seven stories high towered these structures. The well-to-do had their apartments on the ground floor, where there was running water. The upper floors were occupied by the poor. These buildings had an unnerving habit of collapsing abruptly because of shoddy materials and inferior workmanship. The Censors kept passing laws regulating building standards, which the contractors persisted in flouting.

The faint light disappeared as we entered this district, for the *insulae* were so tall, and the streets so narrow, that the moon could only cast its rays from directly overhead, a period of only a few minutes each night.

Perhaps I should explain that in those days we had three types of streets in Rome. The *itinera* were only wide enough for people on foot. The *acta* were called "one-cart" streets because they were just wide enough to permit vehicular traffic. The *viae* were known as "two-cart" streets because it was possible for carts to pass one another on them. In those days, there were precisely two *viae* in all of Rome, the Via Sacra and the Via Nova, neither of which served the Subura. It is not much better now. Our Roman roads are the marvel of the whole world, but they begin outside the city gates. The streets of Rome are nothing more than our old rustic paths paved over. Visitors from Alexandria are always shocked.

Twice we saw wealthy men returning from late dinner parties, accompanied by torch-bearing slaves and bodyguards gripping wooden clubs in scar-knuckled fists. I sighed enviously, wishing that I were rich enough to own such an establishment. Not that I would have taken them on this night's mission.

Abruptly, I felt Chrysis grip my arm and draw me into a recessed doorway. She must have had cat's eyes to find the door, or to see me, for that matter. She scratched at the door, and from inside I could hear bolts being drawn. It opened and light flooded the street. Framed in the light stood Claudia.

"Come in, my dears," she said, her voice a low purr that set my blood racing.

I stepped inside and Chrysis closed and rebolted the door. To my eyes, accustomed to the gloom outside, the light was dazzling at first. Lamps stood everywhere, some of them sporting seven or eight wicks, all of them burning perfumed oil. To make the best use of the limited space available in an *insula*, the apartment was not laid out like a conventional house, but instead had a single large room off the street entrance, with a few smaller rooms opening off the main one.

"Welcome, Decius," Claudia said. She stood by a bronze statue of Priapus. The god's immense phallus jutted forth, gleaming in the lamplight. Such statues ordinarily stood in gardens, but since the god was depicted in the act of lubricating his outsized member with oil from a pitcher, it was obvious that it was intended to be erotic rather than fructifying.

"I rejoice to hear you welcome me," I said. "After our last encounter, I despaired of hearing such words from your lips."

She laughed musically. It did not sound forced, but it did sound practiced. "You must learn that I am not always to be taken so seriously. We women lack the reserve and control wielded by you men. We are more at the mercy of our emotions and express them freely. Aristotle himself says so, so it must be true." Again the musical laugh.

"You sounded most sincere at the time," I said, admiring her dress and makeup. She had made dramatic use of cosmetics, knowing that she was to be viewed by lamplight. She was lightly wrapped in a Greek gown pinned at the shoulders with jeweled brooches. Her breasts moved freely beneath it, showing that she wore no *strophium*.

"I usually do," she said, enigmatically. "Come, sit by me and let me make up for my hard words of a few nights ago." She took my hand and led me to a side of the room that was furnished in the eastern fashion, with thick cushions on the floor near a low table of chased bronze. We sat, and Chrysis came from one of the side rooms bearing a tray of delicacies, a pitcher of wine and several small goblets.

"How do you like my little hideaway?" Claudia asked me as Chrysis filled the goblets. "Even Publius doesn't know about it."

"Unique," I said. I had been studying the decorations, and they were indeed not what one would expect to find in the apartment of a patrician lady. Nor of a plebeian lady, either, for that matter. The frescoes on the walls, exquisitely rendered by one of the better Greek artists, depicted couples and groups performing intercourse in every imaginable position. The couples were not always of opposite sex, and one astonishing scene depicted a woman entertaining three men simultaneously. This sort of decor was quite common in brothels, although seldom of such high quality. It was not unknown in the bedrooms of the more uninhibited bachelors. It was not at all common in the main room of houses, respectable or otherwise. We Romans are seldom shocked, except by the doings of our women.

"Yes, isn't it? I have decided that since life is terribly brief, there is little point in stinting oneself on its pleasures. Besides, I love to shock people."

"I am shocked, Claudia," I assured her. "Generations of ancestrial Claudians are shocked as well."

She made an impatient face. "That's another thing. Why should we conduct ourselves to please a lot of dead people? Anyway, most of my ancestors were scandalous when they were alive, so why should their being dead make them such paragons of righteousness?"

"I am sure I do not know," I told her. She handed me one of the small goblets.

"This is the rarest wine of Cos. It dates from the Consulate of Aemilius Paullus and Terentius Varro, and it would be a crime to water it." I accepted the goblet from her hand and sipped at it. Ordinarily, we regard drinking unmixed wine as barbarous, but we make an exception for exceptionally rare wines, drunk in small quantities. It was indeed rich, so full-flavored that even a small sip filled the senses with the ancient grapes of sunny Cos. It had a strange, bitter undertaste. At the time, I thought that it might be from the evil that cursed the year of its making. Paullus and Varro had been the Consuls whose army had met Hannibal at Cannae. The wily Carthaginian had chosen to fight on a day when the incompetent Varro was in command, and the Roman army had been all but annihilated by the much smaller mercenary force commanded by Hannibal, the most brilliant general who ever lived. It was the blackest day in Rome's history, and there were still some Romans who would touch nothing made during that Consulate.

"I am rather glad it has fallen out this way, Decius," Claudia told me, "in spite of our misunderstanding. Isn't this much better than meeting in a house full of overfed and drunken politicians?"

"I couldn't agree more."

"You are the first man I have invited to my little refuge from the sordid world." This, at least, I was happy to hear.

"I trust that you will remain discreet," I said.

"As long as it suits me," she said. "No longer than that."

"Yet I urge you to be cautious. Periods of license are always followed by periods of reaction, when the Senate and People reassert their virtue by persecuting those who were not discreet in their debaucheries. The Censors love to publicly condemn highborn men and women who have lived too loosely."

"Oh, yes," she said, bitterness in her voice. "Especially women. Women who live to please themselves disgrace their husbands, don't they? Men don't dishonor their wives. Well, Decius, let me adopt the sibylline mantle and show you the future. Someday, my brother Publius will be the greatest man in Rome. No man, whatever his office, will dare to condemn me to my face then, and I care not at all for what is said behind my back."

Truthfully, in that moment she resembled a sibyl. The exaggerated cosmetics she wore made her face a hiero-phantic mask, but I hoped that this was a mere effect of the light. The prospect of Publius Claudius wielding real power in Rome was horrifying in the extreme.

She relaxed from the rigid pose. "But we are being too serious. I did not invite you here to argue. I will make a bargain with you: If you will refrain from passing judgment on my chosen means of relaxation, I will not bore you with predictions of my own or my brother's future prominence."

"Agreed," I said. Indeed, it seemed a fine idea. My mind had entered an odd state, free-floating and de-tached, in that degree of preternatural receptiveness which the more lurid Epicurean philosophers agree is the best for indulging in pleasure, without the distrac-tions of everyday life or the fears of future conse-quences. "Let us carve this night from the fabric of our lives and hold it separate forever."

"I could not have put it better. Chrysis, perform for us."

I had all but forgotten the girl, and was a bit surprised to see her sitting on a cushion, sipping from a goblet, as if she were an equal. This was yet another indication of her uncertain status. She rose and went into one of the

other chambers, to return holding a coiled rope. One
end of this she affixed to a bronze ring set into one wall
of the room. She stretched it across the room and fastened it to another ring in the wall opposite. It was not
taut, about four feet from the floor. It was only about
the thickness of a man's smallest finger.

"Chrysis has so many talents," Claudia whispered,
leaning close so that our shoulders touched. "She has
been a professional tumbler, among other things." What
other things? I thought. But then my attention was taken
once more by Chrysis. Her hand went to her shoulder
and her dress fell to pool around her bare feet. She stood
dressed only in the briefest of loincloths and her body
was almost that of an adolescent boy. Only her large nip-
ples and the rondure of her buttocks attested to her sex.
I found this androgyny strangely stirring. It was especially strange since I had the utterly feminine Claudia so
near me. I decided that it was an effect of the rare wine,
and I sipped more of it.

With an adroit leap, Chrysis sprang onto the rope and
crouched with her knees deeply bent, her arms spread
for balance. Slowly, she straightened until she was standing, one foot poised delicately before the other. Then
she began to bend backward, her hair falling to touch
the rope as her spine bent like a full-drawn bow. Her
hands touched the rope and her pelvis arched upward
like, it seemed to me, that of a woman offering herself
to a god. The image, bizarre as it was, seemed pleasing
at the time.

Her feet kicked free of the rope and she was standing
on her hands. Slowly, she raised her head and bent her
spine until the soles of her feet rested against the back
of her head. Then, impossibly, her feet slid past her ears
and continued downward until her toes dangled an inch
or two above the rope. Her body was now bent backward
into a near-circle. I could scarcely believe that a human
spine could be so flexible.

"She can play the double flute in that position," Claudia whispered. "She can play a harp with her toes and shoot a bow with her feet."

"A many-talented girl," I murmured. Unbidden through my mind went lascivious images of other possibilities of which such a body might be capable. Claudia could read my expression.

"Perhaps later we can have her demonstrate the talents she never uses for public performances."

I turned to her, managing to shake off a bit of Chrysis's spell. "I am not interested in her," I lied. "I am only interested in you."

She leaned even closer. "Why be so quick to dispose of one of us?"

I was not certain of her meaning, but then my mind was playing tricks, disoriented by wine, the unexpected surroundings and the seemingly impossible things Chrysis was doing. One can watch a single improbability without losing equilibrium. Several, either simultaneously or in succession, unsettle the brain.

Chrysis performed a backward somersault from the rope and launched into a series of back handsprings, each time touching the floor so lightly that even these violent exertions were accomplished in the eerie silence that seemed to accompany all her movements. Then she stood before us, her legs spread wide, bending backward until her face appeared between her knees, as if she had been beheaded and now gripped her head between her legs like a ball. Her hands grasped her ankles. Slowly, her head turned and her tongue snaked out to slide upward along her thigh. Her head twisted intricately and she straightened, but now a long strip of white dangled from her mouth. Somehow, she had unknotted her loincloth with her teeth and stripped it off as she whipped her spine back into a more normal position. Now she stood before us dressed only in a fine sheen of sweat. There could be no doubt of her gender now, her smooth-shaven pubis gleaming before us like a pearl. She spat out the loincloth and smiled proudly as she bowed.

I applauded vigorously, the sound of my hands clapping seeming to come from far away. Claudia applauded as well; then she leaned closer and my arms went around her as her lips spread against mine. Our tongues met as our hands explored one another; then she drew back with a look of consternation.

"What's this?" I couldn't guess what she meant; then her hands rummaged in my tunic and came out with the dagger and the *caestus*. For no good reason, I collapsed into laughter.

"Dangerous place, Rome," I gasped. "Especially at night."

She seemed to find this absurdly funny as well, and she tossed the weapons into a corner before she came back into my arms. Our breathing grew ragged and our movements became more urgent. I felt intimately involved yet detached at the same time, and some of the things happening did not seem quite real. When I reached to the shoulder-clasps of her dress, my hands were as clumsy as if they were half-frozen, yet the dress fell away from her shoulders anyway. Another moment, I was dressed only in a loincloth, yet I had no memory of removing my tunic. Gaps began to appear in events, while other things had a clarity such as one ordinarily experiences only when taking part in a unique event, such as an initiation into one of the great Mysteries.

I remember Claudia standing before me naked in the lamplight. Like those of many highborn ladies of that time, her body had been plucked of every hair below the scalp and her skin smoothed by rubbing with pumice. She looked almost like a Greek statue of a goddess, yet I could see every individual pore in her flesh. Slowly she turned and she became my Artemis sculpted by Praxiteles.

Other things were not so clear. Sometime in the night, I felt Claudia's flesh with my palms, but realized that there were too many hands on me. I opened my eyes to see Chrysis lying with us in the welter of cushions, a smile of malignant sensuality on her foxlike features. By that time I was too far gone to protest anything. I had lost all rational faculties and became a being of pure sensation.

The night dissolved into a phantasmagoria of tangled limbs, sweaty cushions, guttering light from untrimmed lamps, bitter-tasting wine. I touched and tasted and thrust and I lost all ability to discern where my own body left off and another began. My world became a place of thighs and breasts, of mouths and tongues and fingers that stroked and penetrated in endless combinations. I would be buried in one woman with the other's thighs gripping the sides of my head and I could not tell which was which. There are libertines who esteem this sort of omnisexual activity to be the most gratifying possible, but I found this occasion not merely confusing but difficult to remember afterward. Since experiences one does not remember might as well not have happened, I have never made a regular practice of such entertainments.

I woke with a ringing head and that much-esteemed gray light of the Roman dawn streaming through the small, high windows onto my upturned face. With loins inert and stomach heaving, I struggled to my feet and fought to keep a precarious balance. My fair companions of the previous night were gone. Standing there, naked, sick and disgusted, I felt thoroughly used. But to what purpose?

I rummaged around the large room, finding my clothes in the oddest places. My weapons were still in the corner where Claudia had tossed them. I tucked them beneath my girdle and looked to see if I had forgotten anything. My memories of the night before were so unclear that I did not remember whether I had been in any of the other rooms, so I decided to explore them just in case.

One room was a tiny, dark kitchen. The stove looked as if it had never been used, although there was charcoal in the storage niche beneath it. Claudia probably had food brought in when she used the place. Next to the kitchen so as to share the same water pipes was a small bathroom, with a lion-footed bronze tub, also looking unused.

There were two small bedrooms, one for Claudia and one for Chrysis, I guessed, although neither contained any personal objects. The last room was a storeroom containing a disassembled litter. I closed the door and turned away, when something about the litter tickled my recently malfunctioning memory. I turned back and opened the door again.

The light was quite dim, since storerooms never have windows, and the windows of the other rooms of the apartment were very small, as is customary with windows opening onto the street. There is no real need to put out a welcome sign for housebreakers. I went back into the larger room and examined the smoky lamps until I found one with a wick still smoldering. With the point of my dagger I teased the twist of tow from its bath of perfumed oil, blowing on it gently until a tiny flame sprang into life. When the flame was well established I carried the lamp back into the storeroom.

The litter was like a thousand others in Rome: a light framework of olive wood with a woven leather bottom like the suspension of a bed. There were leather loops in the sides for the carrying-poles to pass through and spindly rods forming a frame from which to drape the hangings. It was the hangings that interested me. They had probably been wetted by rain on their last outing, because someone had spread them over drying-rods. I pulled a fold close to the lamp and studied it. It was colorfully embroidered with silk thread in a design of twining, flowering vines and stylized birds. This was the Parthian fashion, and I knew where I had seen such a palanquin before. It had been when I left the house of Sergius Paulus and was engaged in conversation by the priest of the little Temple of Mercury. A litter very like this one had left Paulus's house, bearing a veiled person.

I replaced the hanging and the lamp and left the house. Up the street, a barber was setting up his stool and basin, laying out his tools on a folding table. I rubbed a palm over my bristled face and decided it was time for a shave.

In my younger days, most men in public life made a point of being shaved by street barbers like any ordinary citizen. This morning, though, I had a better reason than usual for seeking out one of these humble businessmen. Barbers are, notoriously, the best-informed gossips in the city. Most of them disdain any such luxurious frippery as a shop, and carry out their trade right on the public thoroughfare from which point of vantage they shave half the citizenry while observing the other half.

"A shave, good sir?" the man asked as I staggered up to him. "Please be seated," he said, as grandly as if he were offering the Consul's place to an honored guest. I sat on the stool and braced myself for the ordeal to come. Along with early rising, old Romans professed to find great virtue in enduring the dull razors of the public barbers.

"Had a rough night, eh?" he said, winking and nudging my shoulder. "Shaved many a young gentleman after such a night, I have. You won't be the first, sir, never fear." He stropped his razor on a palm as horny as Milo's. "Now, unlike some, sir, I know what it's like being shaved with a hangover. Like having your skin stripped by the executioner, ain't it, sir?" He chuckled. "Well, rest assured that I do better than that. The secret's in mixing curdled ass's milk with your oil. Leaves your skin smooth as a baby's bottom." So saying, he began to anoint my face with this potion. Every barber had his secret recipe, and this one had an odd yet not unpleasant smell.

"Tell me," I said as he began his ministrations, "how long has that *insula* been there?" I pointed at the one where Claudia had her apartment. Now I could see that it was only four stories high, not large by the standards of the time.

"Why, that one was built only last year." He began to scrape at my beard. Whether it was the sharpness of his razor or the efficacy of his lotion, it was almost as smooth as being shaved by my father's *tonsores*, a Syrian slave of

legendary skill. "The old place on that site burned, sir.
It was a most fearsome fire and had the whole neighborhood in an uproar. Luckily the vigiles were nearby,
though most of the time they're useless. We got the water
pipes up out of the street and had the fire doused before
it could spread. Building was a loss, though."

"Who built the new one, do you know?" I asked as he
scraped his blade down my neck.

"Some freedman. One of the big, rich ones, so they
say. What's his name? Let's see, now." He began to shave
the back of my neck. "They say the bugger's almost as
rich as Consul Crassus, and owns as much property in
the city."

I didn't want to put ideas in the fellow's head, but I
had to know whether my suspicion was right. "I think I
know the one you mean. He has the same nomen as that
old Consul, doesn't he? I mean the one who was Varro's
colleague when Hannibal met the army at Cannae?"

The barber spat on the cobbles. "Curse the day. But
aye, you're right. The fellow's name is Paulus. Sergius
Paulus, that's it. Richest freedman in Rome, they say, and
that's saying something. Owns half the city, including
that *insula* there. Damn shame when freedmen are so
rich and a common citizen has to work all day to make
a living."

"With the legions, were you?" I asked absently. I knew
the type.

"Fifteen years with General Sulla," he said proudly.
"So what if we didn't get the land we were promised?
They were good years. I can see you're no stranger to
the Eagles, either. That's a fine scar you've got there, sir,
if you don't mind my saying."

I rubbed the scar. The man had done a neat job of
shaving around it. "Spain. With General Metellus. Not
the big fights with Sertorius, but the mountain fighting
with his Catalan guerrillas."

The barber whistled. "Rough fighting, that. We had
some like it in Numidia. There, sir, how's that?" He held
out a bronze mirror and I admired myself in reflection.

The man had done a very creditable job, considering the material he had been presented with.

"Splendid," I assured him. "Tell me, that *insula*—do you know anything about the people who live in it?"

The barber finally decided that I was a little peculiar in my interest in that building. "Well, sir . . ."

"I am Decius Caecilius Metellus the Younger, of the Commission of Twenty-Six," I told him. "There have been complaints of irregularities in the construction and leasing of that *insula*, and I would like to know what the neighboring citizens think of it."

"Oh. In that case, sir, we know little. This fellow Sergius Paulus has leased the ground floors to some grand people and the uppers to tradesmen and such. Pretty fair digs, I hear, but they're new. In a few years it'll be a slum like most."

"I daresay. Do you know anything about a lady who owns one of the ground-floor apartments? She sometimes comes and goes in a rich litter carried by Numidians."

The barber shrugged. "You must mean the one who's had the decorators in these last few months. Never seen her myself, but there's some that says she keeps late hours. Never heard of any Numidians, though. Some said she was carried by Egyptians. Others say it's black Nubians."

So Claudia was leasing her bearers rather than using family slaves. There were agencies in the city that did such leasing, but it would be futile to check with them. In all probability, she borrowed litter bearers from friends as well. I would learn little by determining her means of locomotion in any case. I could ask the slaves where they had taken her, but in all likelihood, they would not remember. Why should they? And, practically, what would be the use? Slaves could testify in court only under torture, and nobody believed them anyway.

"I thank you," I said, paying the man an *as*. He was surprised at the munificence of the payment. A quarter *as* would have been more like it.

"Right, sir. Anytime you need to know about this part of the city, just ask for Quatrus Probus the barber."

I assured him that I would always rely upon him and began to make my way home. In future years, the old soldier turned barber became one of my better informants, although he always acted out of a citizen's duty, never as a self-seeking informer.

My clients ignored me elaborately as I staggered into my house. "Not a word," I said to Cato as he rushed up to me. "Everyone, to the praetor's. We are late."

We trotted off to my father's house. Old Cut-Nose himself called me aside as we arrived. "Where have you been?" he hissed. It was unusual to see him so agitated.

"I was out behaving like the worst degenerate," I told him.

"That I do not doubt. Well, the night was not uneventful, however you may have spent it."

"Oh?" I said. "How so?"

"There was a murder last night, and in your district!"

I felt a distinct chill, of the kind I used to feel when, as a boy, I realized that it was time to present my lessons to my Latin master, only to realize that I was unprepared.

"Bad enough that you were out carousing with your friends," he continued, "but you were not even at home to receive the report of the vigiles."

"And what of import did they have to communicate this morning?" I asked impatiently. "There's little enough most mornings."

"Just that one of the richest men in Rome has been murdered," my father said. The hairs upon my newly shaven nape began to stand. "Lowborn though he was, his murder will be a great nuisance."

"And his name?" I asked, already half-knowing.

"Sergius Paulus, richest freedman of the generation. You've no idea how difficult the scum's demise has made my job."

"And how, Father," I said through gritted teeth, "has

this man's death made your task even more complicated?"

"It's Herculaneum," the old man groused. "That was his home town. Like so many of these freedmen, he made up for his humble early years by being a patron to his home town. You know how they do it ... a great, ostentatious amphitheater erected to the memory of his putative ancestors, a theater, a Temple of Juno and so forth. Now all of these local magistrates will be flocking to my court, demanding to know how these projects are to be finished, now that the unfortunate Sergius Paulus is dead."

"Speaking of that unfortunate man," I said, "how did he meet his end?"

Father's eyebrows went up. "How should I know? You're the one who was not home to receive the vigile's report. Go ask the captain. He's here someplace."

I hurried off to push my way among Father's clients in search of the captain of the vigiles of my own ward. I found him sleepily downing some leftover cakes along with some elderly wine, heavily watered. I grasped his arm and whirled him to face me.

"What happened?" I demanded.

"Well, sir, you weren't home and so I came here to the home of the praetor your father, just as you said for me to do, should you not be able to—"

"Splendid!" I all but shouted, drawing some strange looks from Father's other clients. "You've remembered your duty admirably. Now, what happened last night?"

He began to tell me of the events of the night before. He had been stomping through the streets at the head of his bucket-bearing men when a hysterical slave had run up to him and begged him to come at once. An important man had been killed, by violence.

"How was Paulus killed?" I asked.

"Strangled, sir, with a bowstring garrote, it looked like. Just like that freed gladiator a few days ago, now that I think about it."

"Say you so?" I commented. "What was the condition of his household?"

"Didn't check. I posted a guard at the door and ordered that no one was to leave; then I ran to your house. From there I came here. It hasn't been an hour since Paulus's slave stopped me."

I tried to think, a difficult process since I had not yet shaken off the effects of the previous night. What had Claudia slipped into the wine? I recalled the bitter undertaste now. It was just like a Claudian to adulterate one of the finest wines in existence. In an odd way, it was comforting to know that I had been drugged. It gave me an excuse for behaving like a demented satyr.

I returned to my father's side. "Father, I must conduct an investigation at once. May I borrow your lictors? I have to get there before the officials show up. The slaves will have to be confined until the murderer is identified. There will be a terrible scramble to lay hands on Paulus's wealth. I don't believe he had a son."

"Very well." Father gestured and two lictors joined us. "I shall be there myself sometime today, as Urban Praetor. What a tangled mess this will be. It always is when one of these rich freedmen dies. No proper family to lay claim to his property. Had he a wife?"

"I shall find out," I promised.

"Be off with you, then. Have a report ready for me when I arrive."

As we left Father's house, my clients trooping behind, I told one of the lictors, "Go to the ludus of Statilius Taurus and summon the physician Asklepiodes. Fetch him to the house of Sergius Paulus." The man marched calmly away. It is useless to demand that lictors run. They are too conscious of their own dignity.

At least now I had something to distract my mind from my ringing head and heaving stomach. The news would be all over the city soon. Murder was not uncommon in Rome, but the murder of prominent men is always a matter for scandal. There had been a time, not so many years before, when no one would have blinked at this.

During the proscriptions, Senators and *equites* had been slain in droves. Informers had been given a part of the seized property of a denounced traitor, so any rich man was at risk. But men have short memories and more recent years had been peaceful and prosperous. The murder of the richest freedman in Rome would occupy the conversation of idlers for days.

The vigile leaned against the doorpost of Paulus's house, half-asleep when we arrived. Blinking and yawning, he assured me that nobody had been past him since his captain had gone off in search of me. He stood aside and I passed through, along with my lictor and clients. I turned to Burrus, my old soldier.

"Check through every room. Find whether there are other exits or windows large enough for a man to crawl through." He nodded and strode purposefully off. A fat, distressed-looking man came rushing up, bowing and sweating.

"Sir, I am so glad you have come. This is terrible, terrible. My master, Sergius, has been murdered."

"So I've heard. "And you are . . . ?"

"Postumus, the majordomo, sir. Please come—"

I cut him off with a wave of the hand. "Assemble all the house slaves at once in the peristylium," I ordered. "Has anyone left the house since the body was discovered?"

"Absolutely not, sir. And the household staff are already gathered, if you will come with me."

"Excellent. Had Paulus a wife?"

"He had a slave-wife before he was emancipated, but she died before he was freed." Slaves, of course, cannot contract legal marriage, but only the hardest masters fail to recognize these slave liaisons.

"Any free children?"

"None, sir."

The vultures would be gathering with a vengeance, I thought. We entered the peristylium. Paulus's was a colonnaded courtyard without a pool but with a sundial in the center. The space was ordinary for a country house but extremely large for a town house. This was all to the good because there were at least two hundred slaves assembled there.

The tears were copious; the sobbing and shrieking would have done credit to a band of professional mourners. It might have been because Paulus had been a kind master, but more likely because they were terrified, and with good reason. They were trapped in a slave's worst nightmare. If it should happen that the master had been murdered by one of them, and should that slave not come forth to confess, or be exposed, every one of them would be crucified. It was one of our cruelest and most detestable laws, but it stood, and should I not find the murderer, Cato (the repulsive Senator, not my excellent slave) would insist that it be put into effect. He probably would not bother to take into account that the victim had been a freedman rather than freeborn; a master was a master to Cato. He never passed up a chance to be as primitive and brutal as the ancestors he worshipped.

"Who last saw the master alive?" I said loudly enough for all to hear. Hesitantly, a very large, pudgy eunuch came forward.

"I am Pepi, sir," he said in a fluting voice. "I always sleep across my master's doorway, to protect his rest and to come at his call should he need help in the night."

"You were not much help to him this night. Someone got past you."

"Impossible!" he insisted, with a eunuch's childlike indignation. "I wake at the slightest sound. That is why my master chose me for this duty. That, and because I am strong and could easily get him out of his bed and to the chamberpot when he was in no condition to do so himself."

"Excellent," I said. "That makes you the prime suspect." The almost-man went terribly pale, already feeling the nails in his flesh. "Was there anything unusual last night when he went to bed?"

"N-nothing, master. He had drunk much wine, as on most nights. I undressed him, put him into his bed and covered him. He was snoring before I left the room and closed the door. I lay on my pallet and went to sleep. Like every other night."

"Was there nothing unusual? Did nothing wake you? Think hard, man, if you fear the cross."

He thought, sweat coming forth on his pale brow. His eyes widened a bit as a thought came into his dull mind. "Yes, there was something. Once, in the very early morning hours, something caused me to wake. I thought that the master might have called me, but there had been no sound. Then I knew that the master was no longer snoring, and that was why I woke. That happens sometimes. I went back to sleep."

"It makes sense," I said. "Dead men seldom snore. How did you know what the hour was?"

"From my pallet I can see down the hall into the peristylium. There was a very faint light, the light of the hour before dawn."

I addressed the slaves. "All of you are to stay in the house, and stay calm. Should anyone try to escape, that will be a confession of complicity and you will be crucified. Be of good heart. I will have the murderer soon, and I do not believe it is one of you." I had no such assurance, but I could not afford to have mass panic here. They looked at me gratefully, and with hope, making me feel like a wretched fraud.

Burrus entered the peristylium. "No other doors but the street door, sir," he said, then chuckled. "And we always wonder why so many die in fires. All the windows are too small for any but a child to pass through, like in most town houses. Of course"—he jerked a thumb at the wide opening over the courtyard—"you could drop an elephant through this *compluvium.*"

I crooked a finger and the majordomo sprang to my side. "Have a ladder fetched," I said. "I want to examine that roof." He snapped his fingers and a slave went running.

"Now I want to see Sergius Paulus," I said. I followed the majordomo down a short hall to an open door. The eunuch's pallet still lay on the floor, shoved aside and forgotten. Before going inside, I swung the door back and forth. It opened outward, into the hall. Eunuch and pallet would have to be moved before anyone could get in. Also, it creaked loudly on unoiled hinges.

Inside, the room was surprisingly spare and unadorned for a man so rich. There was a small table and a low bed just large enough for his corpulent body. I have noted this about ex-slaves many times. A bedroom is no more than a place for exhausted sleep. Paulus's pleasures were those of the table and the bath.

He lay on the bed, his face contorted, a deep, livid line encircling his neck. Despite his expression, there were no signs of a struggle. He had gone to bed drunk and probably never woke up. The cord had not been left in place.

High on the wall opposite the door was a window which measured no more than a foot on each of its four sides, perhaps even a little less. Only a boy could have entered that way. I suspected that one had. I left and gave orders that no one was to enter.

I was standing on the ladder, examining the roof, when I heard someone call my name. I looked down and there stood my father with a knot of other officials.

"Why are you standing on a ladder like a housepainter when you should be attending to official business?" he demanded.

"I am attending to official business," I said. "I am examining this roof. It's in shocking condition. Decrepit tile and moss everywhere. Why be as rich as Paulus if you can't have a decent roof?"

"Approving of construction standards may be your duty when you are a quaestor. Not now."

I took a tile at the edge of the *compluvium* and shook it. Fragments of decayed tile dropped into the gutter that drained rain from the courtyard. There were no other fragments on the ground. I descended the ladder. "Whoever it was didn't come in over the roof. The moss and the tiles would show that."

"Why this philosophical interest in such details?" someone asked. I saw that it was my colleague Rutilius. Opimius was there as well.

"I want to find out who the murderer was."

"It's obvious," Opimius said. "That fat eunuch killed him. The window's too small to let in a housebreaker, and the slave slept across the door. Who had a better opportunity?"

I looked at him disgustedly. "Don't talk like an idiot."

"What do you mean?" he demanded.

"Even a blockhead like that would know better than to use a garrote," I said. "Or a dagger or any other weapon. You've seen how big he is. With Paulus in a drunken stupor, he'd just smother him with a pillow. The next morning it would look like he'd died naturally, the way fat men who drink too much often die. I'll bet many a master who was too free with the whip was helped along in such a fashion."

"Don't speak so!" said Rutilius, deeply shocked.

"Why not? We all live in fear of being murdered in our beds by our own slaves. Don't tell me you haven't thought of it. Why else do we crucify a whole houseful of them for one murder? Why else did Crassus crucify six thousand rebel slaves last year?"

They were all shocked and deeply offended. I was speaking of something far more sensitive than their wives' chastity. It was the secret fear we all live with and deny. On a better day, I would not have spoken so loosely, but this was definitely not one of my good days.

"If not the eunuch, then who?" my father said, dragging us back to the matter at hand.

"I don't know, but . . ." I realized that I was admitting uncertainty at the wrong time, to the wrong people. I sought to cover my gaffe. "I have strong, almost certain suspicions. However,"—I looked around and lowered my voice—"now is not the time or place to say anything, if you know what I mean." Of course they didn't, but they nodded sagely. All Romans love a conspiracy.

"Carry on, then," Father said. "But don't take too long

at it." He turned and bellowed, "Secretary!" in the voice
that had once struck terror into a veteran legion. An ink-
fingered Greek came running. "Did Paulus leave a will?"
Father demanded.

"Yes, Praetor. Copies are filed at the Archives and in
the temples of Vesta and Saturn. The master always made
out a new will in January of each year."

"A new one each year?" Father said. "Had a hard time
making up his mind, did he? Well, a testament will sim-
plify things greatly."

Rutilius snorted. "Forgive me, Praetor, but it will do
no such thing. If he'd come from a great family, with
many important relatives to uphold it, who would contest such a will? But when it was a mere freedman, and
so much property at stake? The fighting will be vicious
and will go on for a long time."

"You are probably right," Father said. "Perhaps we can
get the reading delayed until after the new year and the
next board of magistrates can handle it. I'll be in Hither
Spain and out of all this." In those days, when the new
praetors for the year entered office, the Senate decided
what their propraetorian provinces should be when they
left office. They would govern these provinces for a year,
or perhaps two or three years. Even for an honest administrator, there were legitimate opportunities for
growing very rich in such an office. Father had drawn
Hither Spain as his province. It wasn't one of the real
plums, but it wasn't bad at all.

Father indicated, in that way that powerful men have,
that he would rather be alone, and Rutilius, Opimius
and the others went off, pretending to be investigating.

"Son," said Decius Caecilius Metellus the Elder to Decius Caecilius Metellus the Younger, "perhaps you should
come to Spain with me. Serve on my staff. This is not a
bad time to be out of Rome. Besides, a little experience
in provincial administration will be good for you. Best
to see some work in the lower levels before the Senate
drops a whole province on your shoulders."

The old man was, in his way, being solicitous. He

wanted to spare me the consequences of my own folly, as long as it could be done under the aegis of duty.

"I'll consider it, Father," I said. "But first I have a murderer to catch, perhaps several."

"That's fine," he said. "But keep a sense of proportion. You have some murder victims in your district, but what are they? A manumitted gladiator, the lowest of scum; an obscure Greek-Asiatic importer, now a freedman. Admittedly a rich freedman, but an ex-slave nevertheless. Don't endanger your career, your future, your very life, for the likes of these."

I looked at him, and for the first time saw a rather frightened old man, but still a man who cared about his son. "Free citizens have been murdered in the Subura, Father," I said. "The Subura is my district. I will see justice."

There was nothing he could say to that. A Roman magistrate could no more deny duty than he could deny the gods. It was unfair of me, of course. I had no stake in the Roman order in those days, without wife or children or high office. I belonged to the most expendable group of citizens—the wellborn young men who traditionally made up the junior officer corps. But in that moment I felt quite virtuous, and so miserable that I cared not whether I lived or died. I do not know whether this was because of my heedless youth, or was just the spirit of the times. Most of the rising men of my generation behaved as if they held their own lives as cheap as they held the lives of others. Even the richest and best-born would resort unhesitatingly to desperate action, knowing that their lives would be the forfeit of failure. In that moment, I was as reckless as any.

A few minutes later Asklepiodes arrived. The place was growing as crowded as the Senate chamber during a war debate. Two quaestors had arrived with their secretaries and were making an inventory of the house with the aid of the majordomo. Two lictors had arrived to take the unfortunate eunuch to the prison beneath the Capitol, there to await his fate.

"Another murder?" Asklepiodes asked.

"And an odd one," I told him. "Please come with me." We went to the bedroom, the only part of the house that was not swarming. Asklepiodes knelt by the bed and examined the victim's neck.

"I would like to see the back of his neck, but I will need aid in turning him."

I turned to my clients, who stood just outside the doorway. "Help him lift the body." They shook their heads and backed away. Romans will do awful things to a live man's body, but they are afraid to touch a dead one, for fear of some unspecified contamination. "Fetch some slaves, then," I ordered. A few minutes later they had the body on its side and Asklepiodes exclaimed triumphantly and pointed at a round indentation in the ring of darkened skin encircling the neck.

"What is it?" I asked.

"The knot. It is typical of the bowstring garrote, as used by the Syrians."

A new shadow blocked the doorway and I turned to tell whoever it was to be off, but I wisely refrained from doing so. It was the Consul, Pompey the Great. With all of *his* lictors and attendants, I thought, the house must be about to erupt like a volcano, its walls bursting outward onto the streets outside.

"Greeting, Metellus the Younger," he said. Pompey was a handsome, square-faced man of excellent bearing, but he always looked uncomfortable in a toga, as if armor suited him better.

"Your Honor," I said, straightening from where I crouched by Paulus. "I didn't expect to see you here at a murder investigation."

He barely glanced at the corpse. "When one as rich as this one dies, the whole Roman economy is in danger. There's a great crowd out in the street. Now they've seen me here, things will calm down. The citizenry are like troubled children. When they see one who is known as a successful general, they think everything will be all right."

It made sense. "Will his death cause such an uproar?" I asked.

"When I passed through the Forum, the slave speculators were already asking each other what it would do to the price of slaves. The man must have owned thousands. If they all go on the market at once, the prices will plunge. No one yet knows how much land and livestock he owned, how many ships and cargoes. I know he had an interest in some mines in Spain, although he owned none outright."

Pompey, who owned many such mines, would be in a position to know. He glanced at Asklepiodes. "A trifle late to summon a physician, isn't it?"

"He is not here to treat the victim, but to examine him," I explained. "Master Asklepiodes is an expert in all manner of violent wounds. I've found his expertise to be most useful in my investigations."

Pompey raised his eyebrows. "That's a new idea. Well, carry on." He turned to leave, then turned back. "But I shouldn't waste a great deal of time on this. The real problem will be for the quaestors and praetors to sort out. The man himself amounted to nothing. The eunuch killed him. My advice is, just leave it at that."

"I will leave it," I told him, "when I am satisfied that the murderer has been caught."

"As you will." His look was not hostile, his words were not loud, but his tone was bone-chilling. He left a great silence behind him when he walked out of the bedroom.

VII

"I still cannot understand it," I said to Asklepiodes. We sat in his spacious quarters at the Ludus of Statilius Taurus. I had never been in a physician's quarters before, and I suspected that his decor was odd by the standards of that profession. Every manner of weapon hung on his walls or stood in racks around the rooms. Many of them had scrolls affixed describing the various wounds they could inflict.

"That a man was strangled?" Asklepiodes said.

"No. I have three murders here, and one break-in and robbery, all of them somehow connected. And an arson, let's not forget that. Sinistrus undoubtedly killed Paramedes, but who strangled Sinistrus? And I can't believe that it was the same person who killed Sergius Paulus. Do we have three murderers here? And who broke into my house, cracked me on the head and stole that amulet? Macro said that must have been done by a boy, and he seems to be a foreigner." I paced the floor and walked to a window. From below came the clattering, the shouts and the labored breathing of the fighters practicing in the palaestra.

"It is a difficult problem." Asklepiodes toyed with a decorated silver stylus. "But why do you think it was not the same person who killed Paulus and Sinistrus?"

I sat on a fine couch and rested my chin on a fist. "You were in Paulus's bedroom. You saw the window. I don't believe that the eunuch killed him. And I doubt that he would have let anyone else past, knowing that it meant his own crucifixion. So the murderer came in through the window. The boy who broke into my house might have done it. Very well, there is nothing logically wrong with that. It would be no great task to strangle a drunken, snoring fat man."

"I follow you so far," Asklepiodes said. He was wearing the plaited silver hair-fillet I had given him on the last occasion. I reminded myself to choose another present for him.

"But the boy could not have strangled Sinistrus, who was a large, powerful man and a trained fighter. So there must be two murderers, both expert with the bowstring."

Asklepiodes set down the stylus and gave me a superior, knowing smile. "Why do you think that a man of exceptional strength must have strangled Sinistrus?"

This drew me up short. "Why, it seems ... how could it not be so?"

The physician shook his head. "The garrote is not the same thing as simply wrapping your hands around a man's neck and squeezing. Allow me to demonstrate." He got up and crossed to one of the walls and took a short bow from a peg. It was unstrung, the stout cord wrapped around the lower limb. Stripping the string from the bow, he stood before me with the string draped between his hands. "This is the most conventional way to use the garrote," he said, wrapping a turn of the cord around each hand. "You are far larger and stronger than I am. Even so ..." He stepped around behind me. A hand flashed in front of my face and I felt the cord biting into my neck. Even though I had been expecting it, I panicked immediately. There is no more shocking sensation than having a breath cut in half and knowing that you cannot breathe. I reached behind me and I could feel the physician pressed tightly against my back. I could grasp his clothes, but I could not secure a strong grip on his body to pull him loose. I began to charge at a wall, ready to twist so that I could crush him between my body and the wall, but instantly both the man and the cord were gone.

"You see?" he said as I sat and drew in great, ragged

breaths. "One need not be terribly strong to throttle even a powerful man. Unconsciousness comes in less than a minute. Death in five or six."

"But why," I said when I had breath, "did Sinistrus not crush the boy against a wall?"

"He may have been too shocked, or too stupid, but I think it may have been another reason." His fingers worked nimbly on the string, fashioning a knot. "You remember the spot on the back of Paulus's neck I showed you?"

I nodded. Asklepiodes stepped up to me and his hands moved swiftly. Then I was strangling again, only this time the Greek was standing before me, hands behind his back and smiling. My hands went to my neck, clawing at the cord, but it was buried in the flesh and I couldn't get them under it. Black spots appeared before my eyes and the inside of my head thundered like the Nile cataracts. I could feel the strength draining from my knees and I fell to all fours, no longer able even to feel my hands. I felt hands at the back of my neck and, suddenly, breath filled my lungs, sweet as water to a man dying of thirst.

Asklepiodes helped me to the couch and handed me a cup of watered wine. "You see," he said, holding the bowstring before my clearing eyes, "it is a noose rather than a true garrote. The Syrian slipknot tightens and will remain tight after it is released. Yet one who has the skill may loosen it in an instant."

"You must be the terror of your students," I croaked. "I hope you don't demonstrate the sword that way."

"I have found that a strong object lesson need not be repeated."

I had indeed learned not one but two valuable lessons, one of which was that it was unwise to rely upon my own limited assessment of any situation in which the circumstances were bizarre or unprecedented. At such times there is always a tendency to give one's own ignorance and prejudice the weight of knowledge. I vowed always to seek out informed and expert opinion, as one customarily does in legal, medical and religious matters.

I thanked Asklepiodes for half-killing me and de-parted. My puzzle had now been simplified to a small degree. The murderer of Sinistrus had also slain Sergius Paulus, and it was the same foreign boy who had broken into my house and attacked me. At this point, even a minor simplification was desirable.

My anger, on the other hand, was growing. Great men were conspiring to thwart my investigation. Claudia had, in some way I could not yet fathom, made use of me. Most illogical of all, I was angry at Paulus's murder. I had met him only once, and I suspected him of involve-ment in conspiracy, but I had liked the man. In a city of self-seeking politicians and military brigands who styled themselves patriots, I had found him a refreshingly hon-est vulgarian, a man devoted to the acquisition of prop-erty and the pleasures of the flesh as only one raised in slavery can be.

I had questioned many of Paulus's slaves before I left his house. They had been, of course, terrified at the pros-pect of crucifixion should the murderer not be found. They seemed to wish the eunuch no ill, but I could tell that they hoped he would be found guilty, because then they might be spared. Through all this, there was a pathetic hope in them, for Paulus had promised many that they would be freed in his will, should he die untimely.

I had not the heart to tell them that their hope was almost certainly futile, that many powerful men coveted their master's property, and they were part of that prop-erty. The will would almost certainly be broken. They had seemed honestly grief-stricken that Sergius was dead, and it takes a man as hard-hearted as Cato (the Senator) to remain untouched by such devotion. He had never remarried after losing his slave-wife, and while he had disported himself freely with his many pretty slave girls, he had never deceived any of them with promises of marriage, as so many heartless men do. He had never produced children by any woman, a curse which he at-tributed to a fever he suffered about the time he shaved his first beard.

To my taste, one Sergius Paulus was worth ten of Publius Claudius, a vicious lout born with every advantage but consumed with the belief that he had somehow been denied something. At least Rome gave a man like Paulus a chance to rise from servile status and make something of himself, as Paulus had. The Greeks have always looked down their Attic noses at us and called us uncouth barbarians, but I never heard of an Athenian slave in the greatest days of Pericles gaining his freedom, becoming a citizen and having a good prospect of seeing his sons sitting with purple-bordered togas in the Curia, debating the high matters of state with the other Senators.

You have to grant us that. We Romans have practiced cruelty and conquest on a scale never attempted by any other people, yet we are lavish with opportunity. We have enslaved whole nations, yet we do not hold a previous condition of servitude as a bar to advancement and high status. The patricians make much of their superiority, yet what are they but a pitiful remnant of a decrepit, priestly aristocracy long discredited?

The sad fact is that in those days we were mad. We fought class against class, family against family. We had even fought a war of masters against slaves. Many nations have been destroyed by civil war and internecine struggle. Rome always emerged stronger from each of these conflicts, another proof of our unique character. At this time, the infighting was between two parties: the *Optimates*, who thought themselves made up of the best men, an aristocratic oligarchy; and the *Populares*, who claimed to be the party of the common man. Actually the politicians of both parties had no ideals beyond their own betterment. Pompey, a former colleague of Sulla, was a leader of the *Optimates*, while Caius Julius Caesar, although a patrician, was a rising leader of the *Populares*. Caesar's uncle by marriage had been the great Marius, and the name of Marius was still revered by the *Populares*. With leaders like these, the fact that Rome was not easily destroyed by foreign enemies must prove that we enjoy the unique favor of the gods.

All these thoughts came to me at that time, but they did nothing to help solve my problem. And now I had another thing to consider. My father's wistful hope that the whole affair would be passed on to the next year's magistrates had reminded me that time was getting short. I had only about a month before the new magistrates took office. The committee positions are by appointment, not by the annual elections, but I had a strong suspicion that the next set of praetors would have their own favorites to appoint, and I would be out. This was when we were still using the old calendar, which would get out of order every few years, so that the *Pontifex Maximus* would have to declare an extra month. That year, the new year would begin on about the first of January, as it does now. The new calendar was one of Caesar's better ideas. (At least, he called it his calendar. It was Cleopatra's court astronomer, Sosigenes, who actually created it, and in truth it was Caesar's own neglect of his duties when he was *Pontifex Maximus* that got the old calendar into such dreadful shape in the first place. That's something you won't find in the histories written later by his lackeys.)

The oddest thing was that Pompey, or Crassus, or any of the praetors could have ordered me to cease my investigations, or to turn in a false report. Undoubtedly they wanted to do just that. After the chaos of the past years, however, our rulers were determined to follow constitutional forms, and to avoid any stigma of tyranny at all costs.

That did not mean, of course, that they would not stoop to any underhanded way to sabotage my work. Assassination was not out of the question. I was convinced that the only thing preserving me from these more extreme measures was my family's prestige. Both parties were courting the Metellans. We had an ancient reputation for moderation and levelheadedness in government. Metellans had always opposed the fanatical extremes of the various parties. As a result we had an enviable reputation with aristocrats and commoners alike, and only someone bent on political suicide would attack one of us too blatantly.

Still, I did not take great comfort in this knowledge. I have already mentioned the extreme recklessness of our politicians, and I did not yet know how desperate this vat of corruption might make them. So far, each man who might have led me to the solution of this puzzle had been murdered.

Then I remembered that there might be another. The merchant Zabbai had said that the pirates maintained an agent at Ostia. The port town was not more than fifteen miles from Rome, using either the river or the Via Ostiensis. There was a chance that he might be able to supply me with some much-needed information. It was worth a try, anyway. I determined to go immediately.

I returned to my house and filled a small purse from my chronically underweight money-chest and found my traveling-cloak, the same close-woven woolen garment I had worn when campaigning in Spain. I left word with Cato not to expect me back until late the next day and left my house.

I had only the slightest knowledge of Ostia, so I decided to take a guide with me, and I knew just the man for the job. I went to pay a visit to Macro.

He was surprised to see me. "Decius Caecilius, I was not expecting you. I still haven't received word of that estate manager in Baiae. I should know in two or three days."

"Excellent. As it occurs, I'm here about something else. I have to go to Ostia immediately and I need a guide, since I'll be calling on some less-than-official people. Lend me your boy Milo. I'll have him back to you by tomorrow evening."

"Certainly," Macro said. He sent a slave running to fetch Milo.

"Possibly you could help me further. I need to contact the agent who negotiates for the pirates in Ostia. Do you know his name and where he's to be found?"

Macro shook his head. "My territory stops at the city

walls. Milo should be able to tell you." He looked at me with a puzzled expression. "What happened to your neck?"

"My neck?"

"Yes. It looks like you tried to hang yourself. Are things that bad?"

My hand went to my throat. I could feel nothing, but I knew that it bore a mark like that around Sergius Paulus's neck. "Oh, that. I just had some lessons on the garrote. It's getting to be quite the fashion in Rome lately."

"So I've heard. It was Sergius Paulus this morning, wasn't it? Damned Asiatics. The city's filling up with them. Bad enough when they were just bringing in their foul gods and cults. Now they're using their strangling cords, as if Roman steel weren't good enough."

"Another sign of the times," I agreed. A few minutes later young Milo arrived and I explained what I wanted.

"Can you help him?" Macro asked.

"Certainly. We can catch a barge going back downriver empty and be there before nightfall. It's Hasdrubal you want to talk to. He's a Phoenician out of Tyre. He used to have a shop down by the Venus dock."

"Let's be off, then," I said. We left Macro's house and went to the river dock, a walk of only a few minutes. I had tucked the scarf Zabbai had given me inside my tunic and now I knotted it around my throat, soldier-fashion. I needed no more questions concerning the condition of my neck. As we walked, people waved to Milo and called his name. He waved back, smiling.

"You've become well-known in your short time in the city," I said.

"Macro's had me at work organizing the vote for the next elections."

"That's months away," I said. "It's early to be out wardheeling."

"That's what Macro said. I told him that it's never too early. He still thinks like an old-fashioned man. Most of them do. They think it's like public service or the religious calendar, where there are days for business and days for sacrifice and holidays and such. I say you take care of business every day, all year. Just in the time I've been here, I've done twice the work of any ten of Macro's men combined."

"Be careful with Macro," I cautioned. "Men like him can turn against young men who rise too fast." Then I saw three men walking toward us. We were passing near my house on our way to the river when one of them saw us and they walked toward us, their three bodies blocking the narrow street. In front was Publius Claudius.

"Now this is fortunate," Claudius said. "We were just at your house and your slave told us you had left town."

"I am on my way to catch a boat right now," I told him. His two companions were hulking brutes, scarred arena veterans whose tunics bulged with weapons. "Was it a social call?"

"Not precisely. I have certain advice for you, Decius, advice that our Consul Pompey is too polite to voice strongly enough. I want you to terminate all this snooping about in the doings of that Greek importer. Turn in a report stating quite truthfully that you were unable to find out who killed him and burned his warehouse."

"I see," I said. "And Sergius Paulus?"

He spread his hands. "The eunuch killed him. What could be simpler?"

"What, indeed? Oh, and Marcus Ager, alias Sinistrus? What of his murder?"

He shrugged. "Who cares? I warn you, Decius, turn in your report and no one will pursue the matter."

"You warn me, eh?" I was growing very tired of him and dangerously angry. "And under what authority do you make these demands, or should I say threats?"

"As a concerned Roman citizen. Will you heed my warning, Decius?"

"No. Now, get out of my way. You're interfering with a Roman official in the pursuit of his duties." I began to brush past him.

"Strabo, Cocles." At Publius's words, the two thugs reached into their tunics.

"Claudius," I said, "even you won't attack a public official in daylight."

"Don't tell me what I can do in my city!"

I realized then, for the first time, that Publius Claudius was mad. Typical Claudian. The thugs were bringing daggers from beneath their tunics and I knew that I had misjudged the situation. Even Pompey would not move against me directly, but Publius would. Belatedly, I began to reach for my own weapons.

"Excuse me, sir." Milo stepped past me and slapped the two strong-arm men. Just that, openhanded slaps, one to the right and one to the left. The two massive men went down like sacrificial oxen beneath the priest's ax. The sound of the two impacts was like breaking boards, and the men's faces were bloodied as if by spiked clubs. I have mentioned the hardness of Milo's palms. He pointed to Publius, who stood trembling with frustrated rage. "This one, too?"

"No, he's a patrician. You can kill them, but they don't take humiliation well."

"And who is this?" Publius hissed.

"Oh, forgive me. Where are my manners? Publius Claudius Pulcher, allow me to introduce Titus Annius Milo, late of Ostia and now a resident of our city, a client of Macro's. Milo, meet Publius Claudius Pulcher, scion of a long line of Consuls and criminals. Was there anything else, Claudius?" I considered telling him what I had been doing with his sister, just to see if I could induce apoplexy, but I really wasn't sure what I *had* done.

"Don't depend on your family to save you this time, Decius. This is no game for boys who aren't willing to play it seriously, to the end." He glared at Milo. "As for you, I suggest you go back to Ostia. This is *my* city!" Publius always spoke of Rome as if he were its sole proprietor.

Milo grinned. "I think I'll kill you now and save myself the trouble later."

"Not in front of me, you can't!" I told him. "Just because a fool deserves to die doesn't mean you can do it yourself."

Milo shrugged and flashed his smile at Claudius once more. "Later, then."

Publius nodded grimly. "Later."

We walked the rest of the way to the river without further violence. In later years I thought of how much trouble and grief I could have spared everybody by letting Milo kill Claudius that day. Even augurs cannot foresee the future, but can only divine the will of the gods through the signs they send. None but sibyls can look into the future, and they only speak gibberish. To me, on that day, Claudius was little more than a highborn nuisance, and Milo just an amiable young thug on the rise.

At the docks we asked a few questions and found a barge about to head downriver after discharging its cargo. We went aboard and found seats in the bow. Soon the bargemen cast off and we were drifting downstream. The rowers maneuvered the craft into the swiftest part of the stream and then concentrated on keeping us in a favorable position, letting the Tiber do most of the work.

This was a far more pleasant way to travel than by road. The wind was damp and chilly, but it would have been the same on the road, and there I would have been getting a sore backside riding a horse. The Via Ostiensis, like all highways near the city, was lined with tombs, as if reminders of mortality were really necessary. As if the tombs weren't mournful enough, most of them were covered with the painted advertisements for political candidates, announcements of upcoming Games and the declarations of lovers.

The river presented no such vulgar display. Once we were beyond the city, the Tiber floodplain was embellished with beautiful little farms, the occasional country houses of the wealthy and here and there a great latifundium with its own river wharf. After the continual uproar and clatter of the city, this travel by water was most restful. A following wind blew up, and the bargemen hoisted up their single, square sail, so that our progress was swifter and even more silent as the oars ceased to work against their tholes.

"Is he typical?" Milo asked. "That fool Claudius, I mean. Is he what most of the Roman politicians are like? I've heard of him before. They say he wants to be a tribune."

I wanted to say no, Claudius was an aberration, that most were conscientious servants of the state who desired only to be of honorable service to the Senate and People. Unfortunately, I couldn't.

"Most are like him," I said. "Publius is perhaps a little more ruthless, a little more mad."

Milo snorted. "I already like Rome. I think I'm going to like it even better."

We reached Ostia in late afternoon. I had only the sketchiest knowledge of the city, having embarked from there to go to Spain, at which time my friends had carried me aboard the ship quite drunk, so that my memories were very hazy. I had come back by the slower but less perilous land route. I determined to learn a little about the city on this trip. When I reached the minimum age, I would stand for the quaestorship, and each year one quaestor was stationed in Ostia to oversee the grain supply. The many long wars had stripped Italy of most of her peasant farmers, and the latifundia were inefficient, so that we had come to rely on foreign grain.

We passed the great naval harbor built for the wars with Carthage and now fallen into decay. In their sheds, beneath falling roofs, the old warships lay like dead warriors long after the battle, their ribs thrusting through rotting skin. A few sheds were kept up, and the ships inside were in good repair, stored for the winter with their masts, spars, sails and rigging removed. As we drifted past the commercial docks Milo named them for me: the Venus dock, the Vulcan, the Cupid, the Castor and the Pollux, and some half-dozen others.

Dominating the city stood the great Temple of Vulcan, dedicated to the patron god of the city. From the Venus

dock we walked to the city Forum, where two fine bronze
statues of the Dioscuri stood, patrons of Ostia as they
were of Rome. Indeed, Ostia was a more attractive city
than Rome, far smaller and less crowded. The streets
were broader and most of the public buildings were
newer, many of them faced with gleaming white marble.
The other buildings were constructed for the most part
of brick. The Ostians eschewed plaster and whitewash,
delighting in intricate and attractive brickwork.

"It's getting late," Milo told me, "but we can get a few
questions answered. Come on, let's go to the theater."
From the Forum we took a broad street that led to the
building in question. It seemed like an odd destination
for men on our mission, but he was the guide.

The theater was an imposing structure, constructed of
marble-faced stone, semicircular in the Greek fashion.
Rome at that time had no permanent theaters, having to
rely on extremely flammable wooden buildings where
the Senate met from time to time in hot weather.

As it turned out, all the guilds, fraternities and cor-
porations concerned with sea-commerce had their offices beneath the three-tiered colonnade of the theater.
It was an admirable use of a public space, centralizing
the organizations, each of which paid a contribution for
the upkeep of the building. As we walked beneath the
arches, I admired the mosaic pavement of the curving
walk that ran around the building. Before each office,
the mosaic depicted the activity of the fraternity within.
There were crossed oars for the rowers' guild, amphorae
for the wine importers, sails for the sailmakers and so
forth. One mosaic depicted a naked man in the act of
swimming. I asked Milo about this one.

"*Urinatores,*" he said, "salvage divers. They're a very
important guild here. Storms and accidents sink ships
here every year. There's always lots of salvage and
channel-clearing to be done. Their work is necessary and
quite dangerous, so they're respected men."

"I should imagine," I said. Only fourteen miles away,
and yet so different from Rome that the two cities might

have been at opposite ends of the sea. "Where are we going?"

"Here." He stood on a mosaic depicting the three Fates at their loom: Clotho, Lachesis and Atropos.

"This needs some interpretation," I told him. "Surely Ostia doesn't receive cargoes of fate."

Milo threw back his head and laughed. He laughed better than any man I ever knew except Marcus Antonius, the triumvir. "No, this is the headquarters of the cloth importers' guild."

We went inside and a clerk looked up from his desk, where he was tying up a bundle of scrolls, no doubt looking forward to his dinner. "I was just closing the office. Please come back tomorrow ... Oh, hello, Milo."

"Good afternoon, Silius. We won't keep you long. This is Decius Caecilius Metellus, of the Committee of Twenty-Six in Rome."

"Afternoon, sir," he said without awe. He knew perfectly well that I had no authority here.

"We just needed to know if Hasdrubal's still about, and where he's doing business these days."

"Oh, is that all? He has a new place, just inland of the Juno dock, between the merchant of used amphorae and the rope loft."

"I know the place. He's still in the old business, isn't he?"

"You mean ..." Silius made a throat-cutting gesture. Milo nodded. "Yes, he's still their Ostia agent."

"Good. Thank you, Silius. Come on, sir." I followed him from the theater. I could have gone to the quaestor's residence to ask for a place to stay the night, but I didn't feel like socializing with someone I didn't know, and making a lot of explanations as to why I was here, so I asked Milo if there was an inn where we could stay.

"I know just the place," he said. Soon we were walking into the precincts of a large temple. Well, in a city where the businesses had their offices in a theater, why not an inn at a temple? Instead of going into the handsome, columned temple, we went down some steps that led us to a tremendous underground crypt where hundreds of men and women sat at long tables. I had never seen anything like this. Rome is a city of small wineshops and modest taverns. Not Ostia. There were four or five large fireplaces supplying light and warmth, and serving-girls hustled among the tables bearing trays of food and pitchers of wine.

Greetings were called out to Milo as we passed among the tables looking for a place to sit. I could hear a dozen languages being spoken, and could see the peculiar tunics and headgear of as many guilds, each congregating at its special table. At one I could see men with palms like Milo's; at another sat a number of sleek, huge-chested men, who I decided had to be divers.

We found seats at a small table jammed into a corner. By this time my eyes were accustomed to the limited interior light, and I could see that this place had been hewn from the solid rock below the temple. As the servers brought us a platter of steaming fish and sausages along with cheese, onions, bread, fruit and a pitcher of wine, I asked Milo about it.

"Been here since the founding of the city, they say. It was a natural cave beneath the temple, used for a storehouse. Then it was enlarged and the god up there"—he jerked a thumb upward, toward the temple—"Mercury, it was, came to a priest in a dream and told him to establish a great wineshop down here."

"Mercury. That makes sense. The god of profit would be the one to tell his priest to establish a business beneath his temple. And do they rent rooms as well?"

"Behind the temple they have an inn. Decent lodgings, if you aren't picky."

"This is convenient," I said. The wine was not bad, either, for a public house. The crowd was interesting and varied. The sailors and rivermen of Ostia were as hard-bitten a lot as I had ever encountered anywhere. They were loud and fairly boisterous, but I saw no fights breaking out. I asked Milo about this and he jerked his chin toward a huge, shaven-headed man who sat on a stool in a corner, an olive-wood club propped against the wall next to him.

"They keep experts here to maintain good order. I've worked here as chucker-out in the off season, when there was no rowing to be done."

We concentrated on our dinner for a while. When we had wrought sufficient devastation, a server took the platter away and left a bowl of figs and nuts. While we munched on these, sipping our wine, Milo began sounding me out.

"Not meaning to pry, sir, but visiting a pirate's agent doesn't seem the sort of thing an official in your position ought to be doing."

"It isn't one of my regular duties," I agreed.

"And that man Claudius," he went on, "he was trying to force you to drop an investigation. What was that all about?"

"And what is your reason for asking?" I demanded.

His eyes went wide with injured innocence. "Why, I'm a concerned citizen, just like your friend Claudius." He held his look of innocence just long enough, then he laughed his great laugh again, and this time I joined him. It was an impertinence, but Milo had such an easy and ingratiating manner that I found myself telling him the whole story. Well, not every little detail. I left out my tryst with Claudia and Chrysis, for instance. I saw no real need to reveal that incident, which was still somewhat mysterious even to me.

I actually felt a great sensation of relief in explaining these matters to Milo. Of my peers and colleagues, none seemed utterly trustworthy. Most of my superiors in office turned out to have some nefarious interest in the case, some secret guilt to hide. Telling Milo of my woes and my bewilderment seemed to clear the air of a maddening vapor. He listened quietly, with great attention. Only a few times did he interrupt with questions, usually to clarify some point about the political standing of some of the men I mentioned: Caesar, Claudius, Hortalus, even Cicero.

"So," he said when I was finished. "It's all about this stolen amulet?"

Once again, I was impressed by his quick intelligence. "It can't be entirely about that. But the amulet is some sort of key that could unlock this whole chest of secrets."

"You want to be careful of boxes like that. Remember Pandora, and Ulysses's men and the bag of winds."

"You don't need to remind me. However, having pried it open a little, I don't intend to stop until I've sifted through to its bottom." Pleased at having extended the metaphor so far, I took another drink of Mercury's excellent wine. A sudden thought struck me. "I wonder if Lucullus's statue here was really struck by lightning a few days ago. Ask somebody."

"How could it have been?" Milo asked. "It was never erected. A few years back the city proposed to honor Lucullus with a bronze statue, but they never got around to paying for it. They never got further than putting up the marble pedestal at the Juno dock."

"I might have known. Now Claudius is making up his own omens."

"That would be a handy political device," Milo mused. "Just spread false stories of terrible omens about your opponents. Who ever looks into the truthfulness of those things?"

I shrugged. "It would only add another type of lying to an activity already heavily burdened with them."

"Odd," Milo said, "that even after the rebellion of Sertorius, they want to maintain contact with the pirates. Those pirates love to slap the Roman face. Last year we could see their sails from the docks as they cruised past, unconcerned as you please, and our fleet laid up in the sheds, doing nothing."

"It's a disgrace," I agreed. "It's possible that some of them are accepting bribes to keep the fleet laid up so the pirates can operate without interference. That would surprise me little."

Milo tossed a handful of nuts into his mouth and washed them down with wine. "I doubt that. Those pirates aren't afraid of the Roman fleet even when it's at full strength. Why pay to be rid of it?"

"You're right. It could be some of them plan to hire the pirates as an auxiliary fleet; that's been done before, in past wars." At this, the beginning of a thought began to form somewhere in the back of my mind, where the worst ones always take shape. "No," I muttered, "even they wouldn't stoop to that."

Milo's interest brightened. "You've made it plain that there isn't much that our more ambitious men won't stoop to. What is it that seems so unlikely?"

"No, this I can't even speculate about. It will have to wait until I have some sort of evidence."

"As you will," Milo said. "Come, are you ready to find a room for the night?"

"Might as well." Only when I rose from my seat did I realize how tired I was. It had been another incredibly long and eventful day, beginning with my waking in Claudia's getaway, still in a drugged stupor. There had been the murder of Paulus, my near-strangulation by Asklepiodes, the encounter with Claudius and his thugs, the trip downriver and my brief tour of Ostia, ending in this underground tavern. It was indeed time to find some rest. We ascended to the fresh air and Milo found a priest to show us to our room, which I did not even examine before crashing onto my cot.

VIII

I woke feeling immeasurably better. The light coming through the door was that of dawn just before the sun appears. I could see someone standing outside the doorway, leaning on a balustrade. I climbed from my cot and found a basin of water with which I splashed my face liberally. Milo turned as I came out of the little room.

"About time you were up, Commissioner. Rosy-fingered Aurora rises from the bed of her husband Tithonus, or whatever his name is."

"You're another of the early risers, I see." I walked out onto the gallery that ran along the front of the inn. We were on the fourth floor. I didn't even remember climbing the stairs the night before. From our vantage point we could look out over the roof of the temple and see the harbor just a few hundred paces distant. The growing light revealed a myriad of details, and a fresh wind brought us the smell of the sea. The markets of the town were beginning to send up their daily din like an offering to the gods. Smoke rose from before the great Temple of Vulcan, probably a morning sacrifice. It was time to begin another overlong day of doing my duty by the Roman Senate and People.

"Let's go," I said to Milo. We descended the rickety steps and began to make our way toward the Juno dock, first stopping for a shave from a street-corner barber. Milo was frequently hailed, and I wondered what had caused him to leave a place where he was plainly so popular. Probably Ostia was too small for him, I decided.

We found the shop we needed without difficulty. It lay, as promised, between the rope shop and the used-amphorae-dealer's establishment. From the stacks of jars in the latter's yard came the reek of sour wine lees. The interior of Hasdrubal's shop had a different smell, odd but not unpleasant. I found that it was the characteristic odor of cloth colored with the murex dye. It was tremendously popular in the East, but in Rome we used it mainly for the broad stripe on the senatorial tunic and the narrow border on the equestrian tunic. Only a general celebrating a triumph was permitted to wear an entire robe dyed with it, in the fashion of the Etruscan kings. There could not have been a great demand for triumphal robes, but Italy was full of old priesthoods and cults demanding their own regalia, and I presumed that Hasdrubal did the bulk of his business keeping them supplied.

Hasdrubal himself was in the front of the shop, arranging the drape of some of his rich cloth to show it to best advantage. He looked up smiling, but the smile wavered slightly when he recognized Milo. He was a tall, lean man, dark of complexion, with a black, pointed beard. He wore the conical cap of his nation.

"Welcome, my old friend Titus Annius Milo. And you, sir . . ." He trailed off interrogatively.

"I am Decius Caecilius Metellus, of the Commission of Twenty-Six, of which I am part of the Commission of Three, in Rome, Subura district." Hoping he was impressed by my long-winded title, I pressed on. "I am investigating the untimely demise of a colleague of yours, one Paramedes of Antioch."

"Ah, yes, I had heard that he was dead." Hasdrubal made some complicated hand-gestures, undoubtedly placating the spirits of the dead or some foul Oriental god. "I knew him only slightly, through our mutual business dealings, but I regret his passing."

"Well, his passing was neither accidental nor voluntary, which is why an investigation became necessary."

"I am of course at your disposal." Hand to breast, Hasdrubal bowed deeply.

"Excellent. The Senate and People of Rome will be most pleased." I could be as mealymouthed as the best of them. "What was the nature of the business you and Paramedes transacted with the pirates?"

"Usually, it involved the negotiation of ransom. From time to time, the pirates would capture a ship or raid an estate that would yield some valuable personage: a wealthy merchant, even"—he allowed himself a faint chuckle—"if you will forgive me, a Roman magistrate. If that person's relatives, guild or corporation were in the Rome–Ostia area, one of us would transact the negotiations for transfer of the ransom. Many of the seafaring guilds here in Ostia, for instance, maintain a ransom fund for members taken prisoner by pirates. In most such cases, the ransom is set by long agreement: so much for a master merchant, so much for a helmsman and so forth. In the case of a wealthy or important person, the ransom must be agreed upon by the interested parties."

"I see. Did you or Paramedes negotiate any really large-scale or special commissions between the pirates and citizens of Rome?"

He was nonplussed. "Special? How do you mean, sir?"

"Well, for instance: A few years back, at the time of Sertorius's rebellion in Spain, certain arrangements were made between that rebellious general and King Mithridates of Pontus, with the pirates acting as intermediaries. Might you or Paramedes have handled such a commission?"

He spread his hands in a self-deprecating gesture. I found these constant gesticulations annoying, and was happy that Romans did not thus supplement their speech. "That is a far larger commission than any I have ever undertaken. We local agents are not really a part of the pirate community. I doubt that anything of such magnitude would be entrusted to one of us."

That didn't sound promising. "And Paramedes?"

"Also unlikely. He had been an agent for longer than

I, and he had operated in other parts of the Mediterranean." He pondered for a moment. "Of course, if a Roman wished to engage one or more of the pirate fleets on such a commission, he might very well approach one of us to arrange the initial contact."

That sounded better. "And have you been thus approached?"

"Such has never fallen my lot. However, I cannot speak for Paramedes."

"Unfortunately, he can no longer speak for himself. Would you happen to know who did negotiate on the pirates' behalf on the occasion of the conspiracy between Sertorius and Mithridates?" This was a wild cast, but I have found that these seem to bag as much game as the aimed sort.

"The pirate captains are an individualistic lot, so it is seldom that one of them is allowed to speak for the combined fleets. Instead, they employ a well-placed and educated person to negotiate for them. I believe that on that occasion the man who acted on the pirates' behalf was young Tigranes, the son of the Armenian king." The expression on my face must have been a sight to behold. "Sir," Hasdrubal asked, "are you well?"

"Better than you can imagine. Hasdrubal, I thank you. The Senate and People of Rome thank you."

He beamed. "Just remember me when you are a Praetor and need a purple border for your toga."

"One more thing, if you please. During the recent slave rebellion, Spartacus arranged with the pirates to ferry him and his army from Messina to some unspecified destination. On the appointed day, the pirates did not arrive. Somebody had bought them off."

Hasdrubal looked uncomfortable. "Yes. Most unlike them, to renege on an agreement like that."

"I won't ponder the ethics of it," I said, "but I would like to know something: Was Tigranes the pirates' negotiator that time as well?"

Hasdrubal stroked his beard and nodded. "He was."

I rose and prepared to leave. "Hasdrubal, I'll never

buy purple from any merchant save you." He saw us out amid effusive farewells and many annoying gesticulations.

"To the docks," I told Milo when we were outside. "I have to get to Rome as quickly as possible."

"No problem there. It's still early enough to catch a barge headed upriver." He grinned as if it had all been his doing. "There, wasn't that worth the trip here?"

"It's beginning to make a sort of sense," I allowed. "And it's even worse than I'd thought. They're both in on it, Milo. Crassus as well as Pompey."

We were only a few steps from the Juno dock and within minutes we arranged passage upriver on a barge carrying amphorae of Sicilian wine. Under no circumstances was I going to travel on one carrying fish. As soon as we were seated in the bow, the barge cast off and we began to move up the harbor to the river mouth, which we had passed the night before. Milo watched the oarsmen critically for a while, then turned his attention on me.

"I'm not certain I want to be so near you," he said. "A man with not one but two Consuls for enemies must draw lightning like a temple roof. Why do you think Crassus was in on it?"

"It was Crassus who had Spartacus boxed in at Messina. As soon as he made the agreement with Spartacus, Tigranes must have gone to Crassus to see if he could get a better offer."

"But Pompey fought the slave army too," Milo pointed out.

I shook my head. "That was later. Pompey was still on his way from Spain when Spartacus was at Messina. He fought the band under Crixus after they broke through the breastwork Crassus built across the peninsula. Besides, who was in a better position to bribe a whole fleet of pirates? Crassus is incredibly rich, while Pompey squanders all his wealth pampering his soldiers."

"It makes sense so far," Milo said. "But that was the slave rebellion last year, and the uprising of Sertorius a few years before that. What has it all to do with what's happening in Rome right now?"

I settled back against a bale of the sacking used to pad the big wine jars. "I don't know," I admitted, "although I'm beginning to entertain some suspicions. The pirates' chief—what shall we call him?—diplomat?—is in Rome right now, in the last month of the joint Consulate of two men he's dealt with before. The pirates' former agent at Rome, Paramedes, was murdered a few days ago. It strains coincidence."

"And Tigranes is the houseguest of your friend Claudius." There are few things more satisfying than unraveling a conspiracy, and Milo was enjoying it. "But where does the murder of Paulus come in?"

"That I have yet to work out," I said, uncomfortably remembering the palanquin I had found in Claudia's hideaway, the one I had seen leaving Paulus's house after my visit. "He was rich, though, maybe even as rich as Crassus. That's enough of a connection for suspicion's sake. As I figure it, Sinistrus killed Paramedes and was killed in turn to silence him."

"Or he might have tried to blackmail his employer," Milo pointed out.

"Even better. Whichever, he was an expendable nobody. I just need to know who bought him out of the Statilian school and then freed him, at a time when it was illegal to do so. The praetor who allowed the transaction must have been in on it as well."

Milo grinned. "You'll have half the Senate involved in this soon."

"It could go that far," I said, only half-joking.

"There is still the matter of the stolen amulet," he said.

"There I am totally mystified. Until it's found, I can't fathom how such a thing could be of any significance."

We were silent for a while, admiring the river. There was no convenient breeze to speed us along, but the rhythmic chant of the rowers was soothing. The dip and splash of the oars was melodious as well.

"Tell me," I said, "how does a strapping young rower

from Ostia happen to arrive in our city with the good
old Roman name of Annius?"

He leaned back against the bale and laced his fingers
behind his head. "My father's name was Caius Papius
Celsus. He was a landowner with an estate just south of
here. We didn't get on well and I ran away to the navy
when I was sixteen. My mother was from Rome and she
always spoke about the city, how big and rich it was, how
even an outsider could become a great man there. So
last year I came to Rome and had myself adopted by my
mother's father, Titus Annius Luscus. Even as an Ostian
I had citizenship, but this gives me a city tribe. I can
attend the Plebeian Council and the Centuriate Assembly. I'm learning street-level politics from Macro."

"And you're learning Senate-level politics from me," I
said.

He laughed his great laugh again. "You're right. And
so far, it looks just like the street."

A trip upstream is, for obvious reasons, slower than
one downstream. Recent rains had made the river higher
and swifter than usual for that time of year. To make
matters worse, there was a constant head wind. We could
have walked to Rome along the Via Ostiensis in about
four hours. This way, it was almost dark when we arrived
in Rome, but we arrived without sore feet.

"I had some calls to make," I told Milo. "Now it's too
late. Well, it hasn't been a bad day's work as it is."

He was less pleased with the prospect. "I wish we could
have got here sooner." His eyes scanned the river docks
with suspicion. "It's going to be chancy, now it's almost
dark."

"What do you mean?" I asked.

"I mean Claudius has had two days to nurse his
wounded patrician pride. He's liable to call on us before
we can reach our homes."

I hadn't considered that. If he was still set upon thwart-
ing me, he would have men stationed at the Ostian gate
and the river docks. I was still armed, and Milo seemed
to have little need of arms, but we were sure to be heav-

ily outnumbered. At that time, it was not unusual for a political adventurer like Claudius to maintain a retinue of twenty or thirty thugs and be able to whistle up a mob of two hundred or more at short notice. Of course, he was just beginning his disreputable career, but I was certain that he could easily have a dozen bullyboys and bravos out looking for us.

"We should have picked up some hooded cloaks in Ostia," I said. "A disguise would be desirable just now."

"If it's dark enough," Milo said, "they may not be able to see us."

I was not certain of that, no matter how dark the Roman streets were. "There is somebody in the city who can see in the dark better than a cat. The break-in at my house, the stranglings of Sinistrus and Paulus, all of those things took place in pitch blackness."

"It could have been a ghost," Milo said. I wondered if he was serious. "But I never heard of a ghost strangling anyone, or stealing things, or taking an interest in politics. No, it must be something more substantial than a ghost."

Darkness comes quickly so late in the year. By the time we tied up at the dock the stars were out, although the moon had not yet made an appearance. There were the usual late idlers hanging about the docks. There was no way to tell if any of them were on the lookout for us. We climbed the ladder to the wharf and walked through the warehouses, alert to any sign of pursuit.

"I'll accompany you to your house," Milo offered.

"I thank you." I wasn't about to let any foolish pride compel me to go alone. "You may stay there for the night, if you wish."

He shook his head, the gesture barely visible in the gloom which deepened with every step we took. "It's you they're after. No one will bother me."

Soon we were feeling our way along like blind men. The feeble light shed by the stars barely revealed the outlines of the larger buildings, and it reflected dimly from pavement wet from a recent shower. I jerked as Milo touched my shoulder. He leaned forward and whispered in my ear: "Someone behind us." We were still several streets from my house.

Quietly, I reached into my tunic. With my right hand I grasped the hilt of my dagger and drew it. On my left I slipped the *caestus*. We walked on for a while and Milo whispered again.

"There were four behind us. Now there are two. Two others have slipped around a block to get ahead of us." Whoever they were, the one with cat's eyes was their guide. I could hear them, but Milo was better at judging their number. He was also a better tactician. "Let's turn and get the ones behind us first," he said, "then tackle the other two afterward."

"Good idea," I acknowledged. We whirled in our tracks and I could hear the two nearing us; then I heard their footsteps falter as they realized that our steps had stopped. There was a whispered consultation between them.

"Now!" Milo said, rushing forward. I heard him collide with one and I rushed in as blindly, leading with my dagger. I could feel someone there, but I wasn't exactly sure where he stood and I was afraid of stabbing Milo. Then there was a face near mine and a blast of winy, garlic-laden breath and I knew this was my target. I thrust with my dagger as I saw starlight glitter on something coming toward me. I managed to bat the sword aside with the bronze strap over my knuckles just as I felt the dagger blade strike home.

At times of such desperation, such urgency of immediate action, all things take on an air of unreality. Time has a new meaning. As the man before me fell, I was whirled around by his collapsing body and saw coming up behind me a faint, diffuse glow, like the marsh-light that flickers over swamps to lure unwary travelers. In that moment, I think I truly believed that there was a ghost after us. But whose? There had been so many new-made lately.

Beside me there were multiple thuds and grunts as Milo took care of his own attacker. Then two more were on us and I reached out, grasped cloth and pulled it toward me, thinking that this was a tunic and I was dragging another man within reach of my dagger. Instead, I jerked a cloak from a lantern held by a man who gripped a sword in his other hand. Another stood crouched next to him, and behind them I could just glimpse a third hanging back. That meant five in all. So much for Milo's superior hearing.

I immediately attacked the lantern-holder, assuming that it would make him a bit more awkward, but he dropped the lantern and came for me. The lantern continued to cast its flickering illumination from the street, making the brutal, violent scene truly eerie and unreal. The sword was real enough as it came for me, though. I dodged aside but bumped into somebody, either Milo or his opponent, and saved myself from gutting only by sucking in my stomach as the weapon lanced inward. Even so, I felt its edge slice my flesh in passing. With my dagger I cut at his forearm, stepping in as I did so, catching his jaw with a neat left cross. I felt the jawbone crack under the *caestus*, but for good measure I ran my dagger through his body as he fell. It is never good to assume that a wounded man is through fighting.

When he was down I whirled to see Milo wrestling his own second opponent to the street. The fifth person was nowhere to be seen.

"Bring the lantern," Milo said. I picked it up by its carrying-ring, carefully so as not to snuff out the light. I opened its gate and with the point of my dagger teased the wick up from its oil reservoir until it was burning brightly, and walked to where Milo held his man in an armlock with one foot on his chest. The handle of a *sica* protruded from the fellow's chest. Apparently, Milo had stabbed him with his own weapon. The other three seemed to be dead. Weapons littered the street: a short *sica* and a long *sica* and even a *gladius*. The sword was smaller than those used by the legions: wasp-waisted with a long, tapering point like an oversized dagger. It was the type used by Roman soldiers a century before and still used in the amphitheater. I recognized none of the

men. Rome was full of such gang-members and they were
of little account.

The one Milo had down was of the usual type: a burly
cretin whose age was difficult to judge through the map
of scars that made up his face. He bore the *caestus* scars
of a pugilist rather than the sword marks of a gladiator,
and men of superior intelligence seldom took up the
profession of pugilist.

"I think this fellow has some things to tell us, sir," Milo
said, giving the arm a twist and getting a groan in return.

"Excellent," I answered. I squatted beside the man,
holding the lantern high. He hadn't long to live and so
I had to ask my question quickly. "Who hired you?"

"Claudius," he groaned as Milo continued the pres-
sure. "He said that you'd be wearing a yellow scarf
around your neck."

I touched the scarf ruefully. I had been talking of disguise, forgetting that I was wearing the conspicuous thing
when Claudius had seen me the day before.

"Who was your eyes tonight, pig?" Milo demanded.
"Who guided you through these streets and kept us in
sight?"

"A boy." He seemed disinclined to say more, so Milo
encouraged him to greater eloquence. "Ahh! It was a foreign boy, eastern. Had an Oriental accent. Said he'd
know our man by sight. Went back and forth all day
between the river and the Ostian gate. Came to join us
when the gate shut for the night, got to the dock just as
you did, says there's our man. Led us through the street
and around in front of you like it was daylight. Eyes in
his toes, that boy has." These last words were spoken in
a whispering mumble and Milo released his arm.

"Well, that's all we'll get from this one. What now, sir?"

"Leave them for the vigiles. I'll make a full report of
it all when I get this case wrapped up. It would just be a
waste of time now. Let's go to my house."

Now that we had a lamp, we made it to my doorway
without difficulty.

"I'll leave you here now, sir," Milo said as Cato opened the door.

"I won't forget your service," I told him. "You were a great deal more than a guide on this little journey."

"Just keep me in mind when you're an important magistrate," he said, then he left. I thought at the time he meant that he was likely to end up before me in court, but young Milo had higher ambitions than that.

I ignored Cato's scandalized protestations about my late hours and dubious companions as I went to my bedroom. I told him to bring me something to eat and a basin and clean towels. Grumbling, he did as ordered. When he delivered what I had asked for, I bade him be off to his bed and closed the door behind him.

I stripped off my tunic and by lamplight examined the cut I had taken in the scuffle. It looked fairly trivial, but it stung when I washed it with wine as best I could, then bandaged it with a folded towel and strips cut from my tunic and tied around my waist. I would have Asklepiodes examine it in the morning.

Drained by the journey and the events in the street, I sat on my bed and forced unwanted food into my empty stomach. I had dealt wounds in battle, but this sort of close-in fighting was something new to me. I decided that it was the aftermath of the sudden, unexpected violence that made me feel dull and melancholy. The men had wished to kill me and they had been the lowest scum imaginable.

Also, I was unhappy that the boy had been so close and once again had escaped me. Only he could lead me to the amulet that had been taken from this very room. With this thought, I looked to make sure that the ornamental bronze bars I had commissioned were in good order. For what it was worth, they seemed to be. I was beginning to believe that the creature was supernatural, though, and that no mere barrier would be proof against him and his strangling cord.

Wincing at the pain, I lay back on my bed and closed my eyes. I had learned much, and yet it was still not enough. Thus ended another day.

IX

The next day I composed a letter. It was something I had been pondering since I had seen the palanquin carrying one of the vestals a few days before. I had toyed with the idea, then discarded it. Now I picked it up again. What I was contemplating was not merely extra-legal, it was sacrilegious. However, I now believed that the good of the state was at stake. Also, my life had been threatened, and that gives one a different perspective on man's relationship to the gods.

"Reverend Aunt," I began. "From your obscure nephew Decius Caecilius Metellus, greeting. I would esteem it the greatest personal favor if you would allow me to call upon you at your earliest convenience. My reasons for wishing to visit with you are twofold: First, I have for far too long neglected my familial obligation toward you, and because of a certain sensitive matter of state which I believe you may be able to help me with, if you would be so kind. If it is at all possible, please send your reply by this messenger." I rolled the papyrus into a scroll and sealed it with wax. On the outside I wrote: "For the eyes of the Reverend Lady Caecilia Metelli."

I gave the scroll to a slave boy borrowed from a neighbor and told him to deliver it to the House of the Vestals and wait there for a reply. The boy scampered off, doubtless wondering what sort of reward he would earn. It was customary to tip generously when you employed somebody else's slave.

The captain of the vigiles had reported the four bodies found in the street that morning, but I was able to delay

151

looking into it since, first, it looked like any other gang killing and, second, I could claim that the murder of Paulus took precedence. The deaths of four more thugs would not reach the Senate even as a rumor and I would only need to find out their identities and scratch their names off the grain dole, if any of them were citizens. In all likelihood, no one would come forward to identify them and in three days the bodies would be taken to the mass burial pits and would be forgotten.

As soon as the early part of the day's business was transacted, I excused myself and went to the Ludus Statilius to call upon Asklepiodes. He was surprised to see me again so soon.

"What?" he said. "Surely there has not been another exotic murder for me to analyze, has there?"

"No, but there almost was. However, the victim is up and walking around this morning, and has come to you for treatment. Are your slaves discreet?"

"Come in," he said, concerned, standing aside as I entered the chamber in which he had nearly throttled me two days before.

"You are the most interesting person I have encountered since coming to Rome," Asklepiodes said. I sat on a stool and dragged my tunic over my head. He stripped off my amateur attempt at wound-dressing and called for one of his slaves. The man came in and Asklepiodes gave him instructions in some language I did not recognize, then he returned to his examination of my wound. "I have lived in some uncivilized places, but I have never known a public official to be assaulted quite so frequently."

"You were among my attackers," I said, wincing at the pain in my flank.

"Purely an educational exercise. But this fellow"—he poked the cut with a finger, drawing another grunt of pain—"clearly intended to take your life. This was inflicted by a *gladius* or a rather large, straight dagger with some curvature to the edge. You note the slight nicking here at the beginning of the cut? That is where the point first pierced the flesh before commencing its incision."

"I know what sort of weapon it was," I said with some impatience. "I saw it myself, along with the thug who wielded it. It was an arena *gladius.*"

"Just as I thought," Asklepiodes said triumphantly.

"I rejoice that, once again, your judgment is vindicated. Now, what may be done about this wound, which I feel this morning may be more serious than it felt last night, when I was exhausted and the light was uncertain?"

"Oh, there is little cause for concern, unless mortification sets in, in which case you will almost surely die. However, that seems unlikely since you are young and strong and the wound is a clean one. If there is no swelling and suppuration in the next few days, all should be well."

"That is comforting," I told him. The slave reentered carrying a tray of instruments and a basin of steaming water. He set it by the stool where I sat and the physician gave him further instructions. He left once more.

"What language is that?" I asked Asklepiodes as he began to scrub industriously at the cut. He used a sponge dipped in the steaming liquid, which was not only hot but full of astringent herbs. It burned like a hot iron laid against my side. I strove to remember the Stoic forbearance of my ancestors. I tried to take courage from the story of Mucius Scaevola, who had shown his contempt for mere pain by holding his hand in a fire until it was burned off.

"Egyptian," the Greek said, as if he were not inflicting pain in which a court torturer might have taken pride. "I practiced for some years in Alexandria. Of course, they speak Greek there, like all civilized people, but the people from farther south, from Memphis and Thebes and Ptolomais, still speak the ancient tongue. They also make the best slaves and servants in the world. So I studied the language in order to learn the medical secrets of the ancient Egyptians and in the process I bought some slaves to assist me. I have made certain that they have not learned Greek or Latin; thus they serve me well and keep my secrets."

"Very good," I said, when the pain had receded enough for me to speak. "I would appreciate it if you would not mention to anyone that you have treated me for this wound."

"You may have total confidence in my discretion." He tried to maintain his bland mask of professional dignity, but soon his curiosity got the better of him. He was, after all, a Greek. "So this was not, shall we say, a casual assault by a common footpad?"

"My attackers could scarcely have been more common," I said.

"Attackers! There was more than one?"

"Four," I said, rolling up my eyes as I saw him pick up a bit of thin split sinew and a curved needle.

"This is Homeric!" he said, fitting the needle to a small pair of ornate bronze pliers. All his instruments were decorated with silver inlay in the form of swirling acanthus leaves. I have often wondered whether the elaborate decoration common to surgical instruments is to distract us from the dreadful uses to which they are put.

"Actually," I admitted, "I was not alone. But I did for two of them." The childish boasting helped me bear the pain of stitching. After all, having thus touted my valor, I could scarcely object to the mere repeated piercing of my flesh by a needle, having sinew drawn through the piercings and the stitches drawn tight, as if my flesh were so much tent-cloth.

"Was this attack politically motivated?" he asked.

"I can hardly believe otherwise," I said.

"The politics of modern Rome resemble those of Athens a few centuries ago. The Pisistratids, Harmodius and Aristogiton and so forth. It wasn't always Pericles and his lot."

"You're the first Greek I've met who admits that Greece isn't always the home of all perfection."

"We are still superior to everyone else," he said, his

eyes twinkling. The slave reentered, this time bearing a bowl that gave off a foul-smelling steam.

"This poultice will help the wound to heal without infection," Asklepiodes said. He spooned some of the loathsome slop onto a gauze pad and slapped it onto my side. Swiftly and with great skill the slave wound bandages around my body, binding the poultice tightly in place yet allowing me to breathe without great difficulty.

"Come back in three days and I will change the dressing," the Greek said.

"How am I going to attend the baths this way?" I asked.

"There are some things even the finest physician cannot answer for you. However, you are a young man of great ingenuity and I am sure you will devise a solution."

"As always, Master Asklepiodes, I thank you. Look for a liberal proof of my gratitude this coming Saturnalia." He looked most pleased. Although lawyers and physicians were forbidden to charge fees, they could accept presents.

"I shall sacrifice to my patron god and pray that you live until Saturnalia. May your next month not go like your last week."

He ushered me out. He was none too subtle in reminding me that Saturnalia was less than a month away, and perhaps hinting that I should put this generous gift in my will. I was too poor for anything lavish, and as I walked home I pondered upon what I might send him. I decided that a physician who was willing to perform what was in effect the work of a mere surgeon was eccentric, so I would give him an eccentric gift.

The slave boy was waiting in my atrium when I reached home. He handed me a small roll of papyrus and I broke the seal. The message inside was brief and simple: "Dearest Nephew: It has been far too long. Come to the visiting-room of the House of the Vestals at about the twelfth hour. Aunt Caecilia." It was, I estimated, somewhere around the end of the ninth hour. Since the winter hours were shorter than those of summer, the twelfth was not all that far away.

She probably meant the twelfth hour as told by the great sundial of Catania in the Forum. Messala had brought it as loot from Sicily almost two hundred years before and it was the pride of the city for a long time. Unfortunately, it was calibrated for Sicily, which is far to the south of Rome, and gives an innacurate reading of the time. The vestals were incredibly old-fashioned and probably ignored the much more modern sundial and water clock of Philippus and Scipio Nasica, which were not even one hundred years old. I decided I would just estimate the time, like everyone else. She had said "at about the twelfth hour." Neither sundial works in cloudy weather, and even the water clock was erratic in winter.

I gave the boy a denarius and he was properly awe-struck by my munificence. He could add it to his *peculium,* with which he might someday purchase his freedom, but far more likely he would use it to bribe the cook for delicacies or wager on the next Games with his fellow slaves.

I decided to go to the Forum. It was the time usually devoted to the baths, but I could not attend the baths bandaged as I was. Rome in winter is like a great, sleepy animal that spends most of the season dozing in its den. The markets are less raucous, the clamor of the builders is quieter, the hammering of the metalworkers more muffled. People even walk more slowly. We Italians need the warmth of the sun to stir us to our customary level of frenetic, if oftentimes unproductive, activity.

In the Forum I lazed among the crowd, exchanging greetings, hearing petitions from dissatisfied residents of my district, most of whom believed, incorrectly, that any public official had the ear of every other, so that I was constantly referring them to the proper authorities.

The Aunt Caecilia whom I was about to visit was one of my many aunts named Caecilia, since women are not given cognomens, thus causing much confusion. This one was known in the family as Caecilia the Vestal, a formidably prestigious lady. She was a sister of the Quintus Caecilius Metellus under whom I had served in Spain, who had been one of our more illustrious generals until Sertorius got the better of him and Pompey, the boy wonder, had arrived to reap all the glory.

As I made my way toward the House of the Vestals, I contemplated upon how to approach her. A woman raised from girlhood within the confines of the vestals' quarters could not be expected to be worldly regarding matters of Roman political life. Chaste and archaic in her attitudes, she would believe and behave as a noble lady descended from a long line of Roman heroes. This shows how inexperienced in the ways of women I was at that age.

The Temple of Vesta was located in the heart of the Forum, and had stood on that spot since the founding of the city, almost seven hundred years before. It was round, in the ancient Italian fashion, because our ancestors had lived in round huts. One of our finest festivals was also the simplest, when, on the kalends of March, all the fires in the Roman community were extinguished and, at first light of the new year (the kalends of March being the ancient new year), the vestals kindled a new fire with wood friction. From this fire, which they would tend ceaselessly for the rest of the year, all the other fires were relighted.

For the last year or more, Caecilia had been *Virgo Maxima,* the head of the college. Though seldom seen, she had prestige and privileges equal to those of any princess of other nations. She alone of all the vestals had the right to visit alone with a man. All others were required to have at least one chaperone. A vestal who was found to be unchaste suffered a uniquely horrible punishment: She was placed in a tiny, underground cell with a little food and water, after which the cell was covered with earth.

Their temple may have been small, but their house, the *Atrium Vestae,* was the most splendid palace in Rome. It lay near the temple and like all Roman residences had a facade as plain as a warehouse, whitewashed plaster over brick. The interior was far different.

A slave girl admitted me at the door—for obvious reasons, all the slaves were female—and rushed off to tell the *Virgo Maxima* that an official had called. The interior was entirely sheathed in pristine white marble. Skylights illuminated wall frescoes depicting the complex rites of the goddess. Everywhere the emphasis was on beauty and simplicity, richness without ostentation. It was as if a fine Tuscan villa had been transported to Rome and enlarged to palace size. I might add that it was and remains the only such palace in Rome. Good taste has never been a prominent Roman virtue.

"Decius, how good to see you." I turned to see my aunt coming through a side door. She was about fifty, but a life free of worldly cares and childbearing had left her looking many years younger. Her face was unlined and preternaturally serene.

"I am most honored that you receive me, Reverend Lady," I said, bowing.

"Oh, let's have none of that. You may be a public official, but you are still my great-nephew."

"You have a great many of those, Aunt," I said, smiling.

"We are a numerous family, it is true, but I get to see so few of them, especially the males. Most especially the young males. If you only knew how your female relatives come here to gossip, though. Now come with me and tell me everything."

To my amazement, she took my hand and all but dragged me to a small visiting room furnished with comfortable chairs and its own fire burning in a central brazier. From a woman of such great dignity I had expected the sort of hieratic behavior one sees the vestals displaying at the great festivals, when they seem to be statues of the goddesses come to life. Instead she was behaving—I could think of no better way to put it—like an *aunt*.

Before we could come to the business at hand, I had to bring her up to date on my own doings, my sisters' marriages, my father's career and so forth. My mother

"It isn't Lucullus," I said. "He seems to be a superior general. For all I know, his soldiers are bandits as bad as any in Pompey's army, and most of them are probably foreigners to boot. But these people have committed three murders in my district. And, I rather liked Paulus."

"And is that all?" she asked.

I thought. Was it just my wounded sense of justice and a random liking for a man I had scarcely known? "No. I don't want to see more than two hundred of Paulus's slaves hanging on crosses outside the city walls."

That seemed to satisfy something in her. "Wait here." She rose from her chair and left the room. After a few minutes, a slave girl came in and lighted the lamps. Then Caecilia returned with a small wooden box, which she placed on a table before me. "I will be back in an hour." She left the room again.

My fingers trembled slightly as I opened the box, breaking the wax seal of the Senate with its embossed letters: SPQR. Inside were three small scrolls of superior papyrus. Each bore the names of the Consuls of the year, the Senator who had been in charge of the investigation, and the scribe. The scribe in each case had been different, and none of them were employed by the Senate. Probably they were the personal scribes of the Senators. Two of the Senators were well-known adherents of Pompey and had served in his legions. They were nonentities who had earned their purple stripes by serving as quaestors and would never be praetors without Pompey's patronage. The investigations went back four years, only the most recent having taken place during the Consulate of Pompey and Crassus. I took the earliest scroll and untied its string.

It was bald and brief. The investigator was Senator Marcus Marius. I knew him slightly. He was a distant relative of the great Gaius Marius, and like him had only two names because the gens Marii did not use cognomens. It stated that the Senator had been told by a quaestor that Paramedes of Antioch, an alien resident in the city, had been visited by several foreign persons who

were under surveillance as suspicious characters. Paramedes was known to be an agent for the pirates, but
these foreigners were in the entourage of the visiting
ambassador from Pontus. The Senator's investigation (a
wretchedly perfunctory proceeding) had determined that
Paramedes was most probably an agent and spy for King
Mithridates of Pontus. As a piece of investigation, it
ranked with what an ordinary citizen says about the
weather when he steps out of the baths and looks at the
clouds.

The second scroll was of considerably greater interest.
The investigator was difficult to make out because of a
slip of the scribe's pen, botching the nomen in a great
smear of ink. Luckily, the praenomen was readable—
Mamercus. This meant that it had to be the Senator Mamercus Aemilius Capito, because only the gens Aemilii
used the praenomen Mamercus. This report related that
the Senator had been directed by none other than the
Urban Praetor of that year, Marcus Licinius Crassus, to
make contact with Paramedes of Antioch. This was, in
fact, not an investigation at all. Crassus wanted to question the man personally, at his quarters near Messina.
Capito was acting merely as an errand boy to bring Paramedes to Crassus.

In those long-ago days of the Republic, the highest
magistrates, Consuls and praetors, were all holders of
the imperium, the ancient military power of kings, and
any of them could take an army into the field. Spartacus
had defeated the consular army under Gellius and Clo-
dianus. Crassus, who had served under Sulla, had been
chosen as the next commander to keep Spartacus occupied while word was sent to Spain to bring back Pompey
and his veteran legions.

Capito reported that he had located Paramedes and
had delivered him, as directed, to Crassus's camp. This
much was of interest, but the next part was even better.
The day after delivering Paramedes to Crassus, Capito
had ridden a short distance up the coast, escorting Paramedes to a small fishing village. There, the Asiatic-Greek

had taken a boat, returning the next day with a very young envoy from the pirate fleet, at that time in the straits of Messina dickering with Spartacus for passage to freedom. No name was mentioned, but the description fitted Tigranes the Younger.

Capito returned both men to Crassus's *praetorium,* but did not attend the meeting which followed. Several hours later he escorted the young pirate envoy back to the fishing village and saw him off on his boat. There the report ended.

I was severely disappointed. Thus far, I had nothing that I did not already know or surmise. The conspirators must have panicked and sequestered anything in the Senate records with the name Paramedes on it. Was it for this that I had made my great-aunt commit sacrilege? I took up the third scroll.

The names of Pompey and Crassus were written on this one, Pompey's complete with his self-chosen cognomen: "Magnus." It was typical of the man's gall that he named himself "the Great," although he later claimed that it was Sulla who had thus hailed him, and that a name granted by a Dictator was legal. To crown it all, he passed the name on to his male heirs in perpetuity, but they never amounted to anything.

The reporting Senator was Quintus Hortensius Hortalus. I put the scroll down and drew a deep breath. Hortalus was my father's patron and, by extension, my own. Disgrace and exile for him would mean severe consequences for us, even though we were in no way involved in this conspiracy. At least, I *hoped* that my father was not involved. I opened the scroll. I read it through quickly, like a man lancing an infected wound, wishing to get the pain over with quickly. This was not as easy as it might sound. Hortalus gave very florid speeches, in what was known as the Asiatic style. He wrote the same way. Even in a confidential report, he wrote as if he were holding spellbound a jury in one of his innumerable defenses of ex-governors charged with corruption. Such writing reads very strangely now, since Caesar's bald and unornamented yet elegant style revolutionized Latin prose. Between them, Caesar's books and Cicero's speeches utterly changed the language as it was taught in my youth. But Hortalus was extravagant even for those days. This report is worth setting down verbatim, as I remember it even after all these years, both for its content and to display Hortalus's inimitable style.

> *In Duty to the Senate and People of Rome*
> *Conscript Fathers:*
> (Actually, this was to be seen by the Consuls alone.)
> *Between the kalends of November, when Jove chastens mortal pride with thunder most terrifying, lightning most deadly, and the commencement of the Plebeian Games, which make gay the hearts of the populace in that season when first radiant Proserpine descends to the bed of her dread husband, Pluto,* (The ink was barely dry on this one, I thought.) *I, the Senator Quintus Hortensius Hortalus, held converse with the royal youth Tigranes, from that land where first fall the rays of Helios, while gloom of night still lies upon the temple roofs of the city of Quirinus.* (So the smarmy little bugger's been in Rome since the first of November, eh? I thought.)
> *Our conversation touched upon the overweening pride of that military brigand, Lucius Licinius Lucullus, and of how that pride may be humbled. Lucullus and his mercenary bands, not content with the spoil of Asia, like the flesh-eating horses of Diomedes, have cast their rapacious eyes upon rich Pontus, and even unto splendid Armenia, seat of the youth's royal father. The valiant Trigranes the Younger, who of choice has forsaken the luxury of a prince's life to seek his fortune upon the wine-dark kingdom of Neptune, has offered the services of his adventurous and high-spirited companions, for the sons of Neptune may venture where the sons of Mars cannot. Under his direction, these bold descendants of Ulysses will harry the transports of Lucullus as they ply the foamy realm of the Earthshaker. In return for this, they are to be free of Roman interference for the space of two years. The prince himself wishes, as a friend of Rome, to be sup-*

*ported in his claim to the jeweled throne of Armenia, from
which his father has debarred him. As he is grandson to
Mithridates of Pontus through his mother, he will be most
pleased to rule that land as subject-king when Roman arms
have prevailed against the perfidious Oriental.* (I'll just bet
he would be, I thought. All of the kingdom and none
of the fighting.)

*To all this proposal I listened with sympathetic ear, and
it is my advice, which you may attend as did the Grecian
chiefs to the advice of Nestor of old, that this plan be adopted.
It seems a simple and efficient means of both subduing the
unruly Lucullus while bringing Roman domination and civ-
ilizing influence to the benighted land of fire-worshipping
barbarians. For, make no mistake, it shall be the seven-hilled
city of Romulus that is supreme lord over all, regardless of
which jeweled and scented pseudo-Greek lounges lethargically
upon the garish and vulgar thrones of those nations.*

*As young Tigranes is not officially recognized in the city,
and as such recognition would be an affront to his royal
father, with whom we are not yet at war, he wears, as it
were, the helmet of Pluto, which grants the wearer invisibil-
ity. He resides for now at the house of Paramedes of Antioch,
whom you know. Should you wish to look with favor upon
his proposal, I shall undertake to provide young Tigranes
with a limited and unofficial debut in Rome, perhaps through
a dinner party attended by a diverse company, drawn from
all parties and persuasions.*

*It is desirable to remove Paramedes from these proceedings
as soon as possible, for I know that he is playing a double
game, in collusion with Mithridates. I have already made
arrangements for this, which shall be executed as soon as I
have your agreement and young Tigranes has removed to his
new quarters. The person entrusted with this delicate mission is well-known to you, having carried out other such
missions in the past.*

I await your reply.

I rerolled the scroll, happy to see that my hands had
stopped shaking. Gradually, things were falling into

place. Paramedes had been murdered as soon as Tigranes had moved to the house of Publius Claudius. It was probably Publius who had been entrusted with the murder, since he was a part of the conspiracy, had his own squad of thugs and simply liked that sort of activity. Something struck me as I closed the lid of the box: The light-footed, nimble-fingered, garrote-wielding foreign boy who was working so much mischief in Rome was probably in the entourage of the versatile Tigranes.

My aunt bade me farewell at the entrance. "Was I justified in letting you see documents entrusted to the goddess?"

"You may have saved Rome," I assured her.

"Then I am satisfied." As I was about to leave, she stopped me. "Tell me one thing."

I turned back. "Yes?"

"That scarf. Is it the new fashion for men to wear them?"

"The very latest," I assured her. "The military look. Our adventurous generals and their troops are all the rage these days. Soldiers wear them to spare their necks chafing from the armor."

"Oh. I was wondering."

I turned and went down the steps, into another dark Roman night.

X

The next day, after my morning duties were taken care of, I sought out expert legal advice. Hortalus was deemed the best lawyer in Rome, but with good reason I was reluctant to seek him out for this, so I looked for Marcus Tullius Cicero, who I was certain was not involved in the conspiracy. My search was made easier because one of the augurs had detected unfavorable omens the night before and had canceled public business for the day.

Thus, I found Cicero at home, the one place a Roman in public life was almost never found in the second half of the morning on a day devoted to public work. Cicero's house was a modest one, although not as modest as mine, and very eccentric in its own way. I found his janitor perusing a scroll as I came to announce myself. All of Cicero's slaves were scholarly-looking men who could read to him on demand when his eyes grew tired. Every room of his house was lined with shelves bearing stacks of scrolls. He was an easy man to buy gifts for on Saturnalia, because he loved books above all things, original manuscripts by preference, but decent copies were almost as good. If you had a famous manuscript in your possession and hired one of his favorite scribes to copy it as a gift for him, Cicero was your friend for life, or at least until you fell afoul of him politically.

The janitor brought a man to receive me and conduct me to the master. He was a slave a few years older than I, dressed as well as any free man. This was the famous Tiro, Cicero's secretary and confidant. He had invented

an abbreviated system of writing specifically to take down
Cicero's incredibly prolific dictation. He taught it to Ci
cero's other slaves and it quickly spread to all Roman
scribes. Its use is now universal. He was one of those
slaves who was never treated as anything other than a
free man by anyone, from cobblers to Consuls.

"If you'll come with me, sir," Tiro said. I followed him
through a hall redolent of papyrus and parchment and
up a flight of stairs onto the roof, where we found Cicero
reading in his splendid little solarium. It was a sunny, if
somewhat chilly, morning and the light fell in oblique
bars through an overhead vine-trellis. Planting boxes
topped the low rampart that ran around the roof and a
few flowers bloomed to defy winter. Cicero sat at a del
icate Egyptian table laden with scrolls, rolls of blank pa
pyrus, pots of ink and a vase full of reed pens. He smiled
and stood as I came onto the roof.

"Decius, how good to see you." He held out his hand
and I took it. Then he gestured to a chair. "Please, sit
down." We both sat, and Tiro took a chair just behind
Cicero, to his right.

"Most generous of you to allow me a little of your
time," I told him. "Your nonstop activity is the stuff of
legends."

He leaned back and laughed gently. "I think at my
birth some malevolent god cursed me with a need to fill
my every waking minute with activity."

"I thought you favored the stars as determinants," I
said.

"Perhaps it was the stars, then. How may I be of ser
vice to you?"

"I need advice concerning some difficult points of
law."

"Then I am at your service."

"Thank you. I know that there is no one in Rome bet
ter qualified to advise me."

"There are those who would hold that Hortalus is a
better counselor than I," Cicero said.

I took a deep breath. "I may have to bring suit against Hortalus."

Cicero frowned. "He is the patron of your father and yourself, is he not?"

"No man is my patron where treason is concerned."

Cicero's face registered shock. "Treason! You use the strongest word in the legal vocabulary, my friend. Were you Metellans not noted for moderation in political matters, I would say that you speak most rashly."

"The rest of what I have to say is stronger than this, so let us use no more names for a while. It is law we need to speak about, not personalities. I have seen certain evidence which indicates that a conspiracy exists to suborn the authority of a Roman general in the field and to attack his shipping, a plan involving collusion with the eastern pirate fleet."

"I will not ask the name of this general, although it is easy to guess. Such an attack could be lawful only if the general in question were to be declared an enemy of the state by the Senate, as was the case with Sertorius."

"There is to be no Senate vote on the matter. It is to remain a clandestine operation known only to the conspirators involved."

"This is an evil business, but so far you have not given me enough cause to bring forth a charge of treason, which is defined by constitutional law as engaging in or conspiring toward the armed overthrow of the government."

I had been afraid of that. "There is more involved: The conspiracy includes a foreign prince. His reward is to be the throne of his father, a monarch with whom we are not at war, and perhaps the throne of another with whom we currently are fighting. He promises for his part to rule both as a Roman puppet."

"Once again there is little guesswork here as to identities. If the monarch in question had been granted the title of 'Friend of Rome' by the Senate, as was the case with, say, Nicomedes of Bithynia, then conspiring to take his throne and grant it to another would be a grave instance of criminal corruption. But even then it would not be treason. Is there more?"

"Thus far, I know of three murders committed for the purpose of keeping this conspiracy secret: two citizens and a resident alien. The last murder involved an arson as well."

He pondered for a moment. "Murder of citizens and arson are both capital offenses. However, both are extremely difficult to prove in court. Do you believe that any of the highly placed conspirators personally committed these acts?"

I shook my head. "One was committed by a freedman, a manumitted gladiator. He himself was the second victim, probably to remove him from the chain of conspiracy as a worthless player. His murderer also committed the third homicide. All the evidence I have indicates that the killer is an Asiatic burglar and assassin in the employ of the foreign prince I mentioned."

"Then you will almost certainly not secure a conviction against any of the plotters. Plus, unless I miss my guess, your third victim was a very rich freedman, not so?"

"That is true."

"So we have as victims two freedmen and a foreigner. One of the freedmen was himself a murderer. A Roman jury will laugh at you if you try to lay such charges at the feet of high officials. What is your chief evidence? Do you have anything in writing?"

"Not in my possession. My surest proof of conspiracy lies in documents placed in the Temple of Vesta."

"Hmm. I won't ask how you got a look at them, but let us pretend that you read them before they were placed there. Documents entrusted to the Temple of Vesta may be subpoenaed by vote of the Senate where imminent danger to the state is involved and with the concurrence of the *Pontifex Maximus*. Since you need the documents to prove danger to the state, I see very little chance for that."

"You are saying, in essence, that I have nothing with which to bring charges against these people?"

"It is, of course, the right of every Roman citizen to bring suit in court against any other citizen. However, no serving Roman magistrate may be charged while in office, although as soon as he leaves office he may be charged with malfeasance. From what you have been saying, I take it that at least one of these conspirators is a serving magistrate?"

"Two, actually," I said.

"And the office they hold?"

"Consul. Both of them."

He paused. "Well. That does remove a bit of the guess-work, doesn't it? Tiro, I can tell you want to say something."

Tiro's waiting for Cicero's permission to speak was the only slavelike behavior I ever detected in him.

"Sir," he said to me, "the Consuls for this year have only a bit more than a month left in office. If you can gather more solid evidence against them, you may bring charges as soon as they step down. Neither has his army with him, and the proconsular command of the greater has not yet been chosen. It would be a good time, if the evidence can be produced."

Cicero nodded. "It would certainly make your name in Roman politics. You'd be singled out as consular material before even serving as quaestor."

"At the moment, I don't find the prospect all that tempting. My recent experiences have made me doubtful of the wisdom of a career in politics."

"Pity. You have what I regard as the highest of qualifications, which is a sense of public duty. A rare commodity these days. Tiro?"

"From what you have said," Tiro commented, "another of the conspirators is a Consul-elect for the next year. That complicates things further. The Consulate is not a judicial office and, technically, he may not interfere, but political reality is otherwise. Since he and his colleague will rule on alternate days, you may try to set your court dates for days when his colleague holds office, but that would be difficult."

"You have my congratulations," Cicero said. "At a very young age, you have acquired not one but three of the most powerful enemies in the world. However, you have asked for legal advice and I shall give it. If you wish to prosecute all the conspirators at once, you must wait until this Consul-elect, who shall remain nameless, is out of office, a matter of some thirteen months and odd days. By that time, the two ex-Consuls will undoubtedly be on foreign soil, in command of very large and powerful armies. Such men may be impeached, as will probably happen to Lucullus. However, I must warn you that, as an exercise in futility, taking legal action against a Roman general in the midst of his legionaries has few peers."

"Is there no hope, then?" I asked, what few hopes I had arrived with already dashed.

"I have spoken as your legal advisor," Cicero said. "Now let me speak as a man of the world." He began ticking off points on his fingertips, lawyer-fashion. "First, the people you wish to prosecute are, for all practical purposes, above the law and the constitution. One of them is the greatest general in the world; another is the richest man in the world; the third is, besides myself, the best legal mind before the Roman bar. Each of the two Consuls commands a party of supporters in the Senate so powerful that they would be safe if they broke into the Temple of Vesta and raped all the virgins. Most importantly, they have the loyalty of thousands of the saltiest, most vicious and battle-hardened troops the world has ever seen. Once, it was unthinkable that Roman generals would lead their troops against Rome herself, but Marius and Sulla changed all that."

Now he leaned forward and spoke most earnestly. "Decius Caecilius, nobody, *nobody*, is going to convict those men for engaging in a bit of conspiracy against an ambitious fellow general or killing a couple of freedmen and a foreigner. I marvel that you are alive at all. This I can only attribute to the fact that these men would like the support of the Metellan family in their future plans."

"I suppose that is true of the highest of the conspirators," I acknowledged. "But there has been one unsuccessful attempt on my life. You see, one of the less highly placed conspirators does not fear the wrath of the Metellans, the laws of Rome or, for all I can tell, the immortal gods."

Cicero smiled wryly. "I think I know who that must be. I believe we had dinner at his table a few nights ago, did we not? Well, him you may protect yourself from. Hire a pack of gladiators from the Statilian school, like all the other politicians. They make good bodyguards."

"Not the family tradition, I'm afraid," I said, rising. "Marcus Tullius, I thank you for your advice. You've given me little cause for hope, but you have clarified some points on which I was unclear, and that will be a great help."

"Will you not drop this matter?" he asked.

I shook my head. "They have murdered people in my district, and I must pursue the case."

He rose and took my hand. "Then I wish you well. I look to see great things from you, if you live." Tiro conducted me out.

Since lawyers, like physicians, were forbidden to accept fees, I pondered what I might give Cicero. I was building up quite a Saturnalia debt lately. As I walked toward the Forum I remembered that I had a rather nice original manuscript of the poet Archias, whom Cicero loved. That should do it. A morning of legal consultation was not quite as demanding as if he had won an important court case for me.

I had other things buzzing through my mind, naturally. Cicero had very aptly and succinctly made my position clear. I was Rome's most unloved investigator and number-one candidate for the next homicide victim. My plans to expose a conspiracy were in ruins. After all, who in Rome *cared* which of several power-mad, plunder-addled generals ruled as cock of the roost? Who *cared* which oily Oriental sat on some eastern throne? Most of all, who cared about a few corpses in the street, where on some mornings corpses were as numerous as peach pits?

I cared, of course, but I found myself in a distinct minority. Very well: I had no chance against Pompey or Crassus, or even Hortalus. I could at least pursue the immediate murderers of the residents of my district. It was a poor accomplishment in light of the larger issues, but it was within my power. If I could stay alive.

The day had warmed slightly, heating the Roman blood to a level of moderate activity. The markets in the Forum were bustling. Some sold country produce, but I noticed an inordinate number of fortune-tellers' booths. Fortune-tellers were periodically banished from the city, but the last such action had been a year or two before, so they had dribbled back in. I noticed that there were long lines at the booths of the various bone-tossers, star-readers, snake-diviners and other such charlatans. It was a sign of unrest in the city. In times of great uncertainty, a single lunatic prophet could send the urban mob into a panic culminating in a full-blown riot.

At the base of the Rostra I saw Caesar talking with a mixed group of Senators and ordinary citizens. He had so far amounted to little politically, but he had demonstrated an extraordinary ability to sway the Centuriate Assembly and had secured himself a quaestorship for the next year. He caught my eye and gestured for me to join him.

"Decius, have you heard?" he said. "A special session of the Senate has been scheduled for tonight." The ban on public business expired at sunset.

"I hadn't," I admitted. "Is it about Lucullus?"

"What else?" said one of the Senators, a man I didn't know. "I suspect that we'll vote on a recall for Lucullus."

"I doubt that," Caesar said. "It would mean handing Pompey the eastern command, and his party is not strong enough to force that through. What we'll see tonight is a senatorial decree ordering Lucullus not to invade Ar-

menia." He spoke as if he were already a Senator, which
he would not be until he finished his quaestorship. In
later years he would not express his opinions so freely
in casual conversation, at least until the time when there
was no man left to gainsay him. At this time, though, he
was as extravagant with his speech as with his debts.

"I suppose I'll hear about it in the morning," I said,
"like the rest of the citizenry."

Caesar took his leave of the others and began to stroll
with me, his hand on my shoulder, head down, a signal
to all that we were engaged in private conversation.

"Have you had any luck in your murder investigation?" he asked.

"Luck was scarcely involved, except perhaps for my
own survival. I have it all now, except for the identity of
the actual murderer of Sinistrus and Paulus." It was reckless to speak thus to Caesar, who I thought was probably
involved in the conspiracy, at least peripherally.

He looked at me sharply. " 'All'?"

"Eggs to apples," I assured him cheerfully. I had just
discovered that I no longer cared whom he talked to.
"All that remains is to find the killer, and I shall make
my report to the Senate, all names included. On that
basis I shall subpoena certain papers deposited in the
Temple of Vesta for extra-legal purposes."

Caesar was thunderstruck. "That would call for a special
instruction to the Senate from the *Pontifex Maximus.*"

"I think he will give that instruction when he under-
stands that a genuine danger to the state exists." The
holder of the high priesthood at that time was Quintus
Mucius Scaevola, who besides his religious office was a
famous jurisconsult. He had trained Cicero in constitutional law. I was speaking with a great deal of bluff and
bravado, but I saw no other way to precipitate events,
having reached a blind alley in my investigation.

"Decius," he said in a low voice, "if I were you, since
it seems you are bent on self-destruction, I would stay in
my house during the hours of darkness. This city is no

longer a safe place for you. It is possible, if you are very discreet, that you may get out of this merely exiled instead of dead. I speak as a friend."

I shook off his hand. "I speak as an official of Rome. I will pursue this until the murderers are brought to justice." I walked away, followed by many curious eyes. Was Caesar trying to be my friend? Even now I cannot say. Caesar was everyone's friend when he was on his way up. It is the politician's art. But he was a complex creature, and I cannot say that he utterly lacked a desire for the friendship of others, especially those who possessed a probity totally absent in his own character. I can only state that, in later years, he more than once spared me when we were enemies and the power, as usual, was all his.

I was not in the Forum long before I noticed that many men, especially Senators, were avoiding me, fading into the crowd if I seemed to be moving in their direction. There was also muttering behind my back. While no one actually pelted me with unpleasant substances, the atmosphere was ugly enough for it. The strangest thing was that scarcely one in fifty of those gathered in the Forum could have known why I was a pariah so suddenly.

I think that, through the years of dictatorships and proscriptions and civil war, the Roman populace had acquired a faculty of mind or spirit that told them when a man was out of favor with the great men of the state, and they would turn on such a man like dogs upon a crippled member of the pack. It signified to me more than anything else how far down the path Romans had gone toward an Oriental slavery of the populace. My spirits have never been lower than they were on that long walk home from the Forum.

When I arrived at my home the light was dimming. I had not been attacked, a matter of some astonishment to me. Cato opened my door, wearing the scandalized look that had grown almost perpetual these past few days.

"Sir, this fellow arrived an hour ago. He insisted he'd wait here until you got home."

I walked past Cato and found none other than Titus Milo lounging in my atrium, munching from a bag of parched nuts and peas. He flashed me his grin as I entered.

"Still alive, eh? Word is out on the street that anyone who comes to your defense proclaims himself an enemy of Claudius and his mob."

"Word is out in higher quarters that anyone who socializes with me risks disfavor from our Consuls."

"The hazards of power," he said. "I have something for you." He held out a scroll and I took it.

"Let's go into my reading-room. Cato, bring lamps."

When I had light, I opened the scroll. It was a certificate of manumission for one Sinistrus, a slave of H. Ager. The date was only a few days from the man's purchase from the school of Statilius Taurus. The ceremony of manumission had been witnessed by the praetor Quintus Hortensius Hortalus.

"How did you get this?" I asked, excited despite my despondency.

"A small bribe to a slave in the Archives."

"The archives in Baiae?" I asked.

"No, the big one here in Rome." He grinned again, loving the role of the man with the answers.

"We've already established that I probably do not have long to live. I would like to hear the end of this before I die. If he was bought for a farm near Baiae, why was his manumission filed here in Rome?"

Milo sat and propped his feet on my desk. "It's complicated, that's why it took so long. Macro's people in Baiae located the estate and questioned the manager. His name is Hostilius Ager and he's in debt to Macro's colleague in those parts—something about a tendency to bet on blue at the races—and so it wasn't too difficult to get answers out of him."

"And the content of these answers?" I asked.

"First, the farm is owned by the family of Claudius

Pulcher. At present it forms a part of the dowry of Publius's sister, Claudia, but Publius has the legal control of it until she marries."

I felt a cold chill washing over me. "And what were the circumstances of this man's purchase of Sinistrus?"

"Very simple. He came up to Rome to give his annual accounting to the master and was sent to the Statilian school to buy this Gallic brute. He says he was terrified that he might have to take the animal back to Baiae and find work for him, but instead he was told to wait in Rome for a few days more. One morning he took Sinistrus to a praetor and freed him and was on his way home the same afternoon.

"That was when the slave rebellion was at its height. It was difficult to free a slave, and it was absolutely forbidden to manumit a gladiator. Transferring ownership of Sinistrus took a special dispensation from a praetor, and his manumission took an extra-legal act by a praetor. Knowing that, the rest was easy. Since the manumission ceremony took place in Rome, the record was in the Archives. And Macro didn't have to think long to figure out who the crookedest praetor of that year was. I was sent to the Archives to look over manumission records from the praetorship of Hortalus. Since there were so few that year, I found it within an hour. Getting it out of the Archives cost four sesterces."

"You shall be reimbursed," I said. "Of course, Hortalus never thought to hide this." I hefted the manumission record. "It was nothing; just a favor to the Claudians, helping them acquire a bullyboy in a year when that was difficult. He had no idea that Sinistrus would attract anyone's attention."

"Does it make your case any easier?" Milo asked.

Disgustedly, I tossed the thing on my table. "No. It's just more evidence. I no longer think that any amount of evidence will allow me to prosecute the people responsible. But now I would just like to *know!*" I slapped the unoffending table, rattling the old bronze dagger. I stared at Milo. "I have to have that damned amulet. It must be the key to all this."

Milo shrugged. "Well, you know where it is, don't you?"

"The house of Publius Claudius, if it hasn't been destroyed already. But there is no legal process for searching a citizen's home."

Milo stared at me as if at some rare new form of idiot. "Surely you don't expect to go about this legally?"

"Well," I began, tapering off uncertainly, "I suppose at this juncture that would be rather futile."

He leaned forward. "Look, Decius, here in Rome we have some of the best burglars in the world. In fact, in some quarters there is resentment that this Asian boy is prowling all over Rome as if he had a perfect right here. I know some good lads. They'll be in that house and toss it from top to bottom, get your amulet and be out by daylight, and nobody will know they were ever there."

I was astonished. "They are that good?"

"The best," he assured me. "The guild's entrance standards are very high."

I was horrified. I was also exhilarated. I, Decius Caecilius Metellus, was contemplating having the house of a citizen burglarized. The prospect of an early and obscure grave made that seem of less account than in better days.

"All right," I said. "Let's do it. Can they find something so small in that great house?"

He spoke as if to a small, naive boy. "The valuable things are always small. No burglar goes in through a window and comes out with a life-size bronze by Praxiteles. These lads know exactly where to look for small, valuable objects. They can steal the jewelry off a sleeping woman without waking her."

"Send them," I said. "Can they be back by morning? I have little time now."

"If it's still there and not at the bottom of the Tiber or cast into a new lamp, I'll have it for you at first light."

"Go," I said.

When he was gone, I prepared papyrus and ink, and

I tried to make out my will. It was appalling how little I had to leave to anybody. Technically, I couldn't own property myself, since my father was still alive, but *patria potestas* was a legal fiction by that time. I made out manumission documents for Cato and Cassandra, and left them the house. I needed very little time to dispose of the rest of my belongings, dividing them among my clients. My field armor I left to Burrus. I knew that he had a son who was about to join his old legion. My farmer I left a small olive grove adjacent to his land. My other possessions I left to various friends. At least, I assumed they were still my friends.

I jerked awake. Sometime during the night, I had nodded off over my table. Someone had thrown a cloak over my shoulders. A dim light just outlined my window and I wondered what had awakened me. Then I heard the scratching at my front door.

I went to my chest and took out my short sword. With drawn steel in my hand, I went to the front door and opened it. Outside stood Milo, grinning as usual. At arm's length, before my eyes, he held something dangling from a ribbon. It was an amulet in the form of a camel's head.

I snatched it from him and turned it over. In the growing light of morning I read the words cut into the flat back side.

XI

———

"Healing nicely," Asklepiodes said. "There is no inflammation, no suppuration. Avoid strenuous movement and it should be fully healed in a few days." His slaves began to rebandage me.

"I may not have much choice about that last part," I told him. "There is a great likelihood that I shall spend the rest of the day running or fighting."

"Well, if it is a matter of preserving your life, do not worry too much about this cut. It will just mean a little more blood and pain."

"I shall try to be Stoic." I stood, feeling almost healthy. "The circumstances being what they are, I've decided not to wait until Saturnalia. Accept this with my thanks." It was a caduceus a foot tall, made of silver and mounted on a base of alabaster. It was not the common one you see carried by Mercury in sculptures, with two serpents twining around the shaft, topped by a pair of wings. Rather it was the older one, the heavy staff wound by a single serpent associated with his namesake, Asklepios, the son of Apollo and god of healing. I had stopped by the quarter of the silversmiths on the way to the ludus in search of an appropriate gift and had fortuitously found this in an antiques dealer's shop.

"Why, this is splendid," he said, and I could tell that his delight was genuine. "I shall have a shrine made for it. I do not know how to thank you."

"A small recompense for the services you have rendered. If I should live through this, be assured that I shall call on you frequently."

He bowed, sweeping his robes gracefully. "I shall always be at your service. I cannot tell you how much more entertaining it is to serve you than to sew up athletes or diagnose the false ailments of healthy aristocrats."

"May we always lead interesting and exciting lives," I said. "Now I must go see whether I can make mine a long one."

On my way from his quarters, I stopped to watch the men practicing their fighting in the exercise yard. Any or all of them could die in the next great *munera*, but they practiced with that inhuman serenity that gladiators always seemed to have. Sinistrus had been one of their number. The old champion Draco watched them with a critical eye, and the lesser trainers shouted out their instructions as to the proper use of dagger, sword or lance. These men never showed the faintest concern for their lives, and I decided that a Roman official, however humble, could scarcely do less.

I walked out through the school's entrance and my old soldier, Burrus, fell in behind me, as did Milo. I stopped and turned to face that remarkable young man.

"Milo, I am sure that Macro does not wish you involved in this."

"I didn't ask him. I have my own reputation to build in this city. I want it known that I don't fear Claudius and I want to be seen publicly as your supporter. After all"—he favored me with that maddening grin again—"they may pretend to despise you, but everyone secretly admires a man who's such a fool for duty that he'll throw his own life away for love of it."

"Here, now!" Burrus said, outraged. He made as if to strike Milo, but I stopped him with a gesture.

"None of that. Milo, you are one of the strangest men I have ever met, but I appreciate your honesty, even if you are a criminal. Honesty is in short supply among the respectable classes these days, so it must be valued, wherever we find it."

"Excellent. Shall we go to the house of Claudius?"

"Not yet. To the Forum first. I intend to make an ungodly show. All Romans love a spectacle, and I shall give them one."

"Wonderful!" Milo said. "May I help?"

"I don't know how you could, but go ahead, as long as you don't interfere and there is no violence on your part."

"Leave it to me," he said.

As we walked toward the Forum, every so often Milo would make a gesture and someone would come from a doorway or a knot of idlers and Milo would whisper to him. They were all rough-looking fellows or else the sort of young street urchins who provided recruits for the gangs the way farm boys provided them for the legions. After each brief consultation the one talked to would run off. I did not ask Milo what he was up to. I was too involved with my own desperation to worry about it.

As I walked, I drank in the sights of Rome, knowing that it might well be for the last time. The whitewashed walls, the little fountains at every corner, the shrines to minor gods in their niches, all stood etched with wonderful clarity, their colors vivid as if seen through the eyes of an infant. The feel of cobbles beneath my sandals, the sound of hammering from the tinsmiths' quarter, the very smell of frying garlic wafting from tenement doorways seemed charged with unbelievable beauty and significance. I would have preferred all this in late spring, when Rome is at its most beautiful, but one can't have everything.

The Forum was simmering when we arrived. Crowds were gathered near the Curia, around the Rostra and before the Basilica Aemilia, where my father held court that day. I could see others coming into the Forum from side streets. I could not believe that it was all on my account. I was simply not that important. At the center of the crowd by the Rostra, though, I saw Publius Claudius. The instant he caught sight of me, he came for me, with his whole mob behind him.

I checked to make sure that my dagger and *caestus* were in place, for all the good they would do me in this situation. No, I thought, this is just *too* public. He won't attack me here. A fat lot I knew about it.

They stormed across the all-but-empty stretch of pavement in the middle of the Forum. Scattering the few pedestrians who stood in their way, the crowd bore down upon us as if to trample us. I knew then that Claudius fully intended to kill me, right in the middle of the Forum with half of Rome looking on. He had scant judgment, but you couldn't fault the man for sheer gall.

As if having collective second thoughts, the crowd broke step, wavered and slowed to a halt a few paces from us. I was under no illusion that they had acquired a respect for the law as they crossed the pavement, so I looked behind me. About thirty young men stood there, hard boys from the gangs. None of them displayed weapons openly, although a large number leaned on perfectly legal walking sticks, as if a sudden plague of lameness had broken out among the youth of Rome. Apparently, Milo was building up his own, independent little mob.

"So the pious and honorable Decius Metellus is not too proud to take refuge among a pack of the city's lowest scum!" Claudius shouted. Considering his own company, this was a weak taunt, but his crowd reinforced it with cheers and shouts of agreement.

"It's never disgraceful to be in the company of Roman citizens," I responded, to much applause from my new following. As a slanging match, this was not up with Cicero and Hortalus in the courts, but we were just getting started.

"Citizens! That pack of slaves and freedmen? They look like they somehow escaped from Crassus's crosses." This was a neat play on words, but it didn't originate with Claudius, who wasn't that clever. Some playwright had used it the year before. There was dark muttering behind me, and it occurred to me that a few of them probably *had* campaigned with Spartacus. Pompey and Crassus hadn't caught all of them.

"At least we're all Romans," I said. "Speaking of which, how is your Armenian guest? Do you two share the same Greek tastes?" No one else knew what I was talking about, but they cheered at Publius's expression of anger.

"Are we to endure this abuse from a mere Metellan," he shouted, "whose kinsman almost lost us Spain?" His crowd jeered loudly.

"This from one who conspires to lose us Pontus and Armenia!" I yelled.

"Cowardly Metellan!" he roared.

"Chicken-drowning Claudian!" I bellowed. The whole Forum roared with laughter and Publius's face flamed. The Claudians will never live that one down.

Screaming with rage, Claudius drew a dagger from inside his toga and charged me. I had already slipped my *caestus* onto my right hand and I stepped forward to meet him. I blocked the dagger with my left forearm and swung a blow that should have taken his jaw off, but somebody jostled me and I only raked the side of his face. He dropped like a stone and in an instant the Forum was alive with flashing daggers, flailing sticks and flying stones. It had been months since the last good riot and winter is a boring season in Rome, so nobody needed much excuse to join in. I dropped two more, men who had been standing close to Publius, then saw five coming for me with daggers. Arms grabbed me from behind and I thought I was done for, but I found myself being dragged away from the riot and into a narrow street. I heard a familiar laugh and I saw that it was Milo and Burrus who had wrested me away.

"No violence, you said!" he choked out between paroxysms.

"I didn't think he'd start anything right there in the Forum!" I protested.

"You still don't know him, do you?" Milo said. "Well, maybe he's dead. That was no love pat you gave him."

"I doubt it," I said. "Claudians and snakes are hard to kill."

"Where to now, sir?" Burrus asked.

"To the house of Claudius," I said.

Burrus was astonished. "But you just dropped the bugger on the pavement back there. His friends will be carrying him home soon!"

Milo smiled. "He's not the Claudian your patron needs to call on just now, am I right?"

"You're right," I said. "And Burrus is right about his men taking his inert carcass home soon. I'd as soon not be there when that happens, so we had best not waste any time." We made a circuit around the Forum, from which we could still hear sounds of riot, and made our way through the maze of cramped streets to Publius's town house. I paused to straighten my disarrayed toga and winced at a pain in my side. I looked inside my toga and saw that blood was seeping through my tunic. Nothing to be done about it now, I thought.

I pounded on the door until the janitor opened it.

"Decius Caecilius Metellus the Younger of the Commission of Twenty-Six to see the Lady Claudia Pulcher," I said, finishing somewhat out of breath. The janitor called a house slave and repeated the message, ushering me inside.

"You two stay here in the atrium," I told Milo and Burrus. "I will interview her privately, but come at once if I should call you." Burrus merely nodded, but Milo spoke in a low voice.

"This isn't very wise. Publius and his mob will be here from the Forum at any minute and your Armenian prince may be here now, with his own band."

I hadn't thought of that, but I was not about to admit it. "Don't worry. He's trying to curry favor with Rome, not to alienate the city by killing one of its officers."

"You constantly underestimate these people," he said, "but have it your way."

The house slave came to fetch me and I followed him. Behind me, I could hear Milo and Burrus arguing quietly. Burrus could not get used to the way Milo addressed me. I nerved myself for the encounter to come. My feelings for Claudia had taken many disorienting turns re-

cently. I had tried to find a way out of this, but I could
find none. Perhaps, I thought, I should have waited, slept
on the problem. I had acted precipitately, without proper
thought or rest. I had, in fact, not acted quite sanely.
Why should I feel afraid to face Claudia with this when
I had walked straight up to her brother and his mob in
the Forum? I could not explain it, even to myself.

She received me in a sitting-room, looking cool and
serene. She sat with her back to a fretted window, so that
the light surrounded her with a nimbus. Her gown was
of some flimsy material, clinging to every curve, a brilliant blue. It complimented her eyes perfectly, as did the
jewelry she wore: gold set with lapis lazuli and sapphires.
She looked every inch the patrician lady, not the wild-
haired maenad she had seemed when I had last seen her.

"Decius, how good to see you," she said, her voice as
low and intimate as ever. It went through me like the
vibration of an overstretched lyre string when it is
plucked.

"I am sorry to appear before you in so unkempt a
condition," I said.

She smiled with one corner of her mouth. "You were
a good deal less kempt when we last parted."

I could feel my face flushing and was infuriated that
this woman could bring out so juvenile a reaction in me.
"There was a rough scene in the Forum, involving your
brother and his thugs."

Her face hardened. "You have not hurt him, have
you?"

"He'll probably live, which is better than he deserves.
His men will probably bring him here soon, although
they may take him to a physician first."

"What do you want, Decius? I have little time for you.
You are no longer a player in the game. You might have
been, but you chose to play the fool. You count for nothing now. Make this brief."

"A game. Is that what it is to you?"

Her look was utter contempt. "What else is it? It is the
greatest game in the world. It is played on a board made

up of kingdoms and republics and seas. The men are just counters. They are placed on the board and struck from it at the whim and according to the skill of the players." She paused. "And there is the uncertainty of luck, of course."

"Fortuna can be a whimsical goddess," I said.

"I don't believe in the gods. If they exist at all, they take no interest in what men do. But I believe in blind chance. It just makes the game more interesting."

"And you have a taste for this sort of gaming? Knuckle-bones and dice and races and the *munera* grew too tame for you?"

"Don't talk like a fool. There is nothing else in the world like this game. The prize is power and wealth beyond dreams. The Pharaohs never saw such wealth. Alexander never wielded such power. This empire we have built with our legions is the most incredible instrument for imposing the leader's will that has ever existed."

"There are no legions of Rome," I said. "They are the personal followers of twenty or more generals. The four or five most powerful generals are always mortal enemies, more occupied with cutting each other's throats and stealing each other's glory than with expanding Rome's empire."

Her smile was dazzling. "But that is what the game is all about. At the end of it, there will be one man who controls all the legions, who controls the Senate, who will be followed by patricians and plebs alike. No more bickering parties and treacherous senatorial votes behind the leader's back."

"You mean a king of Rome," I said.

"The title needn't be used, but the power would be the same. Like the old King of Persia, only much greater."

"It has been tried," I noted. "Marius, Sulla, others. None of them succeeded, no matter how many domestic enemies they killed."

"They were inferior players," she asserted calmly. "They were ruthless, and their soldiers worshipped them, but they were not intelligent enough. Marius tried to

keep playing the game when he had grown far too old.
Sulla had it all won, then he decided to retire. It was the
act of a political moron. We are moving into the final
rounds of a great *munera sine missione*, Decius. When it is
over, only one man will be standing."

"If you will forgive my saying so, this is not a game in
which women compete."

She laughed musically. "Oh, Decius, you really are a
child! Men and women simply play differing roles in this
game. You will not see me in polished armor leading a
legion, of course, but depend upon it, when the game is
ended, I shall be sitting on a throne by the side of the
winner."

I wondered if she was mad. It was difficult to say. The
Claudians were mad almost by definition, but they were
hardly alone in the condition. As I have said, half my
generation seemed to be subject to madness. I was not
immune to the sickness myself. Perhaps Claudia was just
a part of the times.

"In this game, if you lose, you die."

She shrugged. "What is the game if the stakes are not
the highest?"

"And sometimes," I continued, "it's hard to keep track
of all the counters on the board. Ones you thought were
gone turn up again."

For the first time, her self-assurance slipped. She had
thought she had all the answers, and I had said something that indicated otherwise.

"What do you mean?" She frowned. "You make no
sense."

I took out the camel's head amulet and held it before
her, dangling on its ribbon. "It was you, Claudia. I had
thought Claudius, even Pompey or Crassus, but it was
you who had Paramedes of Antioch murdered, and Sinistrus, and Sergius Paulus. In my district."

Her face went white and her mouth began to tremble.
Not in fear, which I do not think she was capable of
feeling, but in rage. "I told that little . . ." She shut herself
off like a tavernkeeper turning a tap.

"There are rules to successful conspiracy, Claudia," I said. "First: Put nothing in writing. Second: Never trust a subordinate to dispose of evidence. They will always keep something back, to blackmail you with later."

She got herself under control. "You have nothing. It means nothing."

"Oh, but I think it does. I think I could take you and this little amulet into court and convince a jury that you are guilty of murder. As far as I am concerned you are also guilty of treason, but expert counsel assures me that, technically, you are not. Not yet, at any rate. So you may escape being hurled headforemost from the Tarpeian Rock. Considering your birth and the influence of your family and the fact that our current Consuls and one of the Consuls for the next year are also involved, you may be let off with mere banishment. Out of Rome forever, Claudia. Out of the game."

"You have nothing," she reiterated, running out of eloquence.

"The remarkable thing," I said, "is that I might never have examined this thing after I took it from the house of the late Paramedes. How could a little bronze amulet be significant? I only became curious after you had it stolen from my room, having me knocked on the head in the process. You shouldn't have balked at one more murder, Claudia; it ill becomes a would-be player in the great game."

I held the amulet before my eyes, watching it rotate on its ribbon. "A token of *hospitium*. A fine old custom, is it not? I received one myself, just a few days ago, from a very honorable and old-fashioned soldier. I suppose only old-fashioned people are honorable anymore. The times really are disgracefully decadent, as my father never tires of telling me. This one identifies you and Paramedes of Antioch as *hospites*. Where did you meet him and exchange tokens, Claudia?"

"On Delos," she said. "As if it makes any difference. You not only have no proof to use against me, you may not live to leave this house. The slave market on Delos.

I was tired of Rome, and my older brother, Appius, was sailing to Asia to join Lucullus. I persuaded him to take me to see the Greek islands. I'd always heard of the great pirate slave market on Delos and I was eager to see it, so when we passed near I asked to be put ashore, to sail home from there."

"Sightseeing in a slave market," I mused. "You really are a woman of unusual tastes, Claudia."

She shrugged again. "Each of us finds his pleasures where he will. Anyway, I met Paramedes there. I saw immediately that, with his pirate contacts, he could be of great use to me. We exchanged tokens and a few months later he arrived in Rome, in the role of an importer of wine and oil."

"But he needed a city patron to hold property and conduct his business here. Since patricians are forbidden to take part in commerce, you sent him to Sergius Paulus. What was Paulus's part in all this? I confess that I haven't been able to puzzle that one out."

"Poor Decius. So something is beyond your logical faculties. I arranged for Paulus to take on Paramedes as patron. He was tremendously rich and had many such clients, so I thought he would take little interest in Paramedes. I gave him some generous presents, told him that he would be doing me a great favor by obliging me in this. Of course, he was to be discreet. He was never, never to hint that there was any connection between the house of Claudius and Paramedes. His activities as a pirate agent were quasi-legitimate, but there are some things that we should not be connected with. Paulus was eager to please. I positively fawned on the man," she said with distaste. "No matter how rich or powerful they get, men like poor Sergius are always flattered by the attentions of patricians."

"Poor Sergius," I said. "Another counter, removed from the board."

"He was nothing," she said. "Just a freedman."

"So it was you who told Crassus about Paramedes when

he needed to spoil Spartacus's arrangement with the pirates?" I asked.

"Yes, for which I would think you'd be grateful, since you conceive yourself to be such a patriot."

"If he'd wanted to, he could have taken Rome," I said. "That Thracian scoundrel and his followers just wanted to get away. I wouldn't have complained. There are too many slaves in Italy as it is."

"You are far too softhearted, Decius."

"I suppose I'll never be a good player in the game. When did it start to go sour, Claudia? Paramedes was useful to you. Did he try blackmail? Co-conspirators often do."

"Yes. He let it be known that Mithridates might make it more than worth his while to keep him supplied with the details of our dealings. Since he fancied that Crassus is even richer than Mithridates, he sought out a better offer."

"And as soon as Tigranes was in Rome, Paramedes was redundant."

"Exactly."

"So you dispatched Sinistrus to kill him. I take it that the arson was a diversion?"

"Partially." She regarded me with some interest. "Your mind works well, Decius. I wish you had decided to throw in with us. My brother and the others are so headstrong and lacking in foresight. Except for Hortalus. Yes, it was decided that, since Romans are far more upset by a fire than by a murder, all the attention would go to the fire the next day. Paramedes was just one more dead foreigner. Also, Paramedes kept little in his house. The fire would take care of any embarrassing documents he might have at the warehouse."

"That brings us to Sinistrus. You acquired him through extra-legal means. A minor bit of corruption, but documents on file at the Archives allowed me to tie Hortalus in with your conspiracy."

"He was just a cheap killer working for me. Bought on the sly and freed so as to have minimum connection with me. I had used him a few times before, usually lending him out to Publius. He was reliable and too stupid to plan a betrayal."

"This time, to make a clean sweep of it, you eliminated him, employing this mysterious Asian boy. I want to meet that enterprising youth, by the way." She smiled at this. At the time, I thought she was just being arch.

"Yes, Sinistrus was at the end of his usefulness to us. There are plenty more of him, and they are much easier to buy, now. We wanted no loose ends at such a delicate stage. It was only later that I realized that Sinistrus had stupidly neglected to fetch that token from Paramedes's house."

"Not the brightest of henchmen, Sinistrus," I commiserated.

"Decidedly not. Of course, by the time we discovered his mistake it was daylight and a guard had been posted at Paramedes's house. Then you came snooping around."

"And inconveniently made off with the token. I must thank you for not having me killed, Claudia. Must have been a wrench for you to leave someone alive."

"It was Hortalus who said you weren't to be killed," she said, shrugging. "He's a dreadful sentimentalist."

"So much for my manly charm." My irony was assumed, but my sadness was real. I had, against all likelihood, cherished the hope that, somehow, Claudia felt something for me. "Why Sergius Paulus? Surely he didn't try to blackmail you."

"Of course not. He was far too rich for that. When I found out you had called on him, I went to see him immediately afterward."

I wondered which of my colleagues had told her I was on my way to the house of Paulus. Rutilius? Opimius? Junius the scribe? Any or all of them, I decided. "I know," I said. "I saw your palanquin leaving his house. Of course, I didn't know it was yours at the time, but I found it in your little hideaway after our memorable night together."

"What a snoop!" she said, indignant. "It was very low-bred of you to go prying like that."

"Each of us behaves according to the gifts bestowed upon us by the gods at our birth. To some is given great strength, to others the ability to lead men, or play the lyre or compose verse. To me was given the propensity for snooping into things others would prefer to remain hidden."

"Just like a plebeian," she sniffed. "Well, Paulus was losing his nerve. Freedmen are always insecure, even rich ones. They know it is possible to lose everything. He was agitated, prattling on about your questioning. I tried to reassure him, but I could see that it was no use. He knew too much and he drank too much. We no longer needed him, since Paramedes had been removed from the board. I decided to remove him, too." She sat back, a puzzled look on her face. "I don't know why I'm bothering to tell you all this."

"But you have to," I said. "Otherwise, who will know what a superb player you are? I'll bet you don't even tell your fellow conspirators everything."

"Don't patronize me!" she hissed. "You aren't half as clever as you think, Decius."

"I suppose not," I admitted. I dreaded the next question. "Now, Claudia, tell me one last thing. I know that the point of all this conspiracy and murder is to secure Lucullus's eastern command for one of the men you plan to manipulate. It hardly matters which one. And that you intend to install young Tigranes on his father's throne as puppet-king, and probably let him pretend to rule his grandfather's kingdom of Pontus."

She nodded. "Very good. And your question?"

I took a deep breath. "Was my father in any way involved in your conspiracy?"

"Don't be ridiculous!" she said scornfully. "Hortalus says old Cut-Nose is more upright than the Temple of Vesta."

Relief washed over me like the cold plunge at the baths. "Well, the old man isn't above taking a bribe now and then, but never over anything important. Certainly nothing touching on state security."

"Then why did you ask?"

"He keeps bad company. Hortalus, for instance." Now for the next unpleasant duty. "Claudia, it is my duty to arrest you and take you before the praetor, to answer charges of murder, arson and conspiracy. However, tradition allows you the honorable option to spare the family name."

I reached inside my tunic and took out the sheathed dagger, tossing it grandly at her feet. She looked down at it, then up at me with secret amusement. "Whatever is this for?"

"I shall retire from the room for a few minutes to allow you to exercise your option."

She smiled with open humor. "Don't bother."

It is a great mistake to make grand gestures at crucial moments such as that one. At that very moment something thin went around my neck and a weight landed on my back. *And here,* I thought, *I've just gone and thrown away my dagger.*

In my lifetime I have been cut, stabbed, speared, shot with arrows, clubbed and half-drowned in rivers, lakes and the sea. I can say with authority that nothing induces instant panic like having one's respiration cut off in midbreath and knowing that there won't be any more coming from where you got that last one. Even drowning isn't so bad, because then there is something to drag into your lungs, if only water.

My mind immediately took leave of me and went into transports of gibbering terror. My eyes swelled to the size of fists and my vision turned red. I tried to reach behind me, to claw the horrible weight from my back, but human shoulders are not articulated to make such a move easy. Legs coiled around my waist and I tried, with great futility, to get my fingers beneath the cord around my neck, but it was drawn too tight against the scarf I still wore to hide the marks left by my last throttling. This was the way Sinistrus had died. What was it I had wondered long ago? Oh, yes, I had wondered why Sinistrus hadn't crushed the throttler against a wall. Because he was stupid. So was I.

With the last of my strength, I rushed at a wall, turning at the last second to smash my would-be murderer against a rather nice fresco depicting Ulysses and the Laestrygonians. I heard a grunt, felt a sudden expulsion of breath against my ear. The cord slipped, loosened slightly. It was not enough to allow a breath through my constricted windpipe, but it gave me the best of news: He was not using the slipknot! If I could just get the murderous little bastard off my back, I might yet live.

The room was too small to start a proper run. Drastic measures were called for. My vision was darkening and I could hear a great rushing sound in my ears. Crouching low, I bent my knees deeply. With all the strength I had left, I sprang up and forward. As my feet left the ground, I threw my body forward so that I hurtled into a forward somersault. Taking flight, I tried to will myself to weigh more, in order to come down harder.

I landed with a gratifying crash, shattering a small table in the process. The cord loosened and I dragged in a great, ragged breath of air more delicious than the finest Falernian. The legs had loosened from my waist and I twisted around, my hand going beneath my tunic and emerging with the *caestus,* which I was about to use for the second time that day. I raised my fist to my ear, then hesitated in amazement.

"Who's this?" said Milo from the doorway. The noise had drawn him.

"This," I said, looking down at my now-unconscious attacker, "is our strangler, our burglar, our 'Asian boy.' Her name is Chrysis and I daresay she's the most multi-talented woman in Rome."

Milo chuckled. "Won't the boys in the Subura be furious when they find out it was a woman doing so well!"

"Sir," said Burrus, "wasn't it the Lady Claudia you were here to see?"

I looked around but she was gone, naturally. I got

shakily to my feet and picked up my dagger from where it lay. "Claudia, Claudia," I whispered. "Such a ruthless player in the big game, and you didn't have the presence of mind to stab me when the little slut gave you the chance."

"Excuse me, sir?" Milo said.

"Nothing. Milo, I don't want that woman to escape before I get her to court. Just tying her up may not work."

"No problem," he said. With one huge hand he grasped both her wrists; with the other, her ankles. He straightened and slung her across his shoulders like a goatherd carrying a strayed kid. "She won't get away from me."

I rubbed my neck. I was alive only because she had not been prepared. She had used her long hair to strangle me, not her usual bowstring. She began to regain consciousness, trying to raise her head. I remembered that there was a formula I was supposed to employ.

Clapping a hand on her shoulder, I intoned: "Chrysis, I arrest you. Come with me to the praetor."

The house was far too large to search for Claudia, and I had already stayed too long. "To the Forum," I ordered.

As we left, we could hear Publius's mob bringing him home, so we took the opposite direction. Romans are accustomed to strange sights in their streets, but we drew our share of wide eyes and dropped jaws. I was noticeably disheveled and the cut in my side had opened, soaking not only my tunic but my toga with blood. My eyes were almost as red from the near-throttling. Behind me walked the grinning, towering young man who carried a wiry woman over his shoulders. Struggle as she might, she wasn't about to escape from those hands. Before me strode Burrus, shoving people aside and bellowing, "Make way for the Commissioner Decius Metellus!"

We walked into the Forum, which was still recovering from the recent brawl. Spilled fruit and rattling teeth still lay on the pavement among splotches of blood and shattered vendors' stalls. We were greeted by cheers and curses, showing that the citizenry were still divided in their affections toward me, although it seemed to me that the cheers predominated. We crossed the Forum and went straight up the steps of the Basilica Aemilia, followed by a growing crowd hard on our heels.

There was a boisterous trial going on when we arrived, but the hubbub quickly died down and all eyes turned toward us. From his curule chair, my father glared at us, enraged.

"What is this?" he shouted.

I stepped forward, bloody toga and all. "Fa-Praetor, I bring the foreign woman Chrysis, resident in the house of Publius Claudius Pulcher, before this court. I charge her with the murder of Marcus Ager, formerly the gladiator Sinistrus, and that of Sergius Paulus, freedman."

Father stood, his face flaming. "If you don't mind, Commissioner, I have another case before me just now. You yourself have already been charged with starting a riot!"

"By whom?" I demanded. "The flunkies of Publius Claudius? Piss on them! This takes precedence." My eloquence received warm applause. Roman jurisprudence in my youth was a rough and colorful business. "This bitch throttled Sinistrus and Paulus, and she just tried to do the same to me!" I tore off my scarf and displayed my luridly marked neck, exciting gasps of admiration.

"I can scarcely wait to find out how *that* came about!" my father said.

"She is an acrobat and contortionist," I said, praying that nobody would ask how I knew of her extreme suppleness. "That is how she was able to insert herself, reptile-fashion, through Paulus's bedroom window. The eunuch is innocent! Turn him loose!"

One of the formerly contending lawyers who had been arguing before my father rose to the bait. "Do you mean to claim," he yelled, "that this little Asiatic bint strangled a very large professional killer?"

I grasped the breast of my toga with one hand and thrust the forefinger of the other skyward, just like Hortalus when he was making his crucial point. "At that time,

What were you doing with a *caestus* anyway? That's not
a gentleman's weapon."

"A sword would have been much better," I agreed.
"But a good citizen isn't supposed to bear arms within
the *pomerium*. The *caestus* is sporting equipment." Perhaps I should explain that in those days the *pomerium*
was still the ancient boundary marked out by Romulus
when he plowed the circuit with a white bull and cow.
Its boundaries are now a mile beyond those in all direc-
tions.

"Hmm. You'll be a lawyer yet."

"The woman, Chrysis," I said urgently, "did she confess?"

"Certainly she confessed. You don't think I'd have
bothered to haul you out of prison if you'd dragged an
innocent woman into my court, do you?"

"Wonderful!" I said. "And has Claudia been arrested?"

"Eh? What Claudia are you talking about, boy? Publius's sister? What has she to do with this?"

My heart sank as suddenly as it had soared. "But what
did she—"

My father silenced me with an impatient gesture. "Quit
babbling. This is important and we have little time. I
have used all my influence to get the charges against you
dropped. I am convinced that you acted out of blunder-
ing stupidity instead of the outright villainy I might have
expected. Young Cicero has told me that you went to
him for advice on points of law. That is good, although
our patron Hortalus knows more of the law than Cicero
ever will, and is bound to give you legal advice without
recompense."

"I didn't want to bother him," I said. Better to leave
Hortalus out of this entirely until I knew where I stood.
I was beginning to feel as if I were standing on thin air.

"How you can get into so much trouble over a dead
foreigner and a couple of murdered freedmen I cannot
understand, but I am trying to get you released from
your committee a few weeks early to precede me to
Hither Spain as my legate. If you can stay out of Rome

and out of trouble for a couple of years, all this may blow over and you can come home when I return to stand for the Consulship."

This was better than nothing—a temporary banishment instead of a permanent execution. I had fantasized about dragging all of them into court and charging them with treason. Now I saw that for just what it was—a fantasy. I would see justice, but I now admitted that it would take years, not just a few days of investigation followed by some flashy jurisprudence. Well, I was only beginning my career; years were among the very few things I had. If I could just live through this.

We reached the Curia and went up the steps. Beneath the colonnade, we stopped.

"I will wait for you here," my father said. "Remember, your very life depends upon how you comport yourself in there." He placed a hand on my shoulder, a rare gesture of affection from him. Roman fathers regard paternal affection rather the way most people regard loathsome, foreign diseases. "Be humble, talk small, swallow your pride. Legal formalities mean little to the men in there. They respect only power, and you have none. Such family influence as you have I have already exercised in your behalf. The men who control the Republic these days may be moved against only from a position of great strength and highest office. That takes a great deal of time and work. Now go, and for once in your life behave wisely."

I said nothing to this, merely nodding before I turned away from him to enter the Curia. I did not hear the usual murmur of subdued talk from the Senate chamber and wondered what was amiss. When I entered the chamber itself, I thought at first that some sort of elaborate prank was being played on me. It was empty.

Then I saw that it was not quite empty. Two men sat on the lowest bench. A single, multi-wicked lamp illuminated them both. They were our two Consuls for the year that was almost over: Marcus Licinius Crassus and Gnaeus Pompeius Magnus. They seemed to be discussing

ome documents that lay on the bench between them.
)ne looked up as I drew closer.

"Ah, young Decius. Come join us." That was Pompey.

Crassus looked up and studied me with chilly blue
-yes. "Now what are we to do with you, Decius?"

"If you have charges," I said, "the proper procedure
vould be to take me to court so that the case may be
xamined."

"You are living in the wrong generation for that, De-
ius," Pompey said. "The courts are well enough for civil
natters, but you have involved yourself with foreign af-
airs."

"It was my belief that foreign policy was the province
of the Senate," I said.

"It still is," Crassus said, "but the Senate votes as we
lirect now."

"If that's true," I rejoined, "then why do you operate
n such secrecy?"

"For some time now," Crassus said heatedly, "your life
las hung by a thread. You have pulled that thread apart
one strand at a time. You are down to your last strand
nd it ill behooves you to tug very hard just now."

Pompey raised a hand in a calming gesture. "Decius,"
le asked mildly, "just what do you think you have on us?
Quite aside from the absurdity of a mere commissioner
ittacking not one but both Consuls, I fail to see that you
ire in possession of any evidence against anybody. Per-
iaps you could explain."

"Murders were committed in my district. I sought jus-
ice."

"And apprehended the perpetrator," Crassus said.
'Most commendable, and I congratulate you. The woman
Chrysis made a full confession of her crimes, how she
:ommitted them and at whose behest."

"Then I wonder that Claudia Pulcher has not been
aken into custody," I said.

Pompey expressed amazement as exaggerated as that
on an actor's mask. "Claudia? Surely you are under some
lelusion brought about by your detestation of the lady's

brother. Chrysis told us she acted under the orders of Prince Tigranes of Armenia, something about sorting out some pirate business, apparently."

"The prince, it seems, has fled the city," Crassus added.

"I want to question her myself," I said.

"You are in no position to make demands," Pompey said. "In any case, you are a bit late for that. The wench is dead. She was being kept in a cell in the old barracks down by the Campus Martius. Hanged herself with her own hair."

"I see," I said. "Resourceful to the last."

"Wasn't she?" Pompey agreed. "Unfortunate, but by then we had the whole story out of her. We made our report to the Senate this morning."

"I take it that you conducted the interrogation?" Both nodded. "And was there a praetor present?"

"Certainly," Pompey said. "All was done according to the law. Marcus Glabrio presided."

Glabrio was one of Pompey's clients and a military subordinate when Pompey was commanding. "And who was the court torturer?" I asked, suspecting that I already knew the answer.

"Marcus Volsinius," Crassus said. "One of my old centurions, a most competent man."

"He's certainly qualified by experience," I said, "having supervised six thousand crucifixions."

"We wouldn't employ an amateur," Pompey said. "Anyway, the case is closed. The woman came to Rome from Delos in the household of Paramedes of Antioch. When Tigranes came into Rome incognito and resided in the house of Paramedes, he suborned her, first with the awe of his birth and rank, then with temptations of wealth. Apparently her talents were well-known among the pirate brotherhood and Tigranes was anxious to have them at his disposal. At any rate, when he went to live in the house of Publius Claudius, she went there with him."

"And why did he go to Claudius?" I asked, knowing

hat they were closing the doors on all of my investiga-
ions.

"Decius, you shock me!" Pompey said. "He couldn't
ery well murder a man while living under his roof. That
ould be immoral. Even a greasy Armenian princeling
as more respect for the sacred laws of hospitality than
hat!"

"He went to Claudius because I sent him there," Cras-
us said, unexpectedly. "I knew the boy slightly from
vhen I had to deal with the pirates during the Servile
Var. He came to me awhile ago and asked if I knew of
 suitable household where he might reside in Rome.
Obviously, considering the delicate state of relations be-
ween the Republic and his father's kingdom, he could
ot very well beg hospitality of a Consul and did not
vant his presence officially recognized. I knew that Pub-
ius had the run of the town house since his elder brother
nd sister were in the East. Lots of room in the house,
nd the Claudians always love to hobnob with royalty.
Seemed perfectly innocent at the time."

"Nothing about the Claudians is innocent," I said.

To my amazement, both men burst into laughter.
They are a difficult lot, to be sure," Crassus said.

"And now Publius is to be your cat's-paw in Lucullus's
rmy, to sow dissent and mutiny among the troops."

"Now, Decius, how do you expect people to believe
hat? The boy needs military experience if he's to stand
or office. What more natural than that he should join
Lucullus? The eastern army is where the action is, where
eputations are to be made. And why should Publius
vant to attack Lucullus's authority? His elder sister is
narried to Lucullus. His elder brother, Appius, has been
vith Lucullus for years and has served loyally all that
ime. All logic says he would serve his own best interests
by pushing Lucullus's fortunes to the best of his ability.
f in spite of all that, Publius should rebel against his
brother-in-law ..." Pompey shrugged and smiled. "Well,
hen, that's just Publius being Publius, isn't it?"

"The night grows late," Crassus said, "and our Consulship grows shorter. Decius, do you really think that you have any evidence of wrongdoing to bring against my colleague or me?"

I thought of the documents in the Temple of Vesta. They could be subpoenaed, of course, but only at the cost of compromising the *Virgo Maxima,* my great-aunt and a lady of such irreproachable worthiness that I would not have endangered her reputation to save myself from the cross. I thought of the document in my house, proving Hortalus's extra-legal freeing of Sinistrus. I dismissed it. As part of a far larger case, that document would have been a solid stone in the wall I was building. By itself, it was proof of a petty corruption too minor to warrant attention.

"There was an amulet among my effects when I was arrested, a bronze camel's head."

"I am aware of no such object," Pompey said. "These items were taken from you." He gestured to my dagger and *caestus,* which lay on the bench beside him. "Quite improper, going armed within the *pomerium,* but we'd have half the population up on charges if we tried to enforce that law strictly." Somehow, I wasn't surprised that the token of *hospitium* had disappeared. They were right. I had nothing. With the two murderers, Sinistrus and Chrysis, already dead and a legal confession from Chrysis, I would look like a fool if I tried to reopen the case. I had no proof of criminal conspiracy, no proof of treason. What I did have, for the moment, was my life. All I could do now was try to keep it.

Crassus studied me with his cold eyes. "Decius, we have tolerated your irrational and pernicious behavior thus far out of respect for your family and your father, the Urban Praetor. He has requested that you be released from further duties and precede him to Hither Spain as his legate. We have decided to grant that request." He handed me a small scroll bearing both the senatorial and the consular seals. "Here are your orders. At first light, when the gates are opened, be on your way to Ostia. You will leave on the first cutter heading west."

I took the scroll. "Taking ship in December might be interpreted as a death sentence," I commented.

"There are less pleasant ways to die than by drowning," Crassus said. "A generous sacrifice to Neptune might help."

"Of course," Pompey put in, "just getting from your house to the gate might be a bit of a problem. Publius Claudius, or rather Clodius, as he's taken to calling himself, is a man who holds a grudge. You might have to make your way through quite a few of his supporters tomorrow."

"And," Crassus said, "I hear that Macro has ordered all his men to stay out of it. He's reined in that rascal Milo. That being the case, you'd better take these." He tossed my dagger and *caestus* to me and I caught them. "You are going to need them at first light."

Pompey returned to his paperwork. "That will be all, Decius. Best of luck."

My father was stone-faced when I came out, but I could hear a muted sigh of relief. To my astonishment, Titus Milo was with him. "I was told you were let out of the Mamertine tonight and came here. Thought I'd join you."

"Does anything happen in this city without your knowledge?" I asked.

"I try to keep up on things."

"What happened in there?" Father asked.

"I received a suspended death sentence, of sorts." As we walked, I explained what had transpired, although for my father's sake I left Hortalus's name out of it.

"Better than you might have expected," Father said. "Sea travel at this season is risky, but you can sail north along the coast and put ashore at the first sign of bad weather."

"I expect to be quite occupied just in getting to Ostia," I informed him.

"I'm afraid I won't be able to help you there," Milo said.

"So I heard."

"Surely Claudius won't try to murder you in public!"

Father protested. Milo and I both got a good laugh out of that one.

"I still wonder why they were so lenient with me," I said. "Granted, I did nothing wrong and pursued my duties diligently, but that never stopped those two from killing anyone."

Milo surprised me by answering. "It's because they're in a good mood. You would be too if you enjoyed their good fortune."

"Yes, that's why I pressed for this interview tonight," Father said. "It seemed a fortuitous occasion."

"What happened?" I asked, mystified.

"The will of Sergius Paulus was read this morning," Father told me. "He left the vast bulk of his estate to the Consuls and the other magistrates, including"—he tried not to gloat—"a rather generous bequest to me."

"And freed all his slaves," Milo said. "Every one of them, and the man owned thousands. He left each one a small cash stake to set them up as freedmen and gave all the rest to the Consuls and praetors."

I let the implications of this seep in for a few moments, then whooped: "Sergius Paulus, you clever freedman bastard! No wonder you filed a new will every year! Cut your estate up among each year's magistrates and no one will question all those manumissions."

Father cleared his throat. "Yes, the will clearly violates the legal limit on testamentary manumissions, but I hardly think there will be any dispute over that."

I laughed until tears rolled down my face. For the first time in days I felt truly fine. Paulus had proved to me that Rome could still produce decent men, even in the form of fat, rich, drunken freedmen.

We left my father at his house. Before bidding me good night, he said, "You've done your duty well, Decius." It was high praise, coming from him.

At my house, Milo took his leave. "I'm sorry I can't help you in the morning," he said.

"I thank you for all the help you've given me so far,"

I assured him. "At worst, I'll get a chance to finish the job on Claudius that I started in the Forum."

I saw his teeth flash in the darkness. "Spoken like a true Roman. I'll pass the word tonight. Who knows, something might turn up."

"Do you never sleep?" I asked.

"I told you before, I get ahead by working when other men rest. I'll be here in the morning, Decius, even if I can't get any of my boys to come." He faded into the dark.

I had a few hours until daylight. Cato and Cassandra were overjoyed to see me, although they were shocked at my appearance. I ordered water heated for a bath and peeled out of my filthy clothes.

At least I had my affairs in order and my will made out. My few belongings went into a travel-chest and I sorted through my *hospitium* tokens for any that might be useful on the journey, assuming I could get out of Rome alive. It was strange to think that all the events of these past few days had turned upon a humble token like one of these. I shook my head at the thought. The ways of men and gods are imponderable, and the most trivial things can loom as large as the greatest. I decided that I would have to take up the study of philosophy, sometime when I was terribly bored with everything else.

Even the prospect of the coming day could not take the edge off my good mood. I sang as I bathed in a cramped tub and didn't even wince when Cato shaved me, inexpertly and by lamplight. Then I lay down and had a few hours of dreamless sleep.

Despite the brevity of my nap, I woke feeling refreshed. I rose and put on clean clothes, belted on sword and dagger and threw a clean toga over all. This was no time for fussy legalities. As the first light of dawn came through my windows, I went out into the atrium. Burrus was there to greet me, and he clinked as he moved. He had put on his armor before calling on me. I was touched that the old soldier had come to meet almost certain death with me, but it would have been inappropriate to make any show of it. He wore an odd smile.

"Good morning, Patron. Wait till you see the street outside. It looks like a meeting of the Guild of Archers out there."

I wondered what in the world he could mean. In the entryway I was further astonished to see my other two clients, both too elderly to be of any use in a street brawl, but serious about their duty to protect their patron. Then I saw what was waiting outside.

A vast throng jammed the street. And almost every head was decorated with a Phrygian bonnet, the pointed cap favored by the mercenary archers who serve the auxiliaries and worn by some priesthoods. It is also worn by slaves who have just been freed. This great mob cheered like maniacs when I appeared. To my intense embarrassment, some of them surged forward and dropped to their knees to kiss my feet.

"What's this?" I demanded.

"They're the freedmen of Sergius Paulus, sir," Burrus said. "I practically had to hack my way through 'em to get to your house this morning. They're grateful to you, sir, and they damn well should be. If it wasn't for you, every buggering one of 'em might be hanging on a cross this morning. That fat eunuch surely would."

A man I recognized as Paulus's majordomo pushed his way up to me. "We heard you might need an escort, sir. We couldn't let you leave Rome without a proper send-off." He turned to a pair of husky youths. "Go inside and get the master's luggage." Cato, confused and muttering, led the two boys to my belongings.

The majordomo turned and shouted to the crowd: "To the Ostian gate!"

With a huge cheer, the mob surged around me and I was hoisted onto their shoulders, and in that fashion I was carried to the gate. Through streets and squares we went, and it seemed to me that half of Rome was out, laughing and pointing at this new prodigy. Even though it was not on the way, the mob of ecstatic freedmen made a detour to carry me through the Forum. In the shadows of an alleyway I saw the heavily bandaged face of Publius Claudius, eyes glaring hate from amid his gang of cut-throats. The Etruscan blood of the Claudian line had come to the fore, since he was reduced to making cursing gestures toward me. I replied with a popular Roman gesture, one which was not supernatural in intent. And so we went, all the way to the Ostian gate.

I have commanded troops, as every Roman in public office must, but I was never a great general and was never granted a triumph by the Senate. However, I do not believe that any *triumphator* who has ever paraded up the Via Sacra to the Capitol could have felt as I felt that morning, borne on the shoulders of freedmen.

At the gate they let me down so that I could continue the journey in a more dignified fashion. The greater part of them would accompany me all the way to Ostia and stay with me until I sailed. Titus Milo waved to me from the top of the gate as we passed through.

Beyond the gate the Via Ostiensis stretched, flanked by tombs and memorials. It was a gray, windy, blustery December morning and we would undoubtedly be rained on before long. But the landscape had never looked so beautiful to me. For once, there were no crosses flanking the road.

These events took place during fifteen days of the year 684 of the City of Rome, the year of the Consulship of Pompey and Crassus.

GLOSSARY

(Definitions apply to the last century of the Republic.)

Acta: Streets wide enough for one-way wheeled traffic.

Aedile: Elected officials in charge of upkeep of the city and the grain dole, regulation of public morals, management of the markets and the public Games. There were two types: the plebeian aediles, who had no insignia of office, and the curule aediles, who wore the toga praetexta and sat in the sella curulis. The curule aediles could sit in judgment on civil cases involving markets and currency, while the plebeian aediles could only levy fines. Otherwise, their duties were the same. Since the magnificence of the Games one exhibited as aedile often determined election to higher office, it was an important stepping-stone in a political career. The office of aedile did not carry the imperium.

Atrium: Once a word for house, in Republican times it was the entry hall of a house, opening off the street and used as a general reception area.

Atrium Vestae: The Palace of the Vestal and one of the most splendid buildings in Rome.

Augur: An official who observed omens for state purposes. He could forbid business and assemblies if he saw unfavorable omens.

Basilica: A building where courts met in inclement weather.

Caestus: The Classical boxing glove, made of leather straps and reinforced by bands, plates or spikes of bronze.

Campus Martius: A field outside the old city wall, formerly the assembly area and drill field for the army. It was where the popular assemblies met. By late Republican times, buildings were encroaching on the field.

Censor: Magistrates elected usually every fifth year to oversee the census of the citizens and purge the roll of Senators of unworthy members. They could forbid certain religious practices or luxuries deemed bad for public morals or generally "un-Roman." There were two Censors, and each could overrule the other. They wore the toga praetexta and sat in the sella curulis, but since they had no executive powers they were not accompanied by lictors. The office did not carry the imperium. Censors were usually elected from among the ex-Consuls, and the censorship was regarded as the capstone of a political career.

Centuriate Assembly: (comitia centuriata) Originally, the annual military assembly of the citizens where they joined their army units ("centuries"). There were one hundred ninety-three centuries divided into five classes by property qualification. They elected the highest magistrates: Censors, Consuls and Praetors. By the middle Republic, the centuriate assembly was strictly a voting body, having lost all military character.

Centurion: "Commander of 100"; i.e., a century, which, in practice, numbered around sixty men. Centurions were promoted from the ranks and were the backbone of the professional army.

Circus: The Roman racecourse and the stadium which enclosed it. The original, and always the largest, was the Circus Maximus, which lay between the Palatine and Aventine hills. A later, smaller circus, the Circus Flaminius, lay outside the walls on the Campus Martius.

Client: One attached in a subordinate relationship to a patron, whom he was bound to support in war and in the courts. Freedmen became clients of their former masters. The relationship was hereditary.

Cognomen: The family name, denoting any of the stirpes of a gens; i.e., Caius Julius *Caesar:* Caius of the stirps

Caesar of gens Julii. Some plebeian families never adopted a cognomen, notably the Marii and the Antonii.

Compluvium: An opening in a roof to admit light.

Consul: Supreme magistrate of the Republic. Two were elected each year. Insignia were the toga praetexta and the sella curulis. Each Consul was attended by twelve lictors. The office carried full imperium. On the expiration of his year in office, the ex-Consul was usually assigned a district outside Rome to rule as proconsul. As proconsul, he had the same insignia and the same number of lictors. His power was absolute within his province.

Curia: The meetinghouse of the Senate, located in the Forum.

Dictator: An absolute ruler chosen by the Senate and the Consuls to deal with a specific emergency. For a limited period, never more than six months, he was given unlimited imperium, which he was to lay down upon resolution of the emergency. Unlike the Consuls, he had no colleague to overrule him and he was not accountable for his actions performed during office when he stepped down. His insignia were the toga praetexta and the sella curulis and he was accompanied by twenty-four lictors, the number of both Consuls. Dictatorships were extremely rare and the last was held in 202 B.C. The dictatorships of Sulla and Caesar were unconstitutional.

Dioscuri: Castor and Pollux, the twin sons of Zeus and Leda. The Romans revered them as protectors of the city.

Eques: (pl. equites) Formerly, citizens wealthy enough to supply their own horses and fight in the cavalry, they came to hold their status by meeting a property qualification. They formed the moneyed upper-middle class. In the centuriate assembly they formed eighteen centuries and once had the right of voting first, but they lost this as their military function disappeared. The publicans, financiers, bankers, moneylenders and tax-farmers came from the equestrian class.

Faction: In the Circus, the supporters of the four racing companies: Red, White, Blue and Green. Most Romans were fanatically loyal to one of these.

Fasces: A bundle of rods bound around an ax with a red strap, symbolizing a Roman magistrate's power of corporal and capital punishment. They were carried by the lictors who accompanied the curule magistrates, the Flamen Dialis, and the proconsuls and propraetors who governed provinces. When a lower magistrate met a higher, his lictors lowered their fasces in salute.

Flamen: A high priest of a specific god of the state. The college of flamines had fifteen members: three patrician and twelve plebeian. The three highest were the Flamen Dialis, the Flamen Martialis and the Flamen Quirinalis. They had charge of the daily sacrifices and wore distinctive headgear and were surrounded by many ritual taboos. The Flamen Dialis, high priest of Jupiter, was entitled to the toga praetexta, which had to be woven by his wife, the sella curulis and a single lictor, and he could sit in the Senate. It became difficult to fill the college of flamines because they had to be prominent men, the appointment was for life and they could take no part in politics.

Forum: An open meeting and market area. The premier forum was the Forum Romanum, located on the low ground surrounded by the Capitoline, Palatine and Caelian hills. It was surrounded by the most important temples and public buildings. Roman citizens spent much of their day there. The courts met outdoors in the Forum when the weather was good. When it was paved and devoted solely to public business, the Forum Romanum's market functions were transferred to the Forum Boarium, the cattle market, near the Circus Maximus. Small shops and stalls remained along the northern and southern peripheries, however.

Freedman: A manumitted slave. Formal emancipation conferred full rights of citizenship except for the right to hold office. Informal emancipation conferred freedom without voting rights. In the second or at latest third generation, a freedman's descendants became full citizens.

Genius: The guiding and guardian spirit of a person or place. The genius of a place was called genius loci.

Gens: A clan, all of whose members were descended from a single ancestor. The nomen of a patrician gens always ended with -ius. Thus, Caius *Julius* Caesar was Caius, of the Caesarian stirps of gens Julii.

Gladiator: Literally, "swordsman." A slave, prisoner of war, condemned criminal or free volunteer who fought, often to the death, in the munera. All were called swordsmen, even if they fought with other weapons.

Gladius: The short, broad, double-edged sword borne by Roman soldiers. It was designed primarily for stabbing. A smaller, more antiquated design of gladius was used by gladiators.

Gravitas: The quality of seriousness.

Haruspex: A member of a college of Etruscan professionals who examined the entrails of sacrificial animals for omens.

Hospitium: An arrangement of reciprocal hospitality. When visiting the other's city, each hospes (pl. hospites) was entitled to food and shelter, protection in court, care when ill or injured and honorable burial, should he die during the visit. The obligation was binding on both families and was passed on to descendants.

Ides: The 15th of March, May, July and October. The 13th of other months.

Imperium: The ancient power of kings to summon and lead armies, to order and forbid and to inflict corporal and capital punishment. Under the Republic, the imperium was divided among the Consuls and Praetors, but they were subject to appeal and intervention by the tribunes in their civil decisions and were answerable for their acts after leaving office. Only a dictator had unlimited imperium.

Insula: Literally, "island." A large, multistory tenement block.

Itinera: Streets wide enough for only foot traffic. The majority of Roman streets were itinera.

Janitor: A slave-doorkeeper, so called for Janus, god of gateways.

Kalends: The first of any month.

Latifundium: A large landed estate or plantation worked by slaves. During the late Republic these expanded tremendously, all but destroying the Italian peasant class.

Legates: Subordinate commanders chosen by the Senate to accompany generals and governors. Also, ambassadors appointed by the Senate.

Legion: Basic unit of the Roman army. Paper strength was six thousand, but usually closer to four thousand.

All were armed as heavy infantry with a large shield, cuirass, helmet, gladius and light and heavy javelins. Each legion had attached to it an equal number of non-citizen auxiliaries consisting of light and heavy infantry, cavalry, archers, slingers, etc. Auxilia were never organized as legions, only as cohorts.

Lictor: Attendants, usually freedmen, who accompanied magistrates and the Flamen Dialis, bearing the fasces. They summoned assemblies, attended public sacrifices and carried out sentences of punishment. Twenty-four lictors accompanied a dictator, twelve for a Consul, six for a propraetor, two for a Praetor and one for the Flamen Dialis.

Liquamen: Also called garum, it was the ubiquitous fermented fish sauce used in Roman cooking.

Ludus: (pl. ludi) The official public Games, races, theatricals, etc. Also, a training school for gladiators, although the gladiatorial exhibitions were not ludi.

Munera: Special Games, not part of the official calendar, at which gladiators were exhibited. They were originally funeral Games and were always dedicated to the dead. In munera sine missione, all the defeated were killed and sometimes were made to fight sequentially or all at once until only one was left standing. Munera sine missione were periodically forbidden by law.

Nobiles: Those families, both patrician and plebeian, in which members had held the Consulate.

Nomen: The name of the clan or gens; i.e., Caius *Julius* Caesar.

Nones: The 7th of March, May, July and October. The 5th of other months.

Novus Homo: Literally, "new man." A man who is the first of his family to hold the Consulate, giving his family the status of nobles.

Optimates: The party of the "best men"; i.e., aristocrats and their supporters.

Patria Potestas: The absolute authority of the pater familias over the children of his household, who could neither legally own property while their father was alive nor marry without his permission. Technically, he had the right to sell or put to death any of his children, but by Republican times this was a legal fiction.

Patrician: A descendant of one of the founding fathers of Rome. Once, only patricians could hold offices and priesthoods and sit in the Senate, but these privileges were gradually eroded until only certain priesthoods were strictly patrician. By the late Republic, only about fourteen gens remained.

Patron: A man with one or more clients whom he was bound to protect, advise and otherwise aid. The relationship was hereditary.

Peculium: Roman slaves could not own property, but they could earn money outside the household, which was held for them by their masters. This fund was called a peculium, and could be used, eventually, to purchase the slave's freedom.

Peristylium: An open courtyard surrounded by a collonade.

Pietas: The quality of dutifulness toward the gods and, especially, toward one's parents.

Plebeian: All citizens not of patrician status.

Pomerium: The line of the ancient city wall, attributed to Romulus. Actually, the space of vacant ground just within and without the wall, regarded as holy. Within the pomerium it was forbidden to bear arms or bury the dead.

Pontifex: A member of the highest priestly college of Rome. They had superintendence over all sacred observances, state and private, and over the calendar. There were fifteen in the late Republic: seven patrician and eight plebeian. Their chief was the pontifex maximus, a title now held by the Pope.

Popular Assemblies: There were three: the centuriate assembly (comitia centuriata) and the two tribal assemblies: comitia tributa and consilium plebis, q.v.

Populares: The party of the common people.

Praenomen: The given name of a freedman, as Marcus, Sextus, Caius, etc.; i.e., *Caius* Julius Caesar: Caius of the stirps Caesar of gens Julii. Women used a feminine form of their father's nomen, i.e., the daughter of Caius Julius Caesar would be named Julia.

Praetor: Judge and magistrate elected yearly along with the Consuls. In the late Republic there were eight Praetors. Senior was the Praetor Urbanus, who heard civil cases between citizens. The Praetor Peregrinus heard cases involving foreigners. The others presided over criminal courts. Insignia were the toga praetexta and the sella curulis, and Praetors were accompanied by two lictors. The office carried the imperium. After leaving office, the ex-Praetors became propraetors and went to govern propraetorian provinces with full imperium.

Praetorium: A general's headquarters, usually a tent in camp. In the provinces, the official residence of the governor.

Proscription: List of names of public enemies published by Sulla. Anyone could kill a proscribed person and claim a reward, usually a part of the dead man's estate.

Publicans: Those who bid on public contracts, most notably builders and tax farmers. The contracts were usually let by the Censors and therefore had a period of five years.

Pugio: The straight, double-edged dagger of the Roman soldiers.

Quaestor: Lowest of the elected officials, they had charge of the treasury and financial matters such as payments for public works. They also acted as assistants and paymasters to higher magistrates, generals and provincial governors. They were elected yearly by the comitia tributa.

Quirinus: The deified Romulus, patron deity of the city.

Rostra: A monument in the Forum commemorating the sea battle of Antium in 338 B.C., decorated with the rams, "rostra" of enemy ships (sing. rostrum). Its base was used as an orator's platform.

Salii: "Dancers." Two colleges of priests dedicated to Mars and Quirinus who held their rites in March and October, respectively. Each college consisted of twelve young patricians whose parents were still living. On their festivals, they dressed in embroidered tunics, a crested bronze helmet and breastplate and each bore one of the twelve sacred shields ("ancilia") and a staff. They processed to the most important altars of Rome and before each performed a war dance. The ritual was so ancient that, by the first century B.C., their songs and prayers were unintelligible.

Saturnalia: Feast of Saturn, December 17–23, a raucous and jubilant occasion when gifts were exchanged, debts were settled and masters waited on their slaves.

Sella Curulis: A folding camp-chair. It was part of the insignia of the curule magistrates and the Flamen Dialis.

Senate: Rome's chief deliberative body. It consisted of three hundred to six hundred men, all of whom had won elective office at least once. Once the supreme ruling body, by the late Republic the Senate's former legislative and judicial functions had devolved upon the courts and the popular assemblies and its chief authority lay in foreign policy and the nomination of generals. Senators were privileged to wear the tunica laticlava.

Servile War: The slave rebellion led by the Thracian gladiator Spartacus in 73–71 B.C. The rebellion was crushed by Crassus and Pompey.

Sica: A single-edged dagger or short sword of varying size. It was favored by thugs and used by the Thracian gladiators in the arena. It was classified as an infamous rather than an honorable weapon.

Solarium: A rooftop garden and patio.

Spatha: The Roman cavalry sword, longer and narrower than the gladius.

SPQR: "Senatus populusque Romanus." The Senate and People of Rome. The formula embodying the sovereignty of Rome. It was used on official correspondence, documents and public works.

Stirps: A sub-family of a gens. The cognomen gave the name of the stirps, i.e., Caius Julius *Caesar:* Caius of the stirps Caesar of gens Julii.

Strophium: A cloth band worn by women beneath or over the clothing to support the breasts.

Subligaculum: A loincloth, worn by men and women.

Subura: A neighborhood on the lower slopes of the Viminal and Esquiline, famed for its slums, noisy shops and raucous inhabitants.

Tarpeian Rock: A cliff beneath the Capitol from which traitors were hurled. It was named for the Roman maiden Tarpeia who, according to legend, betrayed the Capitol to the Sabines.

Temple of Jupiter Capitolinus: The most important temple of the state religion. Triumphal processions ended with a sacrifice at this temple.

Temple of Saturn: The state treasury was located in a crypt beneath this temple. It was also the repository for military standards.

Temple of Vesta: Site of the sacred fire tended by the vestal virgins and dedicated to the goddess of the hearth. Documents, especially wills, were deposited there for safekeeping.

Toga: The outer robe of the Roman citizen. It was white for the upper classes, darker for the poor and for people in mourning. The toga praetexta, bordered with a purple stripe, was worn by curule magistrates, by state priests when performing their functions and by boys prior to manhood. The toga picta, purple and embroidered with golden stars, was worn by a general when celebrating a triumph, also by a magistrate when giving public Games.

Tonsores: A slave trained as a barber and hairdresser.

Trans-Tiber: A newer district on the right or western bank of the Tiber. It lay beyond the old city walls.

Tribal Assemblies: There were two: the comitia tributa, an assembly of all citizens by tribes, which elected the lower magistrates—curule aediles, and quaestors, also the military tribunes—and the concilium plebis, consisting only of plebeians, elected the tribunes of the plebs and the plebeian aediles.

Tribe: Originally, the three classes of patricians. Under the Republic, all citizens belonged to tribes of which there were four city tribes and thirty-one country tribes. New citizens were enrolled in an existing tribe.

Tribune: Representative of the plebeians with power to introduce laws and to veto actions of the Senate. Only plebeians could hold the office, which carried no imperium. Military tribunes were elected from among the young men of senatorial or equestrian rank to be assistants to generals. Usually it was the first step of a man's political career.

Triumph: A magnificent ceremony celebrating military victory. The honor could be granted only by the Senate, and until he received permission, the victorious general had to remain outside the city walls, as his command ceased the instant he crossed the pomerium. The general, called the triumphator, received royal, near-divine honors and became a virtual god for a day. A slave was appointed to stand behind him and remind him periodically of his mortality lest the gods become jealous.

Triumvir: A member of a triumvirate—a board or college of three men. Most famously, the three-man rule of Caesar, Pompey and Crassus. Later, the triumvirate of Antonius, Octavian and Lepidus.

Tunica: A long, loose shirt, sleeveless or short-sleeved, worn by citizens beneath the toga when outdoors and by itself indoors. The tunica laticlava had a broad purple stripe from neck to hem and was worn by Senators and patricians. The tunica angusticlava had a narrow stripe and was worn by the equites. The tunica picta, purple and embroidered with golden palm branches, was worn by a general when he celebrated a triumph.

Via: A highway. Within the city, viae were streets wide enough for two wagons to pass one another. There were only two viae during the Republic: the Via Sacra, which ran through the Forum and was used for religious processions and triumphs, and the Via Nova, which ran along one side of the Forum.

Vigile: A night watchman. The vigiles had the duty of apprehending felons caught committing crimes, but their main duty was as a fire watch. They were unarmed except for staves and carried fire-buckets.